The BONE Shelter

The BONE Shelter

Sue Alcon O'Connor

Bookmite Publishing
Denver, CO

ISBN: 979-8-9869941-0-9

CONTENTS

CONTENTS

ACKNOWLEDGMENTS

I have so many people to thank.

First off, Dario Ciriello, my editor, friend, and biggest cheerleader. None of this could have been possible without your input and patience. My dear husband Mark, who had to look at the backside of a computer from across the kitchen table for months. My kids, Marshall, Logan, and Gina. You always have my back and I love you dearly. And last but not least, the very talented Noelle Nevins at Abbeo Design for her fabulous work on my book cover.

Thank you to all my friends that had to hear me prattle on about monkeys and Elvis for the last six months. I bounced a lot of jokes off you—some of which fell flat. Thanks for being brave enough to tell me when those jokes sucked balls. Kathy, Shelly, Faithie, and Milly—my joke bouncers—who are more bouncy than super balls on a blacktop.

This book is a work of fiction sprinkled with reality. The kid stuff is mostly real. I'll explain later, and you'll probably wonder how they made it to adulthood.

Patton, Colorado is fictional, although if I could find a town for sale (and I had a bazillion dollars) I'd buy it, change my name to Walter, and be its mayor. You're all invited to be my underlings.

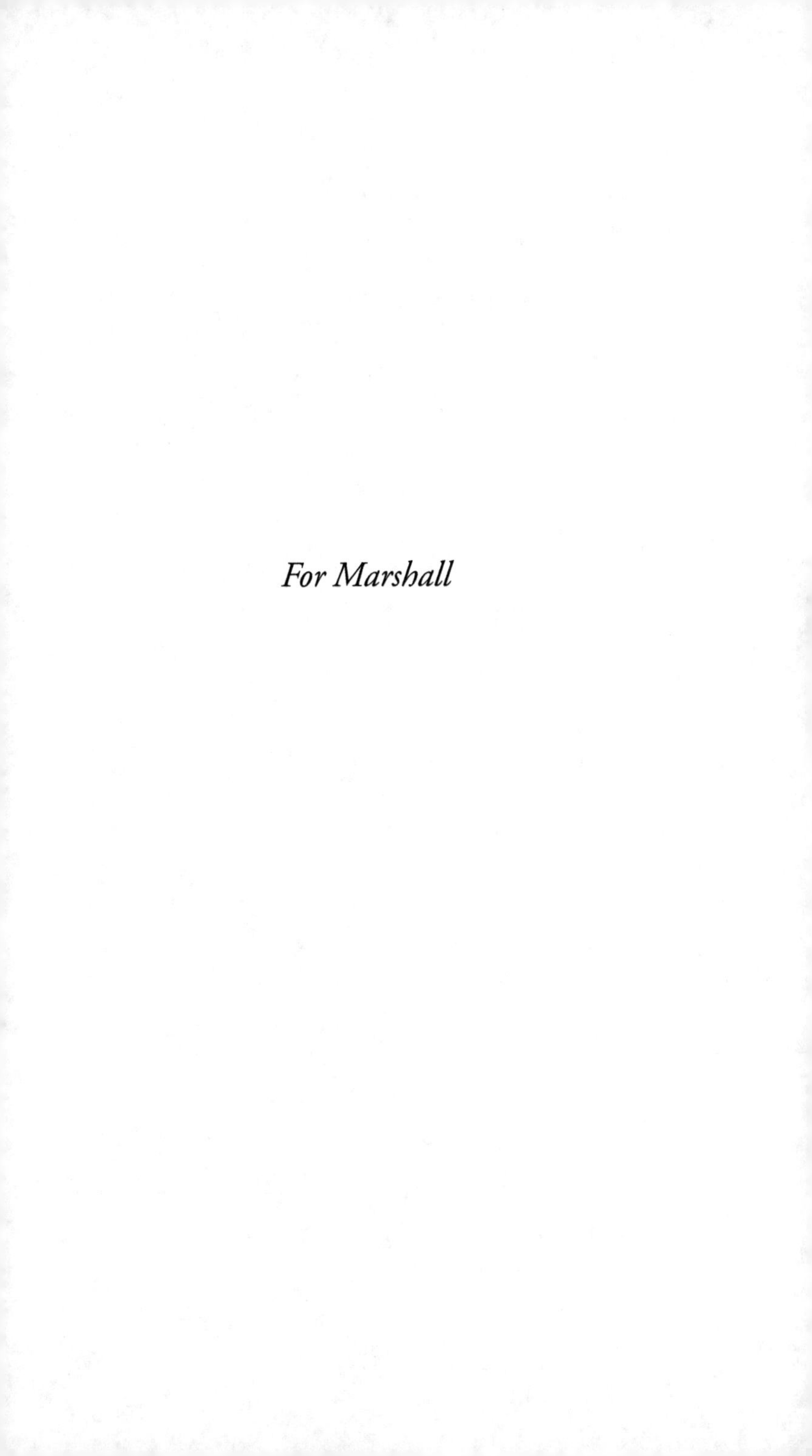

For Marshall

PART I

Chapter One

Murder, Mayhem, & Monkeys

ELVIS LEFT THE BUILDING at 11:15 P.M. and took a right down Pine Street, the silver Colt .45 resting heavily in the pocket of his white fringed coat. A light rain had begun to fall on that moonless night, and he adjusted the collar of his leather jacket to keep out the weather.

He made a brisk pass by Margarita's Hair & Nail Salon, hugging the building and staying in the shadows as he slipped by the Doughboy Bakery, keeping a watchful eye out for anyone who might be out for a late stroll.

Elvis took the next right on First Avenue, past The Liquor Palace, then down the dimly lit alley behind the storefronts, his shoes padding with a graceful ease over the cracked cement as he headed south toward his home.

At the end of the alley and across the street from Patton, Colorado's elementary school, there sat a green dumpster that had seen better days; its sides were rusty and the top bent in such a severe manner it didn't close properly, keeping it perpetually half open and at the mercy of the elements. This particular dumpster backed up to a brick wall, and as he passed by, without missing a step, he shrugged off the slightly damp white leather and gold-sequined jacket, wadded it into a twinkling basketball, and, with an overhead shot, tossed it toward the half open trash bin. It slid over the top and fell with a solid thump between the dumpster and the brick alley wall.

"Hell-fire," Elvis spat, his brow creasing with annoyance. No time to retrieve it now, but he'd been careful about fingerprints, and they weren't an issue. He glanced at his white leather gloves, thinking about how damn canny he was. Careful or not, he knew he needed to dispose of the evidence, but damn, he'd miss that gun—it had cost a fortune and had been worth every red-hot dime.

Feeling safe enough, and having put a good distance between himself and the necessary murders, he removed the synthetic black wig and his gold-rimmed aviator sunglasses. He shoved the glasses into the breast pocket of his red satin shirt, then spun the wig on one finger. He chuckled at how smoothly this evening had gone, and began to whistle. The percentage of simpletons in this town never failed to astound him.

Pleased with himself, Elvis did a little side shuffle and turn, his arms gliding out to his sides. He stood a little taller, his white bell bottoms whispering over the wet sidewalk. He kicked an empty Coke can a scant harder than he should have, and it skittered down the road, startling the black-and-white cat that dashed across the street in front of him.

"I hate cats," he mumbled under his breath, as it slipped behind a hedge and under a fence, "just fucking hate 'em." He spat into the gutter, and made a sharp right onto his property.

Two people were dead, and they deserved to die, he thought, as he keyed open the back door to his house.

"Time for a shower, a sandwich, and a cold beer."

Sam wasn't sure if today would turn out to be the best day of his life or the worst. Smart money was on the worst. He wasn't sure if he'd walk into his house and his parents would think he was the cleverest twelve-year-old who ever lived, or if they'd ground him for the rest of his natural life without the possibility of parole. The jury was out on that one. He bit his lower lip, clutched his English book to his chest, and frowned.

The day had started well enough. He'd walked to school with his friends BJ and Hank; they made it to class on time, which was amazing, since Hank had forgotten his science homework and they had to circle back for it. Sam remembered his lunch, which was a miracle in itself, even if it was only baloney and cheese. To top it all off, that asshole Trevor Becknor wasn't waiting for him at the gate to the baseball field with his fists clenched and murder in his eyes. Yep, it was a pretty good day so far.

Sam shook his head and sighed. The good day had done a mind blowing one-eighty and screeched its way straight into Shitsville.

The trouble began in sixth period English when his teacher, Miss Sharette, dished out the assignment for the day. She was almost seventy-seven years old, and still teaching. She claimed to love her job, but could have fooled him. She either hated her job, hated her students, needed the money, or was just born with an explosive case of resting bitch face. She usually wore glossy pink lipstick and winged eyeliner that smudged in the wrinkles by her eyes and made her look like she was trying too hard. The pink lipstick would bleed into the lines around her mouth by the end of the day. No matter what the weather, she wore a mink coat that smelled a little funky, like someone had tried to set it on fire. Sam's mom said it was because she smoked Camels and that he should mind his own business, but that was hard to do when he sat about three feet from the coat hook, and the room smelled like the time they'd gone camping and Grandpa had accidentally set the tent on fire smoking a cigar. He guessed the coat was mink, but who knew? A lot of cats go missing in Patton, and there were a ton of coyotes in this part of Colorado. Who'd notice if a few dozen mangy coyotes were gone?

Once, on a boring Sunday afternoon, he'd looked up her information online. He'd googled her name, and Miss Sharette's Facebook page popped up. The last entry was 2013, and she had exactly five friends, all of them teachers. It looked as if she had no relatives, no kids, no husband, *no life*, at least as far as Facebook was concerned. Her profile picture was a meme that said, "Teachers! Changing the World One Child at a Time!" Sam thought she needed to click the heels of her sensible shoes together and catch the first rocket to the sun, especially now that she was all but dragging him down the hall to the office. He didn't like her, and he was pretty sure she didn't like him either, although he had once heard her tell his parents at a parent-teacher conference that she was hard on him because she knew he had potential. Yet here he was, standing in front of the principal's office waiting for judgment day.

The assignment for sixth period English was to write a one- or two-paragraph epitaph for a non-human object or thing. Dumb, but easy enough. Sam cursed inwardly at his lack of foresight. Why hadn't he picked a rock, or Jupiter, or a baked potato? He smacked himself on the forehead and tipped his head back with an exasperated grunt. He'd thought he was so smart to have picked a monkey as his subject. In his twelve-year-old boy's mind he had felt the creative juices begin to bubble and churn until he became excited about the assignment. He would write an epitaph for a monkey and compare it to a penis, the monkey-penis still having a bit of a life of its own. In hindsight, he should have known it was inappropriate, but at the time he'd found the idea hilarious and brilliant.

Sam groaned, stopped in front of the principal's office, and hesitated. He had been so sure his ingenious, out-of-the-box thinking would earn him a great grade, and now here he was marching into the lion's den with his slightly smoky-smelling English teacher's hand on his shoulder.

Miss Sharette opened the door, gestured Sam through it, walked straight past the secretary, who looked at them over her half-moon glasses, and barged into Mr. Morrison's office. She thrust his creative handiwork at principal Morrison.

"Read this, Fred."

Mr. Morrison, who looked as if he had no more shits left to give, took the papers from her outstretched hand and sighed. He put on his reading glasses, sighed some more—this time with increased dramatic gusto—and then began to read.

Sam could see the corners of his mouth twitch, and his teeth bite into the side of his cheek. As far as Sam knew, Mr. Morrison never cracked a smile in his life, let alone a laugh. It was as if he'd been born without a personality gene. Was this little smirk a good sign? Sam felt a small tingle of hope.

Fred Morrison finished reading. It didn't take him long, since the masterpiece Sam had written barely an hour ago was only two paragraphs long.

Principal Morrison sat the papers on the desk along with his glasses. He pinched the bridge of his nose. "Miss Sharette," he bemoaned, "it seems to me that Sam has spelled everything correctly." Sam saw a muscle in his cheek twitch. "I don't see a real problem other than his essay being a bit, eh, off-color."

He looked up at Miss Sharette who obviously was not pleased with his response.

"We have bigger fish to fry," he concluded, "than a primate phallus don't we?"

Miss Sharette gave a phlegmy snort and snatched up the papers. "I want to call his parents and read this vulgar essay to them."

There was no question that Sam's mom would answer the phone. She had a decent sense of humor, but you never knew if she was in a good mood. She usually was. She had been when he left for school that morning. Sometimes though, she was in a pissy mood, like when the book she was writing wasn't going the way she wanted, and then little things set her off. Maybe she was day drinking. That'd be a good thing, and Sam said a little prayer to the god of box wine.

Mr. Morrison pushed the phone across the desk and waved his hand in a go-right-ahead gesture, and Miss

Sharette began poking in Sam's phone number on the old landline with her red correction pen, like a miniature game of whack-a-mole. Why the hell did Mr. Morrison still have that old phone, anyway? It had a curly cord and everything. The kids called her pen The Red Pen of Shame, since she seemed to get some weird thrill out of making fancy curlicue Fs on pupils' papers, and now she was using it to call his mom and read her a story about a monkey pecker.

"My mom's gonna laugh," Sam muttered under his breath.

"Hush, Sam," Mr. Morrison said, his teeth still biting the inside of his cheek, making his face look as if his mouth was more on one side than the other. The phantom smile was still on his face, and Sam held his breath. He seemed to actually be enjoying this. Principal Morrison was *enjoying* something.

"Mrs. Hamlin," Sam's teacher, her voice terse, said when his mom picked up, "This is Miss Sharette, Samuel's English teacher. I have him in the office." Sam could hear his mother's mumbled voice come over the phone from where he sat. "No, Sam's fine," she looked directly at him, "*physically*. But he wrote a troubling paper for his assignment today, and I thought you should hear it." Sam's mom mumbled some more, but he couldn't make out what she was saying.

Miss Sharette began a full-on dramatical reading, using the hand that wasn't holding the phone for emphasis; the red pen of shame rolled off Mr. Morrison's desk onto the floor and pinged the side of the metal trash can.

"Peter, the monkey lay stiff in his bed, still throbbing…"

A louder mumble came through the other end of the phone. Sam wasn't sure, but he thought he could make out the word, "Seriously?"

"…By the time the police arrived, the monkey was flaccid, pale and drooling. The veins on his head were standing out and were purple"

More mumbling along, with a very loud, "Oh my God!"

Sam hung his head, his shoulders hitching as he held back laughter. It wasn't that his stupid story was so funny; it really wasn't. What was funny was that his English teacher was being so stinking serious. As if she were Abraham Lincoln reading the Gettysburg Address.

Miss Sharette continued, "It was a schlong way to the cemetery and they rented the Oscar Meyer Weinermobile as a hearse."

Mr. Morrison turned his face toward the wall and away from them.

Miss Sharette ended with a flourish: "No one came to the monkey's funeral," she said, with a final, dramatic pause. "All of his friends thought he was a giant dick."

Miss Sharette pulled the phone from her ear and Sam could hear his mother laughing. Not just normal laughing, but barking. His mom was barking! Sam could hear Mr. Tinkles, their pet dachshund, howling in the background like a renegade fire truck, most likely thinking his mother was having some kind of medical emergency. Yep, Mom was day drinking, thank God.

"I *told* you my mom would laugh!" he said, instantly regretting it. Sometimes it took his brain a while to catch up with his mouth, but Sam knew his mom, and his mom thought weird stuff was funny—and this was as weird as it got.

The principal looked from Sam to Miss Sharette to the phone, where loud braying laughter was still spraying out sounding like a donkey stuck in an electric fence. Mr. Tinkles howled on; Sam could picture him, his head thrown back and his round wiener dog eyes rolling around in their sockets, his mouth a little O at the end of his long snout. Sam's mom was out of control, she was off the rails, she was day drinking! Sam loved his mom so damn much.

Mr. Morrison coughed, covered his mouth, hiccupped, and swallowed a strangled laugh.

Miss Sharette slammed down the phone hard enough to make a framed photograph of Mr. Morrison's family fall over. Sam was pretty sure his mom didn't even notice she'd been cut off.

Mr. Morrison rested his elbows on his desk and laid his head in his hands. "Sam, I think you'll be needing to take tomorrow off to think about all of—" Mr. Morrison made a circular gesture with his hands— "this." He righted the photo of his wife and family and continued, "There's only one period left, so gather your things, get your stuff from your locker, and head out. I'll need a note from your mom on Monday morning." Principal Morrison placed his readers back on his nose, ran his hands through his thinning hair, and pointed toward the door. By the smirk on his face, Sam was pretty sure he didn't trust himself to say another word.

Miss Sharette harrumphed, turned on the heel of her sensible shoes, and stormed out.

"You can go, Sam," Mr. Morrison wheezed. "Oh, and 'flaccid' is a pretty big word for a twelve-year-old."

Sam smiled. "Thanks sir," he said, heading to the door. "Sorry about everything."

Mr. Morrison turned his desk chair to face the wall and nodded without saying anything.

Sam left, quietly closing the door behind himself. As soon as the door clicked shut, he heard Mr. Morrison laugh so hard he thought the frosted glass Principal's Office part of the door would crack and explode like a piano dropped from a second story window. Sam gave a triumphant thumbs-up to the bewildered secretary, opened the outer office door, and headed out to his locker. He was pretty sure he'd be a legend in the teacher's lounge by the end of the day.

Sam's locker was next to the boys' bathroom across from the gym on the first floor. The school was built in the 1940's, with rich, dark woodwork and much newer drop ceilings with God-knew-what behind them; Sam always envisioned spiders and cobwebs and some feral, quasi-human ex janitor with sharp yellow teeth that fed off the blood of the younger kids who didn't do their homework. That was the kind of messed up thing that haunted his dreams sometimes—maybe he was more like his mom than he thought, and would write his own books someday.

Someone in the seventies had thought that painting the lockers bright, electric green was a good idea. The paint was chipped in places, and the dull silver of the original lockers showed through. The color was probably more appropriate for the era it was built, but people in the seventies likely thought lime green would brighten the place up. Most conceivably some old hippies that smelled like weed, or someone who owned a Pinto that hadn't exploded yet. Sam had seen YouTube videos, and those cars were ugly as a dog's butt. Who ever thought they were a good idea? He imagined businessmen in suits sitting around a table trying to design the next big thing in automobiles, and some guy yells, "Hey! Let's make a cheap-ass, homely car that'll take out a whole neighborhood if you run into the back of it with a folding baby stroller!" Anyway, they were obnoxious, old, and green, kind of like Miss Sharette. Beneath the gills of Sam's locker was a section of chipped paint shaped like a pig with five legs and a top hat—at least that was pretty darn cool.

Sam spun the combination into the lock—12-21-48, Samuel L. Jackson's birthday. Sam was a big fan. He knew Samuel L. was an old fart now, but it didn't matter, Sam loved his old movies and watched them over and over when his parents weren't home. Samuel B. loved everything about his namesake, Samuel L., including, much to the dismay of his parents, all his awe-inspiring language. Face it, sometimes "motherfucker" was the only word that worked, and it slipped out before he had time to think. Inside Sam's locker were at least a hundred pieces of chewed gum of various colors and sizes, a photo of Samuel L. Jackson's *Snakes on a Plane* poster that he'd printed out at home, and a picture of his dog, Mr. Tinkles the dachshund, in a birthday hat.

Sam shoved the books he'd be needing into his backpack, added one more piece of chewed gum to the locker door, closed it, and gave the lock a spin. As he turned to leave, Trevor Becknor, the dumb ass he'd avoided this morning by the field, was coming out of the boys' lavatory. Sam could smell smoke, sweat, and unwashed denim as he approached.

"Hey asshole!" Trevor hollered at him, his voice echoing off the rows of lockers as he sauntered over. "What the hell are you doing in the hall between classes?"

Trevor was taller than all the kids in fifth grade; he'd flunked second grade and then fourth. There was a huge difference in size between twelve and fourteen, and the jerk used it to his advantage every chance he got.

Trevor lived with his mom and stepdad on the south side of town, across the street from a store called Dan's Used Furniture and Supreme Meats. His temper was legendary, and most of the kids stayed clear of him; no one really knew him well, as far as Sam was aware. Sam's mom once said Trevor was angry at the world due to his living conditions. All Sam knew about Trevor was that his mom had shot his real dad dead in the street after a big argument. The story grew to legendary proportions over the years, and Sam imagined her shooting his dad in the middle of the road blowing smoke off the gun's muzzle, and twirling it three times before returning it to its holster. He supposed seeing your mom shoot the shit out of your dad would screw anyone up. Sam could appreciate being screwed up by your circumstances, but he didn't appreciate being the screwed up kid's punching bag. Sam had no idea why Trevor had singled him out, so he stayed clear of the older boy's path, and his fists.

"I'm going home," Sam said, shoving the last of his books into his backpack, "family emergency."

Trevor grabbed a fistful of Sam's Dr. Pepper shirt.

"Why?'

"Family emergency!"

Trevor gave him a shake. "Bullshit. Tell me the truth," he snarled, spittle collecting in the corners of his mouth. Sam felt the back of his shirt rip.

The door to the gym opened and out came coach Stephens. Trevor loosened his grasp on Sam's shirt.

"You boys should be in class," Coach said, looking from one to the other.

"Principal Morrison sent me home, Coach, I'm just getting my books."

Trevor glared at him. He'd caught him in a lie.

"Trevor, get back to class, I sent you to the lav twenty minutes ago. Head out, go."

Trevor headed back toward the gym, turned, walked backward glaring at Sam, then pointed two fingers at his eyes and then toward Sam, in the universal *I'm watching you* gesture. He made a slicing motion across his throat. Sam knew exactly what that meant too.

Trevor punched open the double doors to the gym, and the sound of screeching tennis shoes on the polished gym floor punctuated by the dribble of a basketball filled the hallway.

"Best head out now, Sam," said coach Stephens with a grin. "I hope you're not in too much trouble over the monkey thing."

"Me too," Sam said, shaking his head. "Thanks." Wow, news traveled fast.

Sam headed out the school's double doors and down the stairs, found his bike parked in the bike rack, knelt and spun in the lock's combination, which was also Samuel L. Jackson's birthday. "Samuel L Jackson wouldn't take shit like this from some idiot named *Trevor*," he whispered to himself, as he stowed the lock in his backpack.

Sam threw a leg over his bike and pedaled off through the parking lot. He had ten dollars in his pocket from his allowance and he was going to stop and get a soda and some candy on the way home. "I need a drink," he muttered. His mom said that all the time when she had a bad day. Sam squeezed his eyes closed for an instant. Jesus, he was turning into his mother. What a terrifying idea.

The thought of soda and candy brightened him a bit, and he knew he would need some sugar-induced courage to face his parents. He figured his mom was probably still laughing, but that would wear off by the time he got home, and she'd certainly called his dad. Sam pedaled quickly through the parking lot, turned the corner before leaving the school grounds, and threw a mighty middle finger in the direction of Miss Sharette's old black Cadillac.

"Shit."

She was standing right next to the damn thing looking like Smokey the Bear in pink lipstick. Sam peeled out without looking around. He could feel Miss Sharette's eyes burning holes into his back and he pedaled quickly toward town, his feet a blur of motion.

Chapter Two

Sorry, We're All Out of Bratwurst

Main Street in Patton, Colorado was a bustle of tourists and the small businesses that catered to them. Art galleries that featured local artists, craft stores with home-made soaps, candles, stationery, jams, jellies, and shirts that said, "Patton Colorado! Home of the Fighting Panthers!" There were restaurants that made their own craft beers, most of which sucked, according to Sam's grandpa; a trading post that sold things to tourists like taffy, rubber bows and arrows and an assortment of polished rocks; a bakery; a beauty salon; and Sam's favorite store: Mark's Market, the home of all things that could rot the teeth right out of your face.

Sam parked his bike in front of the convenience store, and as he was about to enter, he noticed that Miss Sharette was checking out at the counter. Mr. Bolton, the owner and manager, was handing her a lottery ticket and a pack of Camels. Sam pressed himself against the outside wall and held his breath. He stepped around the corner and waited—there was no way in hell he wanted to see her again today. Not only had his mom laughed in her face, the other teachers were laughing too. It had to be humiliating, and he felt a pang of guilt.

Miss Sharette exited carrying two plastic bags of items. She walked quickly to the crosswalk at the corner and crossed the street. She lived a few blocks from Main Street in a big Victorian house—the largest in all of Patton. It was one of the first brick homes built in the area and had belonged to Walter Patton, who made his fortune in gold, and was later Patton's first mayor.

Patton, Colorado is a small town surrounded by prairie and farms, and about 150 miles northeast of Denver. Its population is just about 3,000 good souls, if you didn't count Trevor Becknor and his crazy mom, Helen. Mayor Walter Patton lived in what the locals call the Patton House until his death in 1939, whereupon his son, Walter Patton II, having made his own fortune in oil, lived there as well. His son, Walter Patton III, was also an oil man as well as mayor in the sixties, and lived in the manor until his death in 1971. Miss Sharette was the next owner, and had called the Patton House home ever since the last of the Pattons' passing.

Seeing Miss Sharette, Sam concluded she must have gone home after sixth period, when he saw her last in the parking lot at school. Her car wasn't in the store parking lot, so she had to have taken her black caddy home and then walked the two blocks to the market for smokes. Lucky, lucky him. This day just keeps getting better and better, he thought, risking a peek around the corner.

Miss Sharette was across Main Street and heading toward her house. Sam inched back to the main door and slipped inside. Whew, that was a close one.

Sam waved to Mr. Bolton, who was manning the counter, and turned into the candy aisle. He picked out a few Twizzlers along with three Milky Way candy bars, and on his way to the counter he grabbed a two-liter Coke from the cooler. He took his items to the counter, and Mr. Bolton gave him a smile. "You're not going to sleep all night, buddy. That's a lot of sugar and caffeine."

"I've had a long day, Mr. Bolton. I'll probably eat them all before I get home." Mr. Bolton smiled and threw in a handful of gum. "A couple for the road."

Sam smiled back and thanked him, pulled the ten-dollar bill from his pocket, and laid it on the counter. Jenny Clark, whom he knew from his math class, came in the door, and as a breeze caught the bill it fluttered to the floor. Sam bent to get it, and noticed that the lottery ticket Mrs. Sharette had purchased was lying on the black-and-white tile floor next to his ten. He picked up the bill and the ticket, looked both ways, shrugged, and shoved the ticket into his pocket. He wasn't about to chase Miss Sharette down, and his grandma said that lottery tickets never win, so he'd give the ticket to his mom and tell her he found it—which was, in a roundabout way, true. How much could it have cost his teacher? A dollar, or at tops, five? He'd had enough trauma that day to earn a few bucks.

Sam paid his bill and turned to leave. "Hi Jenny, bye Mr. Bolton, and thanks for the—"

There was a mad squeal of tires from the street, followed by a crash and a chorus of alarmed screams. Mr. Bolton, Sam, and Jenny ran to the window.

The Dan's Used Furniture and Supreme Meats truck had skidded and slammed into the light pole and was on its side, a dark, oily smoke rising from the front end.

"Someone was hit!" Mr. Bolton slapped a hand to his forehead, gasped, and dived for the store phone to call 911.

Jenny covered her mouth with both hands and muffled a scream. Sam peered around the rack of beef jerky. The delivery van from Dan's Used Furniture and Supreme Meats was a twisted wreck. The tires were still spinning from the collision, and the mangled front bumper clattered on the sidewalk. Next to the back tire he could see lower legs and a pair of feet, one still inside a black sensible shoe. Sam's mouth dropped open and he sucked in a breath. Miss Sharette had been hit by the Dan's Used Furniture and Supreme Meats van. The logo panel on the van, a smiling cow balanced on one hoof standing on a sofa, had lost a bolt and hung upside down by a thread; the cartoon cow creaked and rocked and looked like an upside-down cow bench pressing a sofa.

Why the hell was Miss Sharette in the street? She had been safely across when Sam had snuck into the door.

He groaned. She was coming back to get her damn lotto ticket. Well, shit.

Sam shoved the door open and dashed across the street, his plastic bag filled with candy and soda dropped and forgotten. Pushing his way through the growing crowd, he knelt by his English teacher and looked into her gray eyes, which, still sharp and piercing, bored into his own. Her breath came in shallow, rapid bursts, her chest lifting and falling with each one. The door to the van had fallen open, and there were packages of steaks sealed in white butcher paper laying all around her. Loose bratwursts, free of their paper wrappings, bounced and rolled toward the gutter.

"Oh my God, Miss Sharette!"

"Sam…"

She had blood pooling from behind her head, and her legs were at unnatural angles; more blood dripped from the side of her mouth, and a thin trickle ran from each nostril. Her campfire weasel coat had a jagged tear in it. The blood seeping from the back of her head was growing into a larger puddle by the second, the boundary of the thick red liquid inching its way toward Sam's white tennis shoes. This was bad. Really, horrible, mind blowing bad.

Another package of loose bratwurst rolled past; the wheel of the Dan's Used Furniture and Supreme Meats truck bounced and wobbled by to land with a soft thud in the gutter.

Scared shitless, Sam put his hand on her shoulder. Sirens wailed, first responders on their way to the scene of the accident. He could hear Jenny still screaming in the background, but it was foggy and distant. The driver of the truck, Bobby Ruiz, had gotten out of the van and was also kneeling by Miss Sharette. He'd gently placed his jacket under her head, and it was soaked through with blood. Bobby's eyes were wide, and he seemed to be in shock.

"I'm so sorry," he whispered, tears falling down his cheeks, "I didn't see you; I didn't see you. Oh my God!" Bobby looked anxiously toward the direction of the oncoming sirens. "Hurry!"

This is all my fault, Sam thought. He should have instantly run after her to give back the lottery ticket. He should have gone directly to the door, called out and walked over to hand it to her. What was he thinking? He may write shitty essays about monkey peckers, but he wasn't a thief…or a murderer. Sam knelt next to Bobby, knowing his face was a mirror image of the van driver's. He took the lotto ticket from his pocket and held it out toward her, "You dropped this, you need to take it back, it's yours, I found it, I'm so sorry, I shouldn't have picked it up, I didn't know…"

Miss Sharette lifted her other hand as if the action took the last ounce of energy she had; she grasped Sam's wrist with manicured red nails. Her grip was surprisingly strong, her fingernails cold claws that dug into his skin.

"That's mine," she whispered, in a tone that sounded to Sam as if it were coming from underwater, "mine, Sam." Her eyes bored into him and his blood ran cold. Pink lipstick and blood stuck to her teeth.

Miss Sharette coughed a deep, rattling cough and her hand loosened its grip on his wrist, then dropped heavily across her chest. She hissed out a breath that sounded a lot like the air leaking from the cow truck's tire. Her body shuddered, her eyes focused squarely on Sam, and then they went muzzy, clouded over, aimlessly focused on something behind him. "Is it…you?" she whispered, a small smile on her face. "It is, it's you…"

Sam looked over his shoulder, who was she talking to? No one was there.

Her breath hitched once, twice, and then ceased, her hazy eyes were unfocused, her body still, her face calm. Sam had never seen anyone dead before, but he knew that dead looked just like this. This was some major deadness. Sam could hear her voice in his head, "Teachers! Changing Lives One Child at a Time!"

Sam's face contorted and he started to cry, his brain bouncing from one guilty thought to the next, trying to make sense of everything.

A hand on his shoulder helped him up and off of his knees. It was Jimmy Cruz, the sheriff of Patton. His partner Stan Lender was talking quietly to a weeping Bobby Ruiz. Everyone in town called Jimmy and Stan Andy and Barney. Jimmy hated it. Stan thought it was hilarious and had a Barney Fife shrine in his basement.

"You need to move out of the way, Sammy," Jimmy said gently, when the paramedics pushed their way through to kneel by Miss Sharette's body. Sam hurried back to the sidewalk, nearly tripping over his forgotten snack bag and a few stray sausages. Tears streaked Sam's face; Jenny was still shrieking; another ambulance wailed in the distance. Sam noticed there was blood on his fingers and tennis shoes. He choked down a scream and felt he might vomit. He ran back toward Mark's Market, almost toppling Mr. Bolton in the process. Sam's eyes were blurry with tears, and his heart hammered so hard in his chest he feared it might burst. He mounted his bike and sped off toward home. The voice in his head echoed, "Teachers! Changing Lives One Child at a Time!"

The crumpled lottery ticket was shoved deep into the pocket of his jeans, and later he would notice that there was blood on that as well.

Chapter Three

Wiener Dogs Should Mind Their Business

Beth had called Jack at work. Her husband worked as an assistant manager at the local grocery store. She was put on hold, and the damned Carpenters supplied the wait music. "Hurry up Jack…"

"Hello, this is Jack Hamlin, how may I help you?"

"Jack!"

"Beth? What's the matter?"

"I'm not sure, but you better come home STAT. I just got a phone call from the school and Sam's in trouble."

"What kind of trouble?"

"I don't know! Something about a monkey."

"A monkey?"

"A monkey!"

"Beth, have you been drinking?"

"No! Well, a little, but I can't make this kind of shit up!"

"I'm on my way." Jack set the phone down, rolled his eyes and went to retrieve his jacket. A *monkey?*

Dennis, the store manager, was sorting papers in the office. Jack stuck his head in and said he was leaving early.

"How come, buddy?"

"I have to go home, something about my kid and a goddamn monkey."

Dennis set his paperwork down and yelled after him, "Jack, where in the hell did your kid get a fucking monkey?"

Beth Hamlin was thinking about her goofy kid and his English assignment. She'd laughed so hard that her ribs hurt, and she'd had to wash her face because her mascara had run into her eyes, making them sting. That kid was just like her. The serious tone of Sam's English teacher's voice still rang in her ears. "All his friends thought he was a giant dick."

She shook her head and bark-laughed again. She knew she'd have to punish Sam just because it was rather inappropriate, but in her heart she hoped she could get her hands on a copy of the assignment and frame it.

Beth poured herself a generous glass of Malbec. Mr. Tinkles, their dachshund, watched her intently. "Shut up," she told him, waggling a finger in his face, and booping him on the nose. "Don't judge."

She swirled the red liquid around and sniffed it appreciatively. It was two-thirty in the afternoon and all her housework was finished. The bedding was washed, she had a pot roast in the crockpot, and she'd worked for three hours on her second novel. Her first was a cliche-filled three hundred pages of mommy porn called *His Strong Arms*. She wrote under the pseudonym Blaze Bolivar. It was smutty garbage, really, but had sold quite a few copies to lonely, love-starved housewives. Now she was halfway into her second novel, *His Deep Love*. The protagonist was a Navy Seal named Javier with a heart of gold and a secret bank account worth billions. She hoped it did as well as the first novel, because she couldn't see a third in the series; she was running out of words that meant penis.

Beth was happy with the day's progress and had earned a glass of wine along with a very late lunch, but she'd mostly earned the wine. She drank wine every day. She knew she probably shouldn't, and she wasn't to the point of stumbling around crashing into things. Well, except for that one time at her birthday party with Jack's grandmother's vase.

Beth took a long sip of the Malbec. She couldn't remember a thing about that, but Jack reminded her of it over and over. She was sure he was embellishing a bit more each time he told the story, he had to be. Supposedly, after changing into the outfit she bought for a long-ago belly dancing class, she had been showing off her hula skills in the living room, and Great-grandma's vase had gone flying off the shelf and crashed into a million pieces on the floor. She'd dropped the wine bottle as well. Who needs a glass when it's a party, right?

The only clue to her inebriation was the red splat on the living room rug. When she got up later that morning, Jack had drawn an outline around it with black magic marker, and it looked to her as if there had been a murder, right next to the fireplace. The new rug came out of her private mad money savings account. Beth took another sip and rolled her eyes. So much for the new patio furniture she'd been saving for. It was a hideous vase anyway, and it *was* her birthday. Cutting loose on your birthday was expected, and she'd cut loose to the tune of seven hundred and fifty dollars for the new throw rug.

Beth stretched back in her chair, sighed, and put her feet up. It was a beautiful spring day, and she really should be outside doing some weeding, but that could wait. The baby was sleeping and it was time to take a lunch break and an hour of peace before the boys got home.

The Hamlins' house was clean-ish but not perfect. How could it be with three kids and two bedrooms? It had seemed so much larger when she and Jack moved here ten years ago. Where did all the space go? The kids ate it, she thought. They grew larger and ate it up just as fast as Mr. Tinkles ate up those bacon treats he loved so much.

Sam and Ben shared a bedroom. They were three years apart, and at that age they were best friends one minute and couldn't stand the sight of one another the next. Their bedroom had two twin beds, two nightstands, two dressers and a shared desk: there wasn't much room for more. It was a tangle of mismatched furniture. Ben's side was filled with dinosaur posters, plastic action figures, and dozens of rocks that he'd found in various places. Sam's side had a Samuel L. Jackson poster, video game posters, various band posters—none of whom she was familiar with—and the largest of all, a huge poster from the movie *Alien*. There were dozens of alien action figures beneath it including his favorite xenomorph from that old movie that terrified her. When she'd seen it in the theater, she'd freaked out at one point, her arms had shot up, and unfortunately she was holding a jumbo popcorn at the time. Thank God the man behind her had a sense of humor, because it landed like popcorn snow—right in his lap. She loved Sigourney

Weaver, but, Jesus Christ. Stop running around in your underwear and get out of Dodge.

It was a very crowded, very male-child room that always smelled a little like socks and sweaty kid hair.

Beth thought about refilling her half-empty wine glass, but knew Jack and Sam would be home soon and there'd be "monkey business" to deal with. She laughed out loud, then hiccupped.

As much as she complained, Beth's kids were her life. Boze was the baby. He was a three-year-old explosion of a child. It was almost a good thing that he slept on a toddler bed in the room she'd shared for the last ten years with Jack. If he didn't, they'd find him up in a tree someplace, or out on the highway. That kid was quick. And sneaky.

Beth had come up with both the older boys' names, and Jack had gone along with it. She swore to him that if they had any more kids, he'd get to choose names. After a surprise pregnancy, Jack had chosen the name Boze after his favorite headphones, substituting a Z for the S, which he thought looked weak and lame. He thought it sounded *unique*. Beth wasn't sure what a sixty-year-old Boze would have to say about his name, but in the end, she'd caved. Boze it was.

When Boze was born, Ben had had an issue saying his name, and it came out Bobo; and this, ladies and gentlemen, is how Beth Hamlin, a grown-ass, independent woman of age thirty-nine, ended up with kids named Samuel, Benjamin, and Bobo. She even called him Bobo now.

Beth lifted her glass in a toast. Bobo. Her cousin Dorothy had a dog named Bobo when she was a kid.

Setting the glass down, she laid her head heavily on

the chair back and looked up at the ceiling. Mr. Tinkles the dachshund jumped into her lap, made a circle, once, twice, and plopped down. Beth absentmindedly stroked his head. They needed more room. There was not room for three kids and her sanity in this little house. Once the book sold, once Jack got that promotion they'd promised him for two years, once she robbed a bank, once she found a bag of money buried in the backyard…

Chapter Four

So Much for The Pot Roast

Sam dropped his bike on the front step and blasted through the door. His mother and father were sitting on the living room couch with Ben between them, obviously waiting for him. Bobo, wearing only his Spiderman pullup training pants, bounced on the recliner with Mr. Tinkles looking on and barking. It was loud and crazy and way too normal. The world had changed for Sam, and the fact that his parents and his brothers and his dog were all doing such…ordinary things…seemed unthinkable to Sam. It seemed wrong.

His dad said, "Sammy, I heard about the trouble at school today." He swallowed a laugh. "And even though the whole ordeal is hilarious, we're going to have to talk about—"

"Miss Sharette got hit by the Dan's Used Furniture & Supreme Meats Van! I was there! I saw it! She's dead." Sam started to shake again.

"Whoa!" said Ben, "Like really, seriously, totally dead?"

"Like seriously motherfucking dead, Ben, and I saw it!"

"Dude."

Bobo continued to jump on the recliner. "Motha-faw-king!"

Jack shot Bobo a look, stood and went to his eldest son, and held him at arm's length by the shoulders. "Jesus, Sammy. Are you o—wait, is that blood?"

Beth rushed to her son. "Blood?" She clutched Sam by the arms and gasped as she took in the blood on his hands and shoes. "Is this yours? Oh my God, Sammy! Let me see." She began to examine Sam's face, her hands turning his head from side to side, her brown eyes wide and afraid. "Jack, call an ambulance!"

"No. Mom, stop it!" Sam pulled away. "It's hers! She was bleeding and her legs were backward and bratwursts were rolling everywhere and I think I'm going to throw up." Sam raced to the bathroom and slammed the door shut.

Beth stood there feeling stunned and leaned into her husband, her eyes focused on something beyond the room. "Jesus, Jack, I bought the pot roast I have in the crockpot from Dan's Used Furniture & Supreme Meats…" Her hand shot to her mouth, and she whispered, "I think I bought the crockpot there, too…I don't remember."

Jack nodded at his wife's rambling, and hugged her.

"Jack, I just spoke with her this afternoon. She can't be dead. Maybe she's just hurt or in the hospital…call Andy and Barney and find out? Please call them." Beth began to pace. She picked up her wine glass and gulped the remaining inch. "I mean, she's a strange, bitter old woman, but for God's sake, no one deserves to be taken out by a meat truck."

There was a crash from the kitchen. "I'll get Bobo." Jack made a hasty retreat to the kitchen to retrieve his toddler. "Get out of the microwave!" she heard him yell.

Beth could hear water running in the bathroom. She dropped down onto the couch and put an arm around Ben. "Poor Miss Sharette," she said. "Poor Sam for seeing it all."

"Maybe we should have pizza for dinner, Mom," Ben said.

Beth hugged him tightly. "You're right. Let's go throw out the pot roast, maybe the crockpot too."

Sam closed the door to the bathroom and lunged for the toilet. He retched, and his baloney sandwich from lunch made an encore with a pink splash. *She's dead, and I killed her,* he thought, and retched again. His stomach hurt. His head hurt. And most of all, his heart hurt. Sam couldn't imagine how Bobby Ruiz felt. Together, he and his father Manuel owned Dan's Used Furniture & Supreme Meats—as far as anyone knew, there wasn't and had never been a Dan associated with the company. Today, it had been Bobby driving the white cow truck that struck and killed his teacher.

Sam rested his head on the rim of the toilet and took a few deep, steadying breaths. On wobbling knees, he got to his feet and went to the sink. He turned on the cold water, ran his hands under the stream and splashed his face, took a mouthful of water and rinsed the sour taste from his tongue, and spat into the green sink. The bathroom on the main floor of his house had the original green 1960s-style tile. The tile was behind the shower and wrapped around one wall, bordered in black bull-nose edging. The toilet, the pedestal sink, and bathtub were also green. His mom had gone with that retro look and put up a green-and-orange-flowered seventies-style shower curtain. It was all shockingly horrible and wonderful at the same time.

Sam looked at himself in the mirror. His skin was very pale, and his black curls made his pasty face even more pronounced. His brown eyes looked bloodshot and watery. He studied his reflection and scrubbed his face with both hands, dragging his lower eyelids down and pulling his mouth open. He opened the medicine cabinet to get his toothbrush, and a red pen of shame toppled from the top shelf into the sink along with the toothpaste and a package of dental floss.

Sam stared at the pen in the sink and slammed the cabinet closed. The green and orange curtain rippled behind his reflection. Startled, he spun around, gasped, swallowed a scream, threw open the bathroom door, and dashed into his mother's arms.

Beth looked up as Sam bolted from the bathroom, sending the door slamming into the wall. He ran to her, shaking, and clung to her, burying his head on her shoulder, and suddenly, irrelevantly, aware he was almost as tall as she was.

He was full-on weeping now. Beth hugged her son tightly and stroked his black curls. "Sammy, it's going to be okay," she said, but her voice was shaky.

Sam grabbed Jack's hand, pulled him into the bathroom, and stared into the sink. Nothing.

"I thought I saw something. I thought I saw…" Sam stopped, not wanting to have to explain what really happened that day to Miss Sharette.

"Saw what, Sammy?" Jack grabbed his boy by the shoulders, his face full of concern. "Are you okay? Tell me what's happening."

Sam shook his head and hugged his father. "I don't know, I'm just really freaked out."

Bobo toddled over and hugged Sam around the legs. Sam wiped his eyes and looked down at his baby brother. The worried look on his chubby face made Sam smile despite everything.

Bobo took Sam's hand. "Let's play Legos!"

Sam picked up his little brother. "Okay, Bobo, let's go to my room and play Legos."

Bobo pulled three Legos out of his Spiderman pullup training pants. "Yeah!"

Sam gave the little monster a watery grin and carried him off. Ben followed along, "I'm in!"

Behind them, in the green retro bathroom, the seventies-style shower curtain rippled once more.

Sam, Ben and Bobo sat on the floor, a pile of colorful Legos between them. Bobo's stack of all red Legos was about a foot tall.

Sam looked up at Ben and asked his brother, "Ben? Have you ever seen anything weird happen in the bathroom?'

Ben lifted his head, "Like what?"

"I don't know, like something creepy."

"Well," Ben said lowering his voice, "one time I went in to pee, and I saw the shower curtain moving."

Sam's eyes got wide and he grabbed his brother's arm. "What?"

"Yeah, I ripped it open and it was just Bobo sitting in the tub playing with a jar of mustard."

Sam released Ben's arm.

"Scared the crap out of me."

"Crap!" said Bobo. He knew all the words he wasn't supposed to parrot. It was uncanny.

The doorbell rang, and they knew it had to be the pizza. Bobo was the first up, toppling the red Lego tower and hot-dogging it out of the room toward the kitchen.

"I don't feel very hungry," Sam muttered, looking down at the Lego wreckage.

"It's sausage and pepperoni, extra cheese too."

"Let's go."

Young boys live to eat.

Dinner felt surreal to Sam, even though the pizza was huge and cheesy, and his mom was just drunk enough to be funny. It was all too normal after the day he'd had. He glanced over at Bobo. Bobo was lying back in his booster chair with pepperoni slices on his eyes and his arms in the air. As normal as it gets around here.

Everyone seemed keen on keeping dinner lighthearted, and it was obviously forced. His mom and dad kept looking over at him with worried looks on their faces. Ben babbled on about his Forest Troopers meeting and how they were busy putting together a survival kit. Sam stared down at his pizza and gagged. It was oozing sauce over his plate.

"I'm tired, may I be excused?" he asked.

His mom touched his arm. "Call me if you need me, okay?"

Dad nodded in agreement.

Sam pushed his chair back with a screech, walked to his room, and found some clean pajamas. At least, he thought they were clean. He sniffed them. Maybe they weren't.

As he stepped out of his jeans, the lottery ticket slid from his pocket. He'd forgotten about it. It made him gasp and he bent to get it, wadded it up, and threw it into the trashcan by the desk. He lay back on his bed, and Mr. Tinkles hopped up next to him and curled close to his chest. He stroked his belly and hugged him. "Good boy," he murmured.

Mr. Tinkles had an uncanny way of knowing who needed him most at the moment, and right now it was Sam.

They were both fast asleep before seven-thirty, Mr. Tinkles snoring louder than Grandpa. Witnessing an accidental death takes a lot out of a person.

Javier pulled Alejandra into a tight embrace, his hands tangling in her long, dark, luxurious hair. His tan, muscled body molded to her generous curves, and she moaned. His lips met hers, and her mouth yielded to him, giving way to the only thing she'd wanted for so long. His love. His touch. His hard, girthy...

"His *whatever*," muttered Beth. She shook her head and closed the laptop.

"Girthy." Beth plunked her head twice on the laptop case. "*Girthy*, for Christ's sake." Finishing this novel was going to be harder than Javier.

Beth pushed the laptop aside. She needed a Javier in her life. Actually, she wanted Jack to be her Javier. The billionaire part—their sex life was fine, if not sneaky with three kids in the house.

Bobo was at Beth's parents' house today so that she could get some work done. Her dad had picked him up at about 7 A.M., and they were headed to the park. Grandpa was Bobo's favorite human in the world. Ben was off to school after a big argument and a "stomach ache" brought on by his brother being home that Friday because of inappropriate-essay-induced *monkeypox*, and Sam was lying on the couch with his iPad watching who-knew-what. There was lots of shooting and tires squealing.

She figured a bit of mindless cleaning might clear her head and give her some more ideas on where to go with Alejandra Moreno and Javier Santiago, the billionaire Navy Seal. She gathered the broom, dusting supplies, and window cleaner. She'd start cleaning where it was needed the most—the boy's room.

What a mess. She couldn't tell what was dirty when it came to their clothes, and she refused to sniff them to find out. Beth finally threw it all in the dirty hamper and went from there. The window was covered in boy and dog nose prints; she spritzed it with window cleaner and got to work.

After twenty minutes of tidying, dusting, and polishing, she looked around with satisfaction. She set her hands on her hips. It was as good as it was going to get.

Emptying the trash was last on the list. Coke cans, a few candy bar wrappers, wadded doodling papers, and… what was this? A lottery ticket. The scratch-off kind. Interesting.

Beth propped the broom against the door and looked at it. It had not been scratched. One of the boys must have found it and thought it was junk…which it probably was. She took a fingernail and scratched off a number. Let's see what Mountain Millions had to give her today.

The next number matched. As did the next. Yes! Fifty bucks. She scratched another…it matched. Beth's mouth dropped open. Five hundred dollars! Her hands shook as she scratched the next. It must be a mistake—the next number matched. Fifty thousand dollars?

Beth began to sweat and dropped the dust rag. One more.

She sat on the desk chair and closed her eyes and scratched, afraid to look. She stared at the paper in her hand. Five million dollars. Five. Million. Dollars. It could not be real.

Maybe she was dreaming. Maybe she was drunk. Maybe she was stone cold sober and holding a fortune. It had to be some type of gag ticket because, five million dollars?!

Beth took the ticket and walked onto the porch. She dialed the number on the back. She read them the info and serial numbers. She took a photo and sent it to the woman on the phone. The woman confirmed it was real. It was real. They were rich! Not as rich as Javier, but fuck you Javier and your girthy sexcalibur!

Beth fainted flat out on the porch.

"Mom! Jesus, Mom!" Sam was kneeling over his mother and tapping her cheek. "Talk to me, Mom!"

Beth blinked her eyes open and then slowly sat up. "I'm okay, baby, just got a little lightheaded." She pulled herself up to a sitting position. Then she remembered. In her hand was the lottery ticket. She'd clung to it even in unconsciousness.

Beth grabbed Sam and squeezed him. "I'm okay, Sammy… but we need to make some phone calls. Right. Now."

Sam saw the ticket in her hand and felt lightheaded himself. There was a tiny drop of blood on the ticket. Was Mom calling the police because he killed his English teacher? "I don't want to go to jail, Mom!"

"Jail? What are you talking about? I was thinking more like…Disney World."

Everyone sat around the dining room table at Grandma and Grandpa's house. The lottery ticket was in the center of the table, and they were staring at it like it was a big chunk of radioactive plutonium.

Grandpa spoke first. "I want to buy that dive bar over on Federal Boulevard and call it Al's Beer Joint."

Grandma shot him a look. "I think you should put it all in the bank and not touch it. It'll gain interest, and then when you die it can be your kids' money."

Jack was having none of it. "We need a bigger house. One that fits a pool table and a home theater."

Ben stood up and jumped around. "I want my own room with a fridge in it, my own phone, and a samurai sword!"

Bobo clapped happily. "Legos! I want Legos!"

Sam remained silent, staring at the blood spot on the ticket.

"What about you, Sammy? What do you want?" asked Grandpa

"I want…I want Miss Sharette to be alive again."

Everyone frowned.

"That's really sweet of you, baby," said Beth. She squeezed her sensitive son's hand and pulled him close.

"What about you, Beth, what do you want?" Jack asked her.

She thought about it for a moment, "I have to go with you on this one, Jack. We need a bigger house. One with enough bedrooms and a home office for me. And a wine cellar."

"And enough room for me when I'm old," said grandma.

"What about grandpa?" asked Ben.

"Eh, he'll be dead by then."

"I want to stay in Patton no matter what," Beth added. "I love it here, I grew up here, and it's home." Everyone agreed with that.

"Is that ketchup on the ticket?" asked Grandma.

Sam sank deeper into his chair. Ketchup.

"You better be careful with it. What if it gets lost, or the baby eats it. You can be so careless, Beth. When I was your age—"

Jack stopped her. "We'll cash it in tomorrow, and in the meantime, it will be safe here in my wallet."

The ticket fluttered on the table as if caught by a draft. Jack picked it up, folded it, and placed it behind his driver's license in his wallet.

"Settled. We're house hunting, starting tomorrow."

It was Saturday morning. Beth stared at the online balance of their checking account. $4,200,573 after taxes. It was unbelievable.

She opened Amazon and bought herself an expensive laptop so she could finish the adventures of Javier and Alejandra in style. Guilt flooded her. It was hard to get over spending guilt when being thrifty was a part of your life, and always had been. What the hell. She bought herself an expensive leather case to go along with it.

Beth picked up the phone and called her friend Judy, the realtor.

"Hi Judy, you're not going to believe this, but we need your help, and money is not an issue."

Chapter Five

The Shart Likes Birds?

Saturday afternoon, Sam met his friend Hank at the park. Sam and Hank had known one another since they were babies. Hank's mom, Judy, was a realtor, and good friends with Sam's mom. Sometimes she came over to drink wine, and things got noisy.

Hank flopped down in the grass by the old oak. "What's so important you couldn't tell me on the phone?" Hank said. "You sounded like some guy on a cop show, all secretive and stuff." He pushed strands of sweaty blonde hair out of his eyes. He'd just run six blocks to meet Sam, and Hank was not the athletic type.

"Miss Sharette is dead."

"I know!" said Hank. "My parents were talking about it at dinner. Smashed by the Dan's Used Furniture and Supreme Meats truck." He drifted in thought for a moment, "Does this mean we won't have that stupid test next Wednesday?"

"Jesus, Hank!" Sam said, turning to look at him. "Miss Sharette is dead, and I saw it happen, and I killed her." He looked at his friend, dead serious, "You can't say anything. To anybody."

"You killed The Shart?" Hank said. "Was she flunking you?"

Sam leaned in and whispered, "She bought a lottery scratch-off ticket at Mark's Market, and she dropped it. I saw it and I pocketed it. Next thing I know she's dead on the pavement. She was coming back to get it, and BLAM!" Sam clapped his hands. "Bobby Ruiz plowed into her."

"Whoa, dude," Hank said, staring at his friend. "No one could stand her and she smelled like a weenie roast, but…" Hank shook his head. "Whoa."

"And get this," Sam whispered, "my mom found the ticket in my trash can and it's worth five million dollars." Sam squeezed his eyes closed. "I'm a killer *and* a thief." He fell back into the grass next to Hank. "I'm going to juvie forever."

"Dude. You can buy your way out of juvie for that kind of money! You're rich, buddy!"

"I feel sick."

"Does anyone know? About the ticket and you murdering the Shart, I mean?"

"Not yet." Sam let out a frustrated breath.

Across the park, Jenny Clark and her twin sister Jaimie were spinning slowly on the ancient merry-go-round that they called The Kid Launcher. It had to be the last one on the planet. Weren't they outlawed? The metal squeaked with each turn, and the twins seemed to be deep in conversation.

"Maybe we should tell the Clarks. They're the smartest kids in school, and remember Jaimie's presentation on problem solving got some kind of award?"

Sam peeked over at the Clarks. Jenny had been in Mark's Market the day of the crash. Maybe she'd seen him pick up the ticket. Maybe she could help. Maybe the FBI would use her as a witness to put him away forever.

The Clarks saw Sam and Hank staring at them and they waved in unison, hopped off the Kid Launcher, and walked over.

"I can't believe the Shart is dead," said Jaimie. Jenny visibly cringed. "Our parents want to send Jenny to therapy for being there and seeing it."

"I keep having nightmares about blood and intestines and cows and bratwurst," she whispered.

The Clarks were identical as far as anyone could see, but with one unique, and outstanding, trait. Jenny had one blue eye and one brown eye, as did her sister. They were just reversed. They were mirror twins. It was the coolest thing Sam had ever seen.

Sam and Hank filled the Clarks in on the events of the last two days, leaving nothing out.

"Sam, you're not going to jail," Jenny said. "You didn't push her in front of Manny and Bobby's meat truck. You didn't pick up the ticket knowing she'd be hit and killed in the street. It was a huge, unfortunate series of events and you aren't to blame. I can see how it must make you feel guilty, but legally you are not to blame." She looked directly at Sam. "It was just a terrible accident." She paused and thought for a moment. "Maybe be sure to spend a bit of the money on something Miss Sharette would like. Like… um."

No one said a word. No one had known her well enough to make a suggestion.

"Weasel rescue?" asked Hank, lifting one hand in an I-don't-have-a-clue gesture. "Why don't we walk by her house and see if we can find some clues."

"It's worth a try?" Jaimie said.

Sam stood up and brushed the grass off his jeans, "I think that's a great idea. It's kind of creepy, but," he said, slinging his backpack over his shoulder, "I want to do something nice for her because I feel terrible about what happened. But I can never, ever tell my parents."

The four kids left the park and headed down Main. They turned west on Parker Street, and one block ahead was Mrs. Sharette's old Victorian house. It was two stories tall, painted dark gray with light gray trim, and looked like a ghost factory. The house was surrounded by a black wrought-iron fence, and there was a large front porch that wrapped around almost to the back yard. On the left side of the house was an ornate circular turret. The attic window faced front and was half-moon shaped, and dark. When Jenny pushed open the iron gate, it screamed as if it were being tortured.

"Oil that thing." whispered Jenny.

They dropped their bikes just inside the gateway and walked up to the front door. In the window was a NO SOLICITORS sign.

Jaimie peeked inside. "It's totally dark in there, I can't see anything at all." She walked to the next window. "A fireplace…and a picture of some old guy above the mantle…a couple of chairs that look like spiders would crawl out of them…"

The friends headed around to the back of the house. There was a small table on a brick patio, and from the back wall hung a few metal bird sculptures and an assortment of bird feeders.

"She liked birds. The Shart liked birds." Hank seemed surprised; it was a normal thing to like, and in the mind of a twelve-year-old, teachers weren't supposed to do normal things. They were teachers, not people.

Behind the back lawn was an old-fashioned incinerator and a brick shed that sat under a tangle of vines. The shed's door had a padlock covered in cobwebs. It looked as if it had been there since Columbus discovered America.

Jenny cleaned off a dusty windowpane with the sleeve of her hoodie. "Her old black car is in there." She cupped her hands to help with the glare. "The only other thing I see is a lawnmower, and pegboards filled with hammers and tools."

Sam thought about the last time he'd seen Miss Sharette at school. How he'd shot off a middle finger at her old caddy, and she'd been standing by it. He shuddered, wishing he could take it all back, and started toward the front yard. He'd had enough anxiety for one day. "I better get home, it's almost dinner time."

The other three agreed and promised to meet again by the oak tree in a few days to discuss plans.

"Her funeral is Tuesday, and I think we should go," said Jaimie. As much as Sam didn't want to, he agreed.

"Let's meet afterward at the park."

They gathered their bikes and were about to leave, when Mr. Frank from next door came out of his house, the screen door slapping shut behind him.

Mr. Frank was about Sam's grandpa's age, with balding gray hair that left a perfectly round pancake of bare skin on the back side of his head, and he had a weird mole right in the middle of the bald patch.

"Busted," Jaimie said, throwing a leg over her bike.

"What the hell do you kids think you're doing?" he yelled from across the yard. "You're trespassing," he said, pointing at them. "Olivia isn't even in the ground yet, and you morbid little fuckers are sightseeing?" Mr. Frank was seriously pissed off.

"We were just…" Hank said, and Mr. Frank frowned at them, crossing his arms over his chest. "Leaving."

Hank slammed the gate closed with a squeaky *thwack,* and they sped off, leaving Mr. Frank glaring after them.

Sam gathered the courage to peek over his shoulder. The gate stood open. Mr. Frank was gone. The house stood there, looming dark and gloomy. "I can't believe anyone would want to live in that scary dump," Sam said, pedaling faster. "It's creepy as *fuck.*"

One week later

"We bought a great big new house!" Beth exclaimed, as Sam, Ben, Bobo, and Grandpa Brown walked in the front door. "The biggest house in town!" Sam's heart did a little flip-flop in his chest.

Grandpa set Bobo down, and the little guy ran like a shot to the toy box.

Jack was grinning ear to ear. "It needs some work, but it will be perfect. It's in town, the kids don't have to change schools, and there's room for Grandpa and Grandma if and when they want to move in.

"I want to move in," said Grandpa. "Can we leave Grandma at our old house?"

Beth rolled her eyes. Her parents were something else.

"In three weeks we'll be moving into Miss Sharette's old house: the Patton House is ours as of today!" She held up the keys and jangled them.

"I thought it was haunted?" said Ben.

"It's not haunted, it's just old, big, and needs us to breathe some life into it again," said Jack. "It's a beautiful house with lots of history, lots of room, and you kids get your own damn rooms," he said, pointing at Bobo.

Sam was speechless. It was bought and paid for. He'd be living in The Shart's old house. Maybe sleeping in her bedroom. Using her bathroom…

"*Mom!*" we can't live in The Shart's—in Miss Sharette's old house! We can't!"

"Too late, Sammy. We bought it for cash, it's ours, and I can't wait to gut the kitchen."

Sam sat silently while the rest of the family chattered happily about their new home. Ben wanted to make the attic into a playroom, Dad was talking about how the tower room would make a great office for mom, and Grandpa already had the basement mapped out as his and Grandma's new living quarters.

"All I really want is a giant TV and a bar," said Grandpa.

"We'll do another walk-through tomorrow," said Jack. "Eleven-thirty. You kids can pick your bedrooms then."

A happy cheer went up from the family. All but from Sam, who was convinced this was his punishment for murdering his English teacher. Living in her house and breathing her air…forever.

Chapter Six

Andy Has a Big Fat Ass

MANNY AND BOBBY RUIZ lived in the apartment above Dan's Used Furniture and Supreme Meats. The police had cleared Bobby of all wrongdoing regarding Olivia Sharette's death, and declared it a terrible, unfortunate accident. The delivery truck was fixed and once again usable; it was as if nothing had happened, except for the fact that Bobby felt like hell about it and wondered if he'd ever be able to get behind the wheel again. Manny, his dad, had been so supportive, and at his suggestion, Bobby had an appointment to see a therapist next Friday. Manny thought it was a good idea for his son to talk to someone, and to do it soon. Bobby agreed, since the anxiety was keeping him up nights. He had to sort out the guilt which plagued him and would probably stay with him forever, and talking with someone professional who had no ties to the incident sounded like a good plan. Bobby was a smart enough man to know when to ask for help.

Bobby could hear his dad singing quietly in Spanish in the living room. He was probably working on one of his jigsaw puzzles. Bobby hadn't slept in days, and even though it was just eight-thirty, he was in bed with an open book on his chest.

He felt himself drifting off. Thanks, Nyquil. He sighed, yawned, and rolled onto his side. I have the rest of my life to struggle with this guilt, he thought, laying his forearm over his eyes.

Little did he know how short a time that would be.

Across town, Elvis was preparing for his evening.

He leaned toward the mirror and straightened the black pompadour wig, pulling a lock of hair down over his forehead. His shoes were shiny patent leather, and his white-and-gold bell-bottom pants sat perfectly atop them. The slits on the lower side of his trousers were lined in bright red satin. Elvis's shirt matched the red in his pants, and the spangled white jacket fit him as if it had been tailor-made for him.

He picked up the limited-edition Silver Star government Colt .45 with the ivory grips that he'd purchased for a small fortune and turned it over in his hands. It was magnificent: and more than being an incredible piece of art, it was functional, deadly, and fit perfectly in his large hand, with a serious and reassuring amount of heft. He stuck the beautiful custom piece into his pocket. "An eye for an eye," murmured The King, with a smug half-smile, and strode confidently out of the door, slamming it behind himself.

Manny Ruiz busied himself cleaning his kitchen. Bobby was already asleep. He could hear his grown son snoring in his bedroom. This made Manny's heart happy. It was the first time in days he'd heard the sound of his son snoring in a deep sleep.

He was worried about his boy. The shock of the accident that killed Olivia Sharette was really getting to him, and Bobby's anxiety was visible. He'd jump at any little out-of-place sound. It was getting to Manny as well. Lately, his son just was not up to driving all over town, and Manny wasn't sure if he'd ever drive again. He hadn't pushed the issue, because he knew Bobby was a strong soul and would figure things out; they both needed patience, was all.

Whereas Manny usually ran the store and prepared deliveries, Bobby drove the truck and delivered meats, along with the occasional side table or bed frame to Patton residents; now their roles were reversed, and Manny was feeling the pressure. Not only in his mind, with all the worry for his son, but in his back. Damn, his back was aching.

He reached for the Tylenol and swallowed a couple. Once things were back to normal, maybe the three of them (Bobby's twelve-year-old son Bobby Jr. lived with his mom across town) would go on a little vacation. Maybe to a beach house, BJ loved the beach. Or they could rent a cabin in the mountains and fish or maybe they'd…

Manny heard three swift knocks on the door, and it startled him. He threw the dish towel over his shoulder and went to open the door, hoping like crazy the noise didn't wake Bobby. He unlatched the deadbolt, but left the chain slide engaged. He could barely believe his eyes.

"Elvis?"

"Damn skippy," said Elvis, and kicked his way into the apartment.

Alejandra gasped as Javier pinned her supple body against the wall. Her tiny wrists were trapped above her head, captured in his mighty grasp. Her body shivered and her breath came quick and hot.

"Do you want me, my darling?" he whispered, his eyes dark with lust.

Alejandra moaned softly and nodded her head, her words lost in a sea of desire. His lips crushed hers and his firm body pressed not-so-gently against her willing, warm womanhood. His need was obvious as his _______ began to grind against her thighs.

"Shit," said Beth, throwing her head back and letting out an indignant sigh. There had to be more than four words that meant penis.

"Shit!" said Bobo.

Beth closed the laptop with a soft *click* and picked up the baby.

"Poop," she said. Bobo said nothing.

"Doodoo," said Beth. Still not a sound from Bobo.

"Caca," said Beth hopefully.

"Shit!" said Bobo.

Beth looked deep into his eyes. He had the sweetest face of any baby ever born. "You are a little out-of-control monster, and I am a failure as a mother."

Bobo hugged her neck. "I love you, Mama."

Beth's heart melted and she squeezed him.

"Well, shit," said Beth. She smiled and kissed his nose. Bobo smiled back.

The following day the whole town was abuzz with the news of the double homicide above Dan's Used Furniture and Supreme Meats. Manny and Bobby were well-loved in the town of Patton, and news of their demise hit people hard.

The only homicide in recent history to blacken Patton's crime record was when Helen Becknor shot her husband Mike Becknor right in front of their house. Rumor was that Mike beat the hell out of Helen more than once and put her in the hospital a time or two. He supposedly drank a lot and beat his son Trevor as well. Helen did a year in prison for manslaughter, but it was, for all practical purposes, self-defense. The general consensus in Patton was that Mike had it coming in spades.

Helen married again a few years later. She married Mike's brother Glen, another drunken piece of work. No one knew what Glen did for money, besides keep Coors Lite in business, but hopefully he was smart enough to keep his hands off Helen. The police had been called in a few times for domestic disturbance, but rumor had it that it was Helen did the punching. People knew Glen better mind his manners, because Helen was one hell of a good shot.

A crowd had gathered in the street across from the store. Crime scene tape was flapping in the wind, and the air was crisp with gossip.

"I was just in there yesterday buying a pork butt," said Karen McMurty to Mark Bolton from Mark's Market. "It was kind of fatty, I was going to take it back today."

Andy and Barney were deep in conversation with a petite woman in a Colorado Bureau of Investigation jacket—they'd brought in the big guns, since nothing like this happened in Patton. The CBI gal's hair was pulled back in a tight black bun. She stepped away to take a phone call, one finger on her ear to block out the commotion. She had frown marks between her eyes, and even from a distance you could tell this woman was in total control.

"Hey Andy!" yelled Mrs. McMurty. She gestured him over. Andy whispered something to Barney and came walking across the street.

"Jesus, Karen, don't call me that in public, the feds are on the way and you'll make me look like a fucking idiot."

Karen rolled her eyes. "Sorry, *Sheriff Cruz*. Do you know who killed Bobby and Manny Ruiz? I bet it was that shifty tattooed guy that works at the Dollar Store".

"Did you see or hear something, Karen?" he asked her, all business now.

"No, but you know…tattooed guys."

Andy pointed to the tattoo that covered his forearm.

"Whatever, Andy. He's shifty, that's all I have to say."

Sheriff Jimmy Cruz walked back across the street toward Barney.

Karen turned to Mark and whispered from behind her hand, "Andy's ass is fatter than that pork butt I bought yesterday."

Chapter Seven

No One Knows How to Clean Anymore

Sam and the family pulled up in front of the Patton House. Grandma and Grandpa parked behind them. The yard was a bit overgrown, but other than that it was the same dark, straight-out-of-a-bad-horror movie house that it always had been. The half-moon attic window winked in the sunlight, compounding the ominous feel of the place.

They piled out of Jack's SUV and stood on the sidewalk looking up at their new purchase. Mr. Tinkles christened the mailbox pole in approval.

"The windows are filthy," said Grandma. Grandpa gave her a pained look.

"Glass is cleanable, Elaine."

"You're not getting up on that high of a ladder, Albert. You'll break your neck and maybe your back too. Then I'd have to take care of you more than I do now, and you're so helpless that you can't cut your own sandwich in half."

Grandpa changed the subject. "I've always wanted to go into this place, ever since I was a kid. Me and my friends would ride our bikes up and down the street, and sometimes sneak into the back yard. One time, Mr. Patton saw us and chased us off with a shotgun."

Sam bit his lip. He and his friends had done the same thing. Would he grow up to be just like Grandpa? Would that be better than growing up to be just like Mom?

"That's back when Walter Patton III still lived here. He was a recluse and mean as a wet cat. He'd spray us with the hose." Grandpa paused. "I guess with what happened to his family in the sixties, it's not surprising he was bitter." Grandpa ruffled Bobo's hair. "Now it's ours, and I feel like I'm in some weird, time-warped dream. Let's go inside and see where I'm going to build Al's Beer Joint!"

Grandpa could be a lot like one of the kids.

"The house is huge up close!" Ben ran up and swung open the iron gate and it screamed like a girl.

"That needs oil," said grandma, "Albert, you need to oil that thing." But Grandpa's mind was elsewhere. He was already on the porch, peeking into the window—or he was ignoring her.

They all spilled through the gate, and up to the front porch. Bobo slipped under the lattice railing beneath the decking, and Beth pulled him out by one foot. Jack fumbled with his keys. Mr. Tinkles waddled up the steep porch stairs behind them. Dachshunds tend to be a bit…big-boned and short-legged.

"Mama?" said Bobo. "That little girl wants to play."

"Okay, baby, maybe later." She looked at Jack and shrugged.

Ben peeked under and behind the lattice. "Nothing's under here but an old rake."

Bobo had the attention span of a squirrel, and was now marching back and forth on the terrace with his shirt over his head.

Mr. Frank from next door was on his front stoop, leaning on the railing and observing the invasion of his former, probably quiet, neighbor's home. He put a finger to his forehead in a hat tipping motion when he noticed Beth looking at him, and then took his coffee and cigarette and headed back toward his house. Sam's mom smiled and waved a greeting. Sam watched him tread back through his front door, the sun gleaming off his bald spot, the screen door slapping closed behind him. Mr. Frank was going to love living next to a bunch of noisy kids and their friends, a fat dachshund that barked at the wind even if it came out of his own ass…and Grandpa.

After a juggling act with the keys, Jack eventually got the front door open, and then, for the first time, the family stepped into their new home. The front door was dark wood and opened to a circular reception area to the left. A large living room was to the right.

"Oh, I love the parlor!" said Grandma, hurrying to examine the drapes. Mr. T followed her. "These are ugly as shit, though," she said, touching the thick hunter green velvet fabric. "They have to go, Beth, they make the place look like a funeral parlor." Grandma cackled. "I guess it *is* a parlor and should look like one. Minus the dead people and crying relatives". No one else laughed. "That damn dog better not pee on them," she added, pointing at Mr. Tinkles.

"Mom," Beth said, "we haven't gotten three steps through the front door and you've already complained about ten different things. Have an open mind for once, please?"

"Hrmp," said Grandma, running her fingers over the fireplace mantel and then looking at the dust-covered tips. "No one knows how to clean anymore," she told Mr. Tinkles.

Beyond the circular reception area, an ornate, carved wood staircase ascended gracefully up to the second floor and a long hallway with entrances to the bedrooms. Grandpa flung his hat casually on the newel post, and Grandma glared at him.

Toward the back of the first floor was the kitchen. The appliances looked old, with black and silver accents. Antique and polished, they left Beth completely enchanted.

"That's an old-ass stove," said Grandma, opening it and looking inside. "It's dirty, too."

Beth sighed.

To the left of the kitchen were the back stairs that led upward. They were also wooden, and not as elaborately carved as the entry stairs, but still beautiful even through a light coating of dust. Next to them was a white-painted door with a latch. Sam assumed it led to the basement. A Dutch door led out to the screened-in back porch and the yard. Across the grass was the ivy-covered brick shed, the glass still smudged in the pane where Jenny had wiped the grime to peek inside.

"I wonder if her caddy is still inside," said Sam, and instantly hoped no one heard or was paying any attention to him. They'd know they'd been snooping.

Ben was halfway up the back stairs, "I get first pick of bedrooms!"

Grandpa opened the white basement door and was halfway down the stairs in the other direction. "I'm going to go plan out Al's Beer Joint in the basement!" Bobo and Mr. Tinkles followed him down; Bobo's little shoes had built-in lights which blinked as his heels pounded the stairs.

"Beer Joint!"

"That's my boy!" Grandpa said as Bobo zipped past him, "You can be my bouncer."

Bobo beamed.

"Be careful on the stairs!" yelled grandma. Sam had no idea which of them she was nagging.

Sam, Beth, and Grandma followed Ben up the back stairs. From the back of the house, a large window looked out over the expanse of the back yard. The hallway led in a straight line toward the front of the house. Doors lined either side, and the gleaming wood of the front stairs led down from the opposite end. The hallway with doors on both sides reminded Sam a bit of a fancy hotel, right down to the paisley carpet.

Beth and Jack claimed the front bedroom, which had a circular sitting area that mirrored the reception area below. The room was very large, and in the corner of the sitting area was a spiral staircase made of black iron that twirled up to a round upper room.

Beth ascended the spiral stair to the tower room. It was perfect. It had 180-degree rectangular windows that gave an amazing view of all of Patton and part of the forest behind. It was stunning! The floors were a rich chestnut, and the ceiling had exposed beams which flowed skyward into a graceful point. To the rear of the room was a door that led to the unfinished part of the attic. Storage toward the back, she thought, and the large forward section could be a great playroom when finished.

Grandma huffed up the last of the stairs. "You better be careful not to fall down these stairs and crack your head open. The windows are scary, too. They're too close to the ground." Grandma stood dead center in what was now Beth's office, as if she'd be magically sucked out the windows and fall to a splattery death. That would never happen, thought Beth, she'd mess up her hair.

Beth descended the stairs, her eyes dreamy, already plotting the continuing adventures of Javier and Alejandra. The view from above may just give her creative inspiration and a new, juicy outlook on finding words that meant penis.

"Give me a hand," said Grandma, as she followed her down. Beth extended her hand to help her mother down the iron stairs.

"This is a death trap," said Grandma.

Sam and Ben were exploring the other four bedrooms and decided on the two at the back of the house directly across from one another. The bathroom was next to Sam's room, and he and Ben could share it. Another bathroom was up front, close to their parents' and Bobo's rooms.

"My room's window looks down the street toward Main, and I can see Mark's Market, and the street where The Shart was smashed," said Ben.

Sam cringed and wandered over to his room. His window looked directly into Mr. Frank's back yard.

Grandma picked one of the center bedrooms for her and Grandpa to sleep in while the basement went through its remodel. She wasn't happy with the closet space, but it would do. The remaining room would be a guest room.

Sam lay on the floor where he guessed his bed would go. He stared at the ceiling, where the afternoon sunlight scattered swirls and splotches of gold through the tree branches. There was something lumpy under the throw rug, and he reached under to retrieve whatever it was that was poking him in the back.

It was a Red Pen of Shame.

Chapter Eight

Two Grand for a Coat Baby

The murder of Manny and Bobby Ruiz remained un-solved as of the first of June. The police had questioned Glen Becknor, Trevor Becknor's stepdad. Glen, who'd always had a beef with the Ruizes, was a loudmouthed drunk. He was usually harmless and stupid when inebriated, but he let it be known to anyone within earshot that he hated his neighbors with the smelly butcher shop and the damned noisy cow truck. The shop would get deliveries early in the morning, and it irked Glen to no end. Long nights of drinking made seven in the morning the middle of the goddamned night to him. He was a genuine shit-o for sure, and the police still regarded him as a person of interest, although he did seem to have an alibi that was solid. People continued to look at Glen, and one another, suspiciously, and parents kept a closer eye on their children, but most of Patton had come to the conclusion that it had to be some out-of-town drifter who committed the double homicide.

It was horribly sad to see Dan's Used Furniture and Supreme Meats storefront closed and the van with the happy cow missing from Patton's streets. People hated that cow because it was butt-ugly, but, dammit, it was *their* cow, and it was missed. It had been a proud symbol of their town, as was Casa Bonita in Denver, or Blucifer, that creepy blue bronco with the glowing red eyes at the Denver airport. Casa Bonita had given its customers uncountable cases of diarrhea, and Blucifer crushed and killed the artist who created it. Both were horrible, but don't fuck with them, they are *ours*.

School was out, kids were back outside playing, and some semblance of normal, small-town life was returning. Still, two of their own citizens were no longer with them, and a murderer, maybe Glen Becknor, maybe some stranger from out of town, maybe the tattooed guy at the dollar store, walked free.

Glen Becknor had parked his car and was headed down Pine Street to The Liquor Palace, then took a turn down the alley. It was Tuesday, which didn't really matter; he headed toward The Liquor Palace every day that ended in a Y. He had a plastic bag with him and had been collecting cans to recycle on the way. It was only about a quarter of the way full today, and it pissed him off; most days he had a good, solid full bag of sticky aluminum by then.

Glen passed the green dumpster in the alley and peeked inside. Nada. He gave the dumpster a swift kick in frustration, and something fell with a solid *thunk* between the brick and the trash bin. Glen got onto his hands and knees and peered under the bin. Something white lay on the cement close to the brick wall. Glen lay on his side, his shirt riding up to expose his round, hairy beer belly, and reached his arm under, his sausage-like fingers wiggling and just touching the fabric of whatever it was. In Glen's dim brain, he hoped it was a bag full of money. "Come to Papa," he cooed.

Glen stretched his arm deep behind the trash can until he could just pinch a bit of his prize. He gritted his teeth, stretched a little farther, wished he were taller, and hauled it out toward him.

Glen stared at it. It wasn't a bag of money. It was some sort of sparkly, white leather jacket. He blinked, the gears in his head spinning. What if it wasn't a bag of money after all, but a baby? An abandoned baby left in the alley wrapped in a coat. What if it was a coat baby? He cringed, carefully picked up the coat baby and opened it. Cradled inside was a bright silver, ivory-handled Colt pistol.

Glen blinked, then gave a long, low whistle. "Whoa. Fucking pay dirt!"

He turned the gun over in his hands and swore to hit the pawn shop on the way home.

"Jacket ain't bad either, but it's too small to fit me." Glen was a husky man who stood all of five feet five. "So glad it wasn't a coat baby. I don't need no more police problems, and I sure as hell don't need no more kids".

Glen Becknor stuck the jacket-wrapped gun into the bag with the cans. It was the start of a good day! He headed toward The Liquor Palace, swinging the coat baby bag, whistling and thinking he'd buy a case of Coors Lite *and* a bottle of Jack to celebrate his good fortune.

Al's Beer Joint was coming along nicely. The entire basement of the Patton House was coming along faster than expected. Truth was, when you slipped construction workers thousands of extra dollars for expedited work, things perked along fast. The almighty buck speaks at a powerful volume. Hallelujah.

Although Grandma had worried the basement would be too dark, Jack had had a company from Denver put in six tunnel skylights that angled sunlight from outside, under the basement ceiling and into the rooms. It was like cheerful magic, and gave the basement, once just brick and earth, a warm, sunny feel. The earthen floors were now replaced with cement and topped with a floating wood floor with underfloor radiant heat. It looked wonderful— all rich, warm honey tones and polish. Al couldn't understand why Elaine had insisted on throw rugs covering almost every inch of it, since it was warmed from beneath, but since a happy Elaine was a quiet Elaine, he didn't even mention it.

No throw rugs around the beer joint, though. Grandpa drew the line there. The beer joint had a section of the wooden floor which remained uncovered, and there were three bar tables and chairs, a huge TV, an old-fashioned jukebox, and a pool table. The bar itself, made of wood and leather, stretched the length of his allotted beer joint space and had once sat in a bar in Cripple Creek. In reality, it was half the bar from Cripple Creek; the original bar was twenty-five feet long and had been cut in half. The other half was in a bed and breakfast in Albuquerque.

Behind the bar there was a door that opened to a brick room which was now filled with shelves of various liquors and wines. Beth had helped him out in that department, and it looked just like a wine cellar should look; old and damp, musty and dark. It was perfect. They'd left the earthen floor in this area for ambiance. The wine cellar door was locked with a coded lock so that only the grownups could enter. The last thing Bobo needed was to go on a tequila bender. The Joint was everything Grandpa had imagined. He'd have his Army buddies over soon, when it was finished, and they'd break it in right.

Along with Al's Beer Joint, there was also a living area, two bedrooms, a large bathroom off the master suite, a half bath for guests, and a powder room with a sink and toilet across from the beer joint. Grandma insisted on a separate bar bathroom because she said that Grandpa's friends were all half blind and couldn't hit the side of a barn with a fire hose.

The kitchen was toward the front of the house and was white and new. It had all upgraded (and clean) appliances, and to Grandma's surprise the oven was self-cleaning. She wasn't too sure that she trusted this to happen, so she had purchased oven cleaner and hidden it toward the back of the cupboard above the microwave, just in case. To the side of the kitchen was a pantry and laundry area. If they closed the door at the top of the back stairs, it was a totally private living quarters. Grandpa was happy to be close to his grandkids and have projects to work on. Grandma was glad to have her kitchen far enough away from Grandpa's beer joint that she could have some peace away from him and his rowdy Army pals. She didn't mind them that much, especially Richard Miller.

He'd been pretty darn cute in high school and was easy on the eyes. A few years ago he'd had a stroke, and half of his face dropped a little, but he was still pretty darn handsome.

The upstairs of the Patton House was bustling. It was freshly painted, had all new furniture, the floors had been refinished, and the kitchen had stylish granite counters and updated appliances…except for the antique stove. Beth insisted that that stayed. The furniture in all the bedrooms was new, and Beth's office was equipped with a half-round desk and bookcases. Through the door toward the unfinished attic, a large portion of the back of the third floor had been left open for storage; it was securely partitioned off from the room that butted up to the office. The twenty-by-twenty area that was closest to Beth's office was finished off into a big playroom for the youngest Hamlin. It was a good, safe place for Bobo to play while Beth worked. It was kind of like Bobo jail. Like toddler prison, but safe, secure, and with better toys and snacks.

Life had fallen into a comfortable routine. Everyone seemed happy and busy, and Sam kept his bouts of anxiety to himself. Nothing odd had happened since the first day in his bedroom, when the Pen of Shame that was under the rug had jabbed him in the back. He figured it was just a leftover item from the previous owner. He was beginning to loosen up and enjoy the summer more than he thought he could. Every Friday at therapy, he talked about the guilt he felt regarding the death of Miss Sharette. He was doing better. He liked his room, and he loved the space that the big house gave him. He'd be okay.

As the Hamlins settled happily into their new surroundings, unbeknownst to them, in the musty wine cellar in the basement, a door that they had yet to find silently closed.

Chapter Nine

Murder Makes You Sad and Cranky

A HOT AND DRY JULY had Patton Park swarming with kids and parents. Sam and his friends had taken the Kid Launcher over for their own private meeting area. Parents didn't really want their small kids near it anyway—it was the location of one too many broken bones.

The Clark twins were there, as was Hank. Ben had tagged along as well; he'd been bored out of his mind this morning, and Sam let him come with him as a favor to their mom who was in her office working away. Bobo was with Grandma and Grandpa. Jack was at work at the supermarket.

The Kid Launcher slowly spun, powered by ten white, scuffed tennis shoes. Eight actually—Ben's toes barely touched the dirt. He gave it his all, though.

"Does that big house get scary at night?" asked Jenny. "I mean, I think I'd be petrified to sleep alone." She thought for a moment. "I think you should sage it." She propped herself up on one elbow. "You never know with old houses, and yours has history." She kicked the ground and gave the merry-go-round a spin. "And probably buckets full of ghosts."

"Sage it?" asked Ben. "Like paint it the color Mom painted her office?"

"No, dummy, sage it, like to get rid of ghosts and demons and paranormal shit. I read about it online. You take a chunk of tied up sagebrush and walk through the house, and the smoke clears out haunted stuff."

"Why do ghosts hate sagebrush?" Sam's little brother asked.

"I dunno, they just do."

"Isn't sage in breakfast sausage?" Hank asked "Maybe we should just cook up some Jimmy Dean sausage links. We could make pancakes too. I bet ghosts hate pancakes since they're so good, and they don't have teeth so they can't eat any."

"I think it has to be special dried sage. Maybe it has holy water on it," said Jaimie. "I'll do some research. Why?" she asked, "have you seen or heard something?"

Sam wondered if he should say too much about it, especially in front of his little brother, who, as far as he knew, was innocent enough to still believe in Santa Claus.

"Ghosts aren't real," said Ben. "Like Santa and Bigfoot."

So much for that theory. "Not really, no," Sam fibbed. Better to be 100 percent sure before spilling the beans.

The Clarks were the first to notice Bobby Ruiz Jr., the kid who had lost his father, Bobby, in the Dan's Used Furniture and Supreme Meats murder. Even from a distance he looked sad and alone.

"I'm going to go ask him to join us," said Jenny, and when no one disagreed, she hopped to her feet and ran over to the big oak tree, puffs of dust kicking up from her sneakers.

The group on the Kid Launcher could see Jenny speaking with him. She offered him a hand to help him stand, and they walked back together.

"Hey BJ," said Hank. "Have a seat."

BJ sat on the Kid Launcher between Hank and Jenny. All eyes were on him, and it was obvious he was a little uncomfortable. BJ automatically added to the momentum of the merry-go-round, adding one more pair of white, smudged, high propulsion tennis shoes.

"I know you're all gonna ask," BJ said, "so I might as well get it out of the way." He swallowed hard—this was tough on him. "It sucks without my dad and grandpa, it's all surreal, and I'm having a tough time believing it actually happened. Why would anyone want my dad and gramps dead? The worst thing they ever did was sing off key, drive the noisy cow truck, and drink too many beers at family reunions." He wiped his eyes, "My mom's been trying so hard to make me feel better." He exhaled through pursed lips. "I come here and sit under the tree, listen to music and think." BJ sighed. "I miss them a lot. I'm glad you guys are here today."

Jenny put her hand over his for a moment and smiled softly.

Bobby Jr. looked into her mismatched eyes, blushed, and smiled back. "Thanks."

Patton Park sat squarely on Blair St. and Main. From around the corner, Sam noticed Trevor Becknor approaching them. He had his hands in his pockets and eyes cast down, apparently lost in thought. Trevor lifted his head as he got closer and saw the kids sitting on the Kid Launcher.

"Hey, assholes."

No one said a word. Trevor marched straight over to BJ. "I just want you to know that my stepdad didn't kill your dad and grandpa." Trevor seemed to have all the fight drained out of him. "He didn't like them, but he didn't kill them."

BJ squinted his eyes and gave Trevor an angry stare. "How do you even know that, Trevor? He hated them. Everyone knew he hated them. The cow truck too, he told everyone that would listen that he hated them, and he called them all kinds of fucking names and you probably do too, you micro-dicked squirrel-fucking pendejo." He glared at Trevor, ready for a fight. BJ was small for his age, but man, did he have some balls.

Trevor stared at him blankly. Everyone held their breath. BJ stared right back. Trevor took a seat next to him on the Kid Launcher and sighed.

"I know my asshole stepdad didn't kill them," Trevor said, "because I know who did. I saw it happen."

BJ brought the Kid Launcher to a screeching halt. "What the hell do you mean you know who did it?" he screamed. "What did you see, who did you see? You better not be fucking around with me, Becknor."

All eyes were on Trevor.

"I saw something the night of the murders," Trevor said. "I can't believe what I saw, but I know I saw what I think I saw. See?"

Sam scratched his head trying to follow all that. Trevor wasn't the sharpest tool in the shed, but he seemed genuinely upset.

"Tell us," said Hank. "Start from the beginning."

Trevor stood and began to pace; it was obvious he was struggling with what to say first. He stopped walking and stood facing BJ. "I saw Elvis Presley kill your dad."

BJ was up like a shot and hurled himself toward Trevor. Trevor lost his balance, let out a grunt and fell over onto the dirt. BJ was straddling him and throwing punches left and right. Trevor covered his face with his arms but didn't fight back.

"Elvis killed my dad and grandpa?" BJ was on fire. "What kind of stupid shit are you trying to pull? You. Stupid. Inbred. Fucktard." BJ punctuated each word with a sharp punch.

Sam and Jaimie pulled BJ off him and held BJ by the arms. BJ was breathing hard and swearing, his feet kicking up dust, spit flying from his mouth. "My dad is *dead,* and you're making jokes?" BJ had murder in his eyes. Trevor scrambled back, wiped the blood from his nose, and leaned against the Kid Launcher, uncharacteristically subdued.

"I'm not fucking with you, BJ," Trevor said earnestly. "I was still awake at about eleven on that Monday night, and I heard a gunshot." Blood trickled from his lip where the younger, much smaller boy had punched him. He licked it away. "So, I got out of bed and looked out the window." Trevor looked straight at BJ. "I'm not lying, I swear to God. I looked out the window toward the apartment above Dan's Meats, and I saw a flash and heard another gunshot, so I hunkered down by the window to watch." There was honest fear in Trevor's eyes. "About a minute later I see the door to the shop open and out walks Elvis. Or someone that looked like Elvis. He had on a white leather jacket that looked like my older sister had bedazzled it with my mom's Bedazzle kit from the eighties." Trevor took in a shaky breath. "Then he went to the corner, looked back and forth, up and down, shoved what looked like a gun into the back of his pants, and headed off down the alley."

"So, Elvis isn't a jaywalker." BJ snorted.

Trevor's hands were trembling as he brushed the dirt off his pants. "I haven't told anybody about this until right now."

BJ was shaking but seemed to be calming down. Sam and Jaimie loosened their grip on his arms. "So, you're telling me," BJ said through clenched teeth, "that you saw Elvis leave the cow truck building after killing my dad and grandpa." BJ snarled at him, "My dad and grandpa didn't even *like* Elvis."

"Maybe that's why he killed them," said Ben, shrugging his shoulders.

BJ shot Sam's kid brother a look. Sam caught Ben's eye and shook his head.

Trevor shrugged. "That's all I saw, and that's all I know."

"Did you go to the police?" asked Hank.

"The police? And tell them what? That Elvis Presley walks the streets of this shitty little town and is a homicidal maniac? They're gonna believe me? Except..." Trevor dug into his pocket and pulled out his phone. "I took this that night." The kids gathered around to look at the photo on Trevor's phone.

"That sure looks like Elvis," said BJ. "He's right under the light pole, see the light shine off of the glitter on his jacket?"

"Okay," said Sam, "but still, let's say for the sake of argument that Trevor isn't full of shit this time and not making this up." Sam began to pace. "Even though that's a pretty obvious photo of Elvis, it couldn't be the real Elvis, because he's dead." Sam knew about Elvis because of Grandma. She listened to his music and sometimes made Grandpa dance with her. "So, it has to be someone dressed as Elvis." Sam's eyebrows shot up, "Who in the hell would wear an Elvis costume to a murder?"

"Someone hiding their identity!" said Ben.

"But isn't that kind of…obvious?" said Jenny. "I mean, if I was a serial killer, I'd want to blend in and wear jeans and a black t-shirt."

"Maybe he was a stupid serial killer," said Sam's little brother.

"Shut up, Ben, let me think." Sam huffed out a breath. "I think we should go to the police."

The rest of the kids, even BJ, thought this was a bad idea and argued their point. No one would believe them. They were kids, and walking into the police station announcing to Andy and Barney that Trevor Becknor—of all people—had witnessed two of Patton's dearest citizens murdered by a long dead rock-and-roll star seemed iffy at best.

"I think we should sneak into Dan's Supreme Meats and look for clues," said Trevor. "The cops weren't looking for Elvis, they may have overlooked something important."

They pondered this idea. After a short deliberation, it was unanimous. They'd hunt for clues on their own. If they had the goods on the Elvis imposter, the police couldn't dismiss their evidence.

"That just might work," said BJ, "and I have an idea." He squinted his eyes and looked at his friends. "What are all you clowns doing Friday night?"

Chapter Ten

Holy Shitballs

GLEN BECKNOR DIDN'T KNOW if he could part with it. He'd stood in front of the Easy Pawn for about fifteen minutes debating the issue. Treading up and down the street, Glen was in deep thought.

If he kept the gun, Helen would probably kill him with it. He thought about his dead brother, Mike. He'd had it coming though. Glen himself would never lay a finger on his wife. He loved her and always had. Even when she was married to Mike, his heart would flip-flop every time she was close to him. Her dark blue eyes lined in black, her long, dark, silky hair, the way her perfume smelled of lemon and flowers. When Helen dolled herself up, which wasn't often, she looked like a movie star.

Truth be told, Glen was a little afraid of her. That girl was beautiful, but man! What a temper. Ask his dead brother, Mike. It just about broke Glen's heart to see Helen mistreated the way Mike had done. Glen had offered to go with her to the police, or help her get out, but no, she chose to stay.

Glen peeked inside the plastic grocery bag. The coat baby was snug in the bottom, surrounded by empty Coke, Pepsi, and Fanta cans, with its heavy, silver secret inside.

He couldn't do it. Someday Helen might go on a rampage and he might just need it. He deserved a thing of beauty like this pistol, right? And the jacket was kick-ass, too. He could conceivably wear it next Halloween if he lost forty pounds. Or he could wear it to the bar or bowling alley. Hell, just around the house when no one was home, he wouldn't even need pants. His stepson, Trevor, would laugh if he caught him, but Trevor was an okay kid. Glen knew Trevor thought he was an asshole, but what teenager doesn't think their parents are assholes? Glen insisted Trevor do his homework and get to bed by eleven on school nights: if that made him a giant asshole, so be it.

Still, Glen waffled. What if it was worth some money? Maybe even a couple of grand? Helen made okay money working at Patton Electric, but still. She monitored every penny he spent. That was why he collected cans; he didn't want her to know how much he spent on beer. He clutched the plastic bag to his chest. "I'm keeping it," he said aloud. And with his head high, his heart happy, and his outlook better than it had been in days, he was off to the Liquor Palace. He left Easy Pawn in his rear-view mirror, the coat baby snug beside him.

After a fast beer run, Glen pulled into his driveway, and saw that Trevor's bike was gone. Good timing, kid!

Glen tucked the coat baby under his arm and went in the side door. The house he shared with Helen and Trevor was small and tidy—not perfect, but tidy. Two bedrooms, one bath, a living room, and the kitchen. The furniture was old but in good shape, and the air smelled of bacon from that morning's breakfast. Sometimes Glen thought he should get a real job, but then who the hell would clean, cook, and make sure the kid got to school on time? Who'd go to all the school meetings when the kid got into trouble?

Glen placed the bag of cans and his new-found valuables on the table. He opened the top and peered in. The coat baby was safe and sound, and he knew just where to hide it. He headed toward the master bedroom with the coat baby tucked beneath his arm.

There was a board in the back of the closet, under some boxes that he had carefully pried up, and that was where he hid his beer money. His own secret little place to stash the things that were nobody's business. Glen moved the boxes to the other side of the closet and pulled up the plank that covered his hidey hole. Next to the metal box with three hundred dollars or so of cash, behind the reserve emergency whiskey and right next to his porn collection, he set down the coat baby, as gently as he would an actual infant. Glen closed the hiding spot and placed the boxes back over it.

"Goodnight, coat baby," he whispered, patting the top box. "I'll come visit when I have more time."

After a long day with his friends, Sam blasted through the back door and into his house. They'd hung out at the park awhile, gone down to the creek and climbed a big cottonwood, and then sat on some of the old, sturdy branches and had lunch. The five of them, Sam, Hank, Jennie and Jaime, and BJ, had stopped at the Clarks' house to play video games and watch a movie. Summers were simple fun, laid back and easy—that is, if you didn't count a double murder and accidental death by cow truck.

Ben was off playing at one of his friends' houses, so no little brother to tag along, which was good. Sometimes you just couldn't talk about important stuff in front of Ben. BJ was working on a plan to get the keys to Dan's Used Furniture and Supreme Meats, he just needed to find an opening to go through his mom's purse without her noticing and smacking him with the dreaded chancla—a flip flop. They'd run into Trevor Becknor, but didn't talk much; he had seemed sullen but determined to find some type of evidence that would validate what he had seen. Trevor was still 100 percent on for Friday, though, and seemed nervous about it. He'd even thanked Sam for going along. It was so out of character.

They'd all agreed on meeting at Trevor's house and heading across the street to Manny and Bobby's apartment, which sat atop Dan's Used Furniture and Supreme Meats. They'd hide their bikes and go as a team.

The day was drawing to a close, and Sam was hungry. He pounded up the back stairs and down the hall to his bedroom to drop off the video games, and then he'd raid the fridge. He threw the door open to his room—and came to a hard stop. His mouth dropped open.

There, amongst the dirty laundry and video game controllers, was a bag from Mark's Market sitting squarely in the center of his bed. He walked over, puzzled and a little apprehensive, opened the bag with the thumb and forefinger of each hand, and cautiously peeked inside. He hadn't been into Mark's Market since the day of Miss Sharette's unfortunate accidental splattering in the street. What was this?

"What the actual chicken fried fuck…?" Sam whispered, his eyes wide with surprise and his heart hammering in his chest.

Inside the bag were a few Twizzlers, three Milky Way candy bars, a two-liter of Coke, and a handful of bubblegum. Sam backed up. It was the exact bag of snacks he'd purchased that day of the cow truck accident. There was even dirt on the bag from where he'd dropped it in the street. "Holy—" Sam dropped it again— "Shitballs."

He backed up some more, stumbling over his desk chair. He stared at the bag on the bed with the bright red Mark's Market logo. "How the hell did this get here?" Sam did a double take around his room, searching for answers. He couldn't even remember what had happened to it; he sure as hell didn't go back for it. In all the commotion he'd probably dropped it in Mark's Market's parking lot, or abandoned it in the street. Sam did know that it hadn't made it home with him that day. The only thing that had made it home with him was the lottery ticket. The terrible, wonderful, horrible lottery ticket.

"Mom!" Sam screamed and ran from his room and down the hall. No matter how old a boy might be—they could be forty—they scream for mom first.

His mom was still in her office and came pounding down the stairs holding the baby. From the other end of the hallway, he heard Grandpa's heavy footfalls barreling up the back stairs. Grandpa was at one end of the hall, holding a wooden spoon dripping red spaghetti sauce. His mom was on the other, holding Bobo; the baby was wearing only training pants and a "I Heart My Grandma" shirt. Sam looked from his mother to his grandfather, then back again. It was like a Mexican standoff with really shitty weapons.

"Who the Hell died!?" yelled Grandpa, throwing his arms up, the wooden spoon still in his hand. It was his day to cook, and everyone knew it was going to be spaghetti— it was the only thing he knew how to make.

"What, what, what?" said Sam's mom hurrying toward him. "What's the matter?"

Sam pointed toward his bedroom. "There's a bag of snacks on my bed."

"You screamed like someone was murdering you because there's a bag of snacks on your bed?" said Grandpa, his eyes narrowing. He poked Sam's door with the wooden spoon, opening it a few inches and leaving a spaghetti sauce mark.

Grandma had followed Grandpa up the stairs. "Be careful Albert, maybe it's a bomb."

Grandpa rolled his eyes.

Grandma and Beth peeked around the door and into the room.

"I don't see a bag of anything on the bed," said Grandma, "All I see is a bunch of dirty clothes; I can smell them from here." She grabbed the laundry basket and began gathering his dirty laundry. "I'm surprised you don't have rats. Or ants. God, I hate ants, they get everywhere." She busied herself tidying. "Borax in the dishwasher kills ants."

Sam snuck a cautious look between his grandfather and mother. The bag of snacks from the day of Miss

Sharette's accident was gone. Maybe it had rolled off the bed and onto the floor. Sam frantically went to check, but came up empty.

"I think you better call that therapist of his for an early session," Grandma said to Beth. Grandpa was already half-way down the stairs to finish making dinner.

"I'd sure like someone to leave *me* a bag of snacks," Grandpa muttered as he plodded down the stairs, Bobo running after him.

Ben stuck his head out of his room and took off his headphones, "Did someone say snacks?"

After a spaghetti dinner where everyone looked at him suspiciously and with concern, Sam called BJ and asked if he could come over. They'd become good friends since that day at the park when Jenny had first invited him over, and Sam felt that BJ needed to be filled in about the day Sam found the lottery ticket which had preceded Miss Sharette's unfortunate bulldozing in the street.

BJ dropped his bike on the grass by the front gate and pulled it open; it creaked and squalled in protest, and BJ looked at it.

"Somebody's gotta oil that," he said, pointing at the gate. He walked up the steps and sat by Sam, pulled out a pack of gum, and offered him a stick. Sam took it, thanked him and slowly unwrapped it.

"So, what's up? What's the emergency?" asked BJ. "You sounded pretty darn serious on the phone." He paused, un-wrapped his own gum, and stuck it in his mouth. "Did some-thing go down with Trevor? I knew that jerk was full of shit."

"Naw, nothing like that." Sam popped the gum in his mouth and looked up at his friend. "I think my house is haunted."

BJ stared at him in mid-chew. "It's old and creepy, for sure." He glanced up at the half moon window that led to the attic. "I've only seen windows like that in old horror movies."

Sam filled him in on what had transpired that day at Mark's Market. He told him about the lottery ticket which he had pocketed, and how he'd witnessed Miss Sharette's accident with the cow truck. How his mother had found the winning ticket, and how he now, for some unbelievable twist of karma, lived in his dead English teacher's house. The English teacher whose death was his fault.

Sam laid his head in his hands. BJ touched his shoulder.

"That's just the beginning of it," Sam told him. "I think Miss Sharette is haunting me."

"Whoa," said BJ, his eyes wide. "You seriously think The Shart is haunting you? Does your house smell like burning weasels?"

Sam snorted and told him about the unusual happenings, and how he had blown them off as coincidence. But what happened that day wasn't a coincidence. That sack of snacks had been there. He'd touched it. He'd looked inside, he saw the dirt on the bottom of the bag.

"BJ, we need to go recheck my room," Sam said. "The sack was muddy, maybe there's dirt on my bed, or something rolled under it and I missed it."

BJ followed Sam into the house and the boys ran up the stairs, taking them two at a time. They ran down the hallway to Sam's room and threw open the door. Very carefully, as if they were sneaking up on a sleeping badger, the two of them crept to the bed. Cautiously, they dropped to their knees by the bedside, pushed away all the old socks, and examined the bedspread.

"Right there!" exclaimed Sam, "Do you see it?

BJ bent in and examined the spot where Sam was pointing.

"I'll be damned," BJ whispered. He picked up a crumpled cash register receipt from the bedspread that sat atop crumbs of dirt and unfolded it. It was dated the day of the accident.

BJ turned his attention to Sam, "You either have ghosts or burglars, buddy." He looked Sam in the eye. "I thought it was bad enough having The Shart for English class. Having her pissed-off ghost in your house is about a million times worse." BJ thought for a moment. "Okay, first we have to rule out that it's not a prowler. Someone may have come into your house and prowled, got spooked, and dropped his snacks."

"And come back for them?" Sam added. "They came back for the exact bag of stuff I bought that day at Mark's Market?" Sam shook his head. "That didn't happen."

He was quiet for a minute. "I think that this all boils down to either someone is pranking me, or I have ghosts." Sam raised an eyebrow. "No one knows about this except for my friends. My parents don't know, and I want to keep it that way." Sam smoothed the receipt from Mark's Market flat and noticed that he hadn't been charged for the two-liter of Coke. Sheesh. Add shoplifting to his growing list of crimes.

"The stairs in this house creak like crazy, so we'd know if anyone was in the house. And why the hell would anyone want to prank me?"

"That leaves only one conclusion, Sam-o," BJ whispered. "Your house is fucking haunted."

Sam nodded in solemn agreement. "By The Shart."

Chapter Eleven

Alejandra Ain't Never Gonna Get Laid

FRIDAY MORNING started out as most summer vacation mornings do, bright gold and filled with promise. Sam lay awake in his bed staring at the ceiling, the sound of birdsong coming through the open window. The only thing that tarnished the optimistic outlook of another lazy summer day was that after it was over, after the sun set and the moon came out, six friends would be doing a little bit of B&E at Dan's Used Furniture and Supreme Meats, looking for clues regarding a double homicide. BJ had scored the keys to the back door to Manny and Bobby Ruiz's apartment, everyone had a plan for what to tell their parents explaining their absence, and all systems were *go*.

They had agreed to dress all in black, because that's what you do when you break into a place that doesn't belong to you. They'd also decided to wear gloves. Grandma had a boxful of blue latex gloves in her closet for when she dyed her hair cherry pie red. Sam confiscated just enough of them, figuring Grandma wouldn't miss them. They would all meet at Trevor's house at 9:45 tonight. Trevor's dad bowled in a league on Tuesdays and Fridays and never was home before midnight, usually more than a little drunk. Trevor's mom was working the late shift and wouldn't return until six the next morning. They'd have more than enough time to pull off their plot to do a little detective work and plenty of time after to discuss where to go from there—hopefully with a sack full of evidence.

Sam stretched out on his bed; his mind filled with what-ifs. What if they got caught? What if they didn't find anything? What if they actually *did* find something? Did they go straight to the police?

Sam swung his legs out of his bed and to the floor, stood, and went to the window. Mr. Frank was mowing his backyard with a push mower. It was the old-fashioned kind without a motor. Did they even make those anymore? Mr. Frank looked up and saw Sam at the window; he gave him one of those one-finger-hat-tipping waves, and Sam waved back. Lost in thought, he stood at the window watching Mr. Frank cut perfect lines into his grass with blades that had to be seriously sharp.

Sam smelled bacon cooking from downstairs and headed out to start the day that would end up changing everything.

Alejandra's hands raked through Javier's jet-black mane, his breath sizzling on her neck. She pulled him toward her in a burning kiss that lingered and smoldered with a fire as hot as

the sun. Oh, how she wanted him. She wanted his weight on her, she craved his touch. She wanted all of him, every inch, with everything she had. She hungered for his rigid…

"Mom! Bobo's stuck in the TV stand!" Ben yelled from downstairs.

"He found his way in, he'll find his way out!" she hollered back.

"Mom! Dad's taking pictures and Bobo's losing his shit!"

She could hear her husband and middle son cackling and the baby screeching. Beth sighed, stood, and went to rescue their baby from what she saw as an easy situation to handle. Her train of thought was totally lost.

"Alejandra isn't ever gonna get laid," she muttered, hoping that there was a Bobo picture funny enough to post on Facebook.

It was the longest day of Sam's life. The moments ticked by so slowly that it felt as if time stood still. So slowly that he had to force himself not to look at the clock. Things seemed unnaturally quiet. Ben was at a friend's house, Dad was at work, Mom was upstairs in her office, Bobo was in baby prison next to her in the playroom, possibly napping.

The minutes gradually slid into the afternoon when his dad got home, changed his clothes and started dinner. It was Dad's turn to cook. That meant hot dogs or quesadillas and salad, along with canned soup. Dad wasn't the greatest cook, and every time he tried to cook something a little bit more complicated, Bobo cried. Dad's meatloaf brought on an actual temper tantrum.

Bobo was a mischievous little guy, but all-out, full blown, red-in-the-face temper tantrums were rare.

Sam washed the dishes that night, staring out into the backyard. His mind was elsewhere, still pondering if tonight's scheme was worth it. BJ had a right to know who killed his dad and grandpa. He and BJ were friends. That answered all questions of legitimacy in Sam's mind, but it didn't make B&E any less terrifying.

"You've been rinsing that same glass for the last twenty minutes." said Grandma, making him jump.

Sam placed the glass into the dishwasher. "Sorry Grandma," he said, "I guess I have a lot on my mind."

"What in the world does a twelve-year-old have to be worried about?" Grandma was wiping the counters. "You're not seeing things again, right?" She huffed, looking at him over her glasses, and tossed the sponge into the sink. "You may need medicine for that if you are. I saw this drug commercial on TV. Said it would knock that sort of crazy nonsense clear out." She paused and looked at Sam's mother. "Beth, you may want to ask Sam's doctor about Xacharelto."

Sam's mom shook her head. "You watch too much television, Mom."

"It's good to nip this kind of thing in the bud. When I was in my twenties, maybe my early thirties…" She turned toward Grandpa. "Which was it, Albert?"

Grandpa looked up from the word puzzle he was doing. "Elaine, I don't have a clue what the hell you're talking about." He went back to his game.

"Anyway," Grandma said, "this woman thought cats could talk to her. She'd walk around town talking to cats and swearing they could talk back. She must have had a hundred cats at her house." Grandma paused. "Her family finally put her in a home."

"Put *you* in a home," Grandpa mumbled, but she didn't hear him.

Sam placed the last dish into the dishwasher. "All done," he said. "I'm going outside for a while."

"Don't even think about talking to any goddamn cats," Grandma yelled after him as he walked out the back door and the screen slammed shut.

Chapter Twelve

Breaking, Entering, and a Full-size Bear

There were five bikes stashed behind the bushes in Trevor Becknor's unlit backyard, and the kids had come in through the back screen door. None of the bunch had ever been inside Trevor's house before, and it was remarkably well kept.

It was almost 9:45, and you could cut the tension with a knife: things were about to go down, and they could almost taste the anxiety, bitter and bright.

BJ held up the confiscated keys. "Getting these was harder than I thought, there seemed to always be someone around, but I got 'em," he said proudly. He stuck them safely in his pocket and patted it. "The trick will be getting them back into my mom's purse without her seeing. My mom sees everything. She notices anything out of place. I hope having the keys missing for a few hours won't be one of them."

The kids were dressed all in black, their hands covered in Grandma's blue latex gloves. The Clarks had gone as far as wearing black balaclavas, which highlighted their mismatched eyes.

"That's the weirdest shit I've ever seen," said Trevor, looking into their mirror image eyes. "I love it, but it's totally strange."

The Clarks shook it off; they were used to it.

The crew hugged the side of Trevor's house and kept low until they were directly across from the alley. After crossing the street, they made a stealthy beeline through the alley to the back door of Dan's Supreme Meats. The night was dark except for the streetlight at the end toward the road, which gave off a sick tinge of yellow and flickered from time to time. A poster was stapled to it, offering a reward for a missing dog. Boxes and trash cans lined the brick walls; the trash cans were pretty ripe, since tomorrow was trash day.

The back door to Dan's Used Furniture and Supreme Meats was about twenty yards down the alley on the left, and the group walked slowly toward it, leaving the streetlamp and its flickering shadows behind. They stood in front of the three metal checkerboard steps that led to the back entrance of the shop. The door itself was metal, gray and heavy, and looked like a million other alleyway doors. Beside it was a nine-foot garage door that was used for loading and unloading furniture and larger items. Someone had left an old refrigerator next to it, probably before they knew the Ruizes were no longer with the living, and no one would have seen them dump it. BJ fumbled with the keys, and the metal door opened outward.

Sam had his dad's big Mag flashlight. He turned it on.

"Careful with that thing," said Hank, "don't point it at the windows."

Sam nodded and was grateful that the back storage room only had grimy windows that faced the alley.

The room inside had a concrete floor and unfinished walls and was filled with tables and chairs, sofas and dressers, antiques of various sizes, a taxidermied full-size bear, and a large silver freezer case that used to house various meats and sausages, bacon, and sometimes cheesecake during the holidays. It stood open and was completely empty.

To the right of all the furniture inventory was another door with the words, "Private Residence" engraved on a wooden sign. BJ approached it and opened it with another of the keys on the ring.

Beyond the door was a worn set of stairs that led to a landing with another door. They crept up the stairs, Jenny in the lead. BJ inserted the key into the lock. It wouldn't open. He tried the other key from the ring and it still wouldn't open. He began to look worried. He tried the last key on the ring, and still the door wouldn't budge.

"Shit on a stick," muttered BJ.

"Let me look," whispered Trevor, pushing BJ out of the way. He jiggled the handle, then reached to the top of the door and ran his fingers over the frame. A key tinkled to the floor. "See?" he said, "The cops miss stuff." Trevor bent, retrieved the key, and handed it to BJ. "This is exactly where my mom hides our spare key."

The front door to the apartment opened without issue, and the six of them stepped into Manny and Bobby's former home. The living room was silent and dark except for the yellowish glow from the streetlamps below. Sam aimed the flashlight around, being careful to not point it at the windows.

BJ took in a shuddering breath. There in the corner, in front of the TV, was his grandpa's chair; the table before it still held a half-finished puzzle. His father's coat was draped over the edge of the couch, as if he'd just come in from work. Dust motes danced in the beam of the flashlight, and the air smelled stale and abandoned. Hank put a hand on BJ's shoulder in solidarity. BJ gave him a silent nod, inhaled deeply, wiped his eyes, and continued into the apartment.

The kitchen looked much as it always had. The countertops were cluttered with small cooking appliances and canisters of staples. Manny and Bobby cooked for themselves, it was rare that they went out to eat. BJ recalled how it always smelled vaguely of bacon. He'd come to dinner a few times a week, and the meal was always hearty, spicy and filling. It smelled of home. Now it only smelled heavy and depressed, as if the structure itself was lonely and missing its former inhabitants.

BJ wasn't sure what he had expected when he came in. The shape of a body drawn on the floor? Blood? Bullet holes? He'd worried about this all day. The uncertainty of his reaction to coming into the apartment, to seeing what could have been a messy crime scene, lay heavy on his mind. To his amazement it was quite the opposite. The floor had been scrubbed clean, and the only sign of anything different was the overly clean area in front of the kitchen entryway. He walked over to it, sure that this was where his grandpa had taken his last breath.

The kids scoured every bit of the kitchen looking for

anything amiss. They came up with nothing, and according to BJ, everything seemed to be in its place.

"Let's check out the bedrooms," whispered Jaimie, and led the way to what was once BJ's grandpa's room. The bed was made, and the room looked collectively in order. They searched under the bed and in the closet. BJ could smell his grandpa's cologne when they opened the closet door. It took everything he had to keep it together, but they were on an important quest and today was not the day for mourning—he had to distance himself and think like a detective. He'd absorb the sad parts of their findings tomorrow when he was alone.

The bathroom looked the same, neat and filled with shaving equipment, soap, shampoo, and air freshener. Nothing was out of place, from what they could see.

The second bedroom belonged to BJ's dad, Bobby. It looked quite different. The bedding was missing, the mattresses too. The southwestern rug that had been in front of the bed was also gone, and the lamp lay on the floor, unplugged from the wall. Bobby's books had toppled to the floor along with an empty glass and a bottle of Tylenol PM. The kids looked at each other knowing full well what this meant; that the police had confiscated all the bedding as evidence. BJ's dad had died right where they stood.

Using the flashlight, they searched the drawers and closet, the edges and corners of the room, and still found nothing that stood out as unusual.

Sam ran the flashlight over the back wall and towards the curtains that covered the only window. He pulled back the curtains and aimed the light at the window ledge, careful to not point it at the glass. Something sparkled in the beam, and Sam hunched over to get a better look.

"BJ, did your dad ever wear anything sparkly?" Sam asked. "Did he have any western shirts, or…maybe a girl-friend that wore fancy glittery stuff?" Sam bent closer to the tiny objects on the ledge.

"Glittery?" asked BJ, walking over to peek. "No, he wore work clothes and jeans, and if he had a girlfriend my grandpa would have told me right away. He'd have teased him in front of me just to get a rise out of him."

Jenny, Jaimie, Hank, and Trevor gathered around.

"I think those are sequins," whispered Jaimie. "The kind you sew on clothes, like skirts and jackets and dress-es."

They looked at each other, bewildered.

"You know who wears sequins, right?" said Hank in a hushed voice, gathering the sparkling decorations into a small sandwich bag with his gloved fingers.

"Fat Elvis," whispered Trevor.

Elvis Presley had been in Bobby Ruiz's bedroom, most likely the night of the double homicide.

Chapter Thirteen

Muchachos Con Nachos

Grandpa had the guys over to break in Al's Beer Joint in style. The bar was 100 percent finished and stocked, and fulfilled an old man's dream of owning his own tavern—complete with a pool table, a big-screen TV, and four different beers on tap.

The guys were an eclectic bunch of ex-Army buddies who had known one another for many years. They sat at the bar, and Grandpa was tending, with a towel over his shoulder and a happy grin on his face.

Albert Brown was in his element. Bobo had been appointed honorary bouncer for an hour or so with the one and only purpose of "keeping these jackasses in line." Bobo had his own glass of apple juice that looked like beer, and enjoyed the company of "lots of grandpas!" going from lap to lap and handing out napkins. Beth snatched him up for bed about eight o'clock; he cried when she took him upstairs, and it broke Grandpa's heart a bit as the little guy bawled, "I want more beer, Mama!" holding his arms out toward Grandpa all the way up the stairs. Beth shot her father a look.

"It was just apple juice!" Grandpa yelled after her.

"Say good night to Grandpa and his friends, Bobo," Beth urged him.

"Night Grandpa! Night jackasses!" Bobo said tearfully. The wailing continued up the stairs until it grew distant, and the kid was probably asleep before he'd reached his bed. Being a bouncer was tough work.

"Too bad the little guy couldn't stay up another hour or two," said Grandpa's friend Stumpy Joe, turning down his hearing aid. "Kid sure has some lungs on him."

"Yeah," answered Grandpa, "you know how parents these days are about schedules. It's not like the kid has someplace to be in the morning."

Grandpa had a huge soft spot for Bobo. He even kind of looked like him, and sometimes drew a little mustache on Bobo so they could be twins. Grandpa not only prided himself on being a terrific grandparent, but took great pride on his knowledge of booze. He didn't drink that much, but he knew his spirits.

He poured Richard Miller another beer, and the four of them—Stumpy Joe, who was half deaf and portly, to say the least; Richard, the object of Grandma's little crush; and Shorty, who was six feet four—chatted about their Army days, retirement, sports, and sometimes even their wives.

Grandpa's wife was hiding in the bedroom watching some reality TV show and well out of earshot. The group was rather rowdy that night, and laughter rang out from the walls and up the stairway.

"Hey Sarge," said Richard Miller, "where's that fancy-ass, expensive tequila you've been bragging about for the last week and a half?" Richard was spending the night in the guestroom for sure, he was pretty well pickled.

Grandpa pushed himself up from his barstool.

"I'm on it!" Grandpa stumbled as he stood, happy to have been reminded. None too sober himself, he bumped into the edge of the bar, dropped the towel, swore, and headed into the wine and liquor cellar, reveling in his role as the resident mixologist. Grandpa made for the back shelves where he kept the good stuff. That's odd, he thought. The shelf was a bit askew, and about two inches away from the wall. He pushed it back into place and searched for the tequila. When he turned to go, he noticed something on the earthen floor. A pair of gold aviator sunglasses. He picked them up, puzzled by their presence, and headed back out into the bar.

"Do these things belong to any of you dumbassses?" Grandpa slurred, holding them up.

Everyone shrugged, and Stumpy Joe took them and put them on. Grandpa poured a round of tequila shots for his friends and handed them out.

"Hey *muchacho*, you look like an old bald Elvis," Shorty said.

Stumpy Joe looked over the top of the gold glasses, "What? You want *nachos*?"

"I *said*," Stumpy said, raising his voice, "you look like Elvis in those dumb glasses."

Stumpy adjusted the volume of his hearing aids. "Thank you. Thank you very much."

Sam peeked around the corner of the alley, making sure no cars were coming and that no people were about. Silently, he waved the group forward, and they made a dash for Trevor's house, slipped around the back, and ducked into the door. They looked at one another with disbelief. They'd actually pulled it off without being spotted, and with evidence in hand.

Trevor pulled a couple of the dining room chairs into the living room and everyone had a seat. Jaimie pulled off her balaclava and Jenny followed suit, their hair standing out wildly from the static of the material sliding over it.

"You two should join the fucking circus," said Trevor, and BJ punched him in the arm. "Sorry," Trevor said, apologizing and rubbing his arm. "You're both great, and seriously pretty, but damn…those eyes."

Jaimie and Jenny looked at him and rolled their eyes at the same time. The sisters stood next to one another, electrified red curls framed their faces making them look like a pair of radioactive dandelions. Jaimie covered her right eye; Jenny covered her left. Two brown eyes looked at Trevor. They switched hands, now two blue eyes stared at him. They'd obviously pulled this trick plenty of times.

"It's called heterochromia," said Jenny, "it means two different colors of irises."

"Whoa," Trevor whispered. "My aunt Linda had a cat like that."

Jaimie shot Trevor a look. "You know you love me," she deadpanned, and Trevor blushed. Trevor Becknor, school bully and badass—blushed. The sisters giggled.

The kids sat for a moment without speaking, the adrenaline of the last half hour dispersing and leaving them shaking and stunned.

"Let's order a pizza," said Jenny, her voice quavering a bit. "I need to process all of this, and the only thing that'll do that is junk food."

The six of them put their money together and came up with five dollars and twenty-seven cents. Not near enough for pizza for them all.

"We need at least another ten bucks," said Hank as he rechecked his pockets.

Trevor's eyes lit up, "I know where my dad stashes the money he hides from my mom," He stood and began walking toward his parents' bedroom.

"Do you really think we should do that?" asked Hank. "Do we really want to add burglary to the laws we already broke tonight?"

Trevor raised an eyebrow at him. "We just unlawfully broke and entered a crime scene and took what could be evidence. I think we'll all be better detectives on a full stomach, and anyway, my stepdad ain't exactly an accountant. He won't notice, and I'll stick the money back when I get my allowance."

Hank nodded in agreement. "I'll pitch in with my allowance too." The rest agreed to pay Trevor's dad back. Pizza was important, and they needed brain food to fuel the detective work that needed to be done.

Trevor continued into the bedroom. "I'll be right back, it'll take me a minute, I have to move a few things."

Hank took the bag of sequins from his pocket, held them up, and looked at them under the light. They sparkled, glinting white and gold in the glow of the standing lamp in the corner. He carefully placed them on the coffee table. "It could be nothing at all, but the fact that Trevor thought he saw Elvis the night of the murders, and even has a picture, makes these little spangly things very important."

Sam picked them up, examined them, then set them back on the coffee table.

"It could be nothing at all, you're right," said Jenny, picking them up and studying them. "But it could be everything. Now we just have to figure out what to do with them; we gotta be smart about how we move forward, because—"

A sound from the bedroom startled them, and they all looked up as Trevor ran back into the living room, eyes wide and breathing hard. In his left hand he held a white sequined jacket, and in the other a silver pistol.

"Fuck me sideways," whispered Sam.

Everyone backed up a step. "Put the gun down, man," said Sam.

Trevor slowly laid it on the table. His face had gone pale, and it was obvious he was stupefied by his find. He looked up at BJ and then back to the gun and jacket.

"I don't know what this is. I don't know how it got into my house! Why would my stepdad have this?"

BJ stepped forward and snatched up the bag of sequins that they had found in Manny and Bobby's apartment. He held it close to the jacket. They matched perfectly.

"My…dad?" stammered Trevor. "He wouldn't!" He looked as if he might just pass out.

"You didn't know anything about this?" BJ hissed, stepping into Trevor's personal space.

"*No!*" Trevor cried, "I've never seen this gun or this jacket in my life!" He stared at the gun as if it might bite him.

"We have to go to the police," Sam said. "This is some important shit, we may just have solved a murder!"

Trevor paled even more, "But, my dad!" he pleaded, "he'll get arrested! He'll go to prison! He wouldn't kill anybody!"

"Fuck your dad," said BJ, snatching up the bag of sequins, the coat, and pistol. "Fuck your dad into next week." He headed to the door and left, slamming it hard enough to shake the walls.

Beth had missed lunch. Her fingers had flown over her keyboard today, and she just couldn't stop while the writing was hot. Alejandra finally got a little nookie from her hot-blooded, handsome, Spanish billionaire Navy Seal. Buying a thesaurus of erotica had been a great idea. Beth fanned herself a little, her own body also craving satisfaction. A sandwich.

She reached over the gate to the playroom and gathered up the baby. He wasn't such a baby anymore, he was a good, solid toddler. Hoisting him onto her hip, she made her way down the stairs, Bobo half asleep on her shoulder. She stopped by his room, placed him into the toddler bed he was outgrowing, kissed his forehead, headed down the hallway, and padded down the back stairs to the kitchen.

Beth stopped in her tracks and sucked in a surprised breath. Every cabinet door was open. The oven was open. The dishwasher too—even the fridge.

She pulled open the back door and yelled for Jack, who was out working on the landscaping around the back fence.

"Jack!" She looked back over her shoulder to make sure she wasn't imagining it. Nope. "Get up here quick!" she called, motioning frantically. "Hurry!"

Jack threw down the trowel he was using and jogged to the door. "What?" he said, peeling off his work gloves. "Jesus, you're white as a ghost, what…" he stopped mid-sentence, staring into the kitchen. He turned his attention to Beth. "Grandpa?"

She opened the door to the basement. "Dad!" she bellowed, "come up here!"

Grandpa's footsteps fell heavily on the stairs. "What? I was watching Jeopardy. What the hell?" Grandpa walked into the kitchen, taking in the fact that forty-two cabinets and drawers stood open along with all the appliances. They could hear Grandma scurrying up behind him.

"Is it a fire?" she asked. "I knew that old stove would burn down the house someday…oh," she whispered. "You've got ghosts. I saw a show about this one time and you absolutely have ghosts…or…" she turned to Grandpa, "Did you do this, Albert?"

"Why the hell would I open all of the cupboards?" He shook his head. "Anyway, I've been downstairs all day."

"True," said Grandma, "I'd have heard him go up the stairs. He huffs like a train." She glanced at Beth. "Where are the kids?"

"Sam and Ben are with friends; Bobo has been with me since this morning. We haven't left the office or his playroom once."

Grandma looked around, "Are you sure?"

"Yes, mother," Beth said, exasperated. She closed the fridge and then began closing doors and drawers. "And right now he's asleep in his room."

"Are you sure?" asked Grandma.

"You can check for yourself, I just laid him down five minutes ago."

"Well, then you definitely have ghosts."

"Ghosts without any imagination whatsoever, or any idea what a creative haunting looks like," said Jack, as he pushed closed the junk drawer. "We have cliché ghosts."

"It's what ghosts do," said Grandma, closing the oven. "I hate this old stove."

Many years before

Olivia Sharette worked as a waitress in a diner in Nashville. She had aspirations of being a teacher someday, and was looking into taking some classes, but she was in no hurry. She was only eighteen, and time seemed like a blurry thing, something without any substance to her teenage self. She had all the time in the world, and besides, she needed to save up for tuition. Her parents wouldn't be any help, so she worked long days and sometimes nights in the diner.

The nights were tough, though; a lot of drunks came through after the bars closed, and she'd had her fill of old and young men making passes at her. But the tips were good, and she put up with more than her older self would have ever dreamed of putting up with.

Olivia's hair was long and black back then, and she pulled it back into a high, tight ponytail. Her eyes were gray and smokey, and they sparkled with all the keenness of youth. Her red uniform had white buttons up the front and a crisp, white collar. On her feet were bobby socks and white Keds tennis shoes. It was the standard diner uniform and she owned two uniform dresses, both with her name embroidered on the breast pocket. One dress was a size smaller and seemed to get her better tips with the drunk crowd. Men could be awful; it was a shame boys couldn't grow up into something else.

One very slow, humid night, two men in suits came in and spoke to her manager, Beverly. There was a whispered exchange of hushed words, and Beverly approached the only occupied booth. She leaned in and spoke with the couple sitting there, then handed them a few bills. Olivia couldn't tell how much money it was from where she was standing, but the pair rose and exited the diner in a rush. After the booth was cleared, the men opened the front door, with Beverly standing close by.

In a cloud of bodyguards, in walked Elvis Presley. *Elvis* Presley.

Beverly locked the door and pulled the front shades as Elvis walked past the freshly bussed booth and took a seat at the counter where Olivia was refilling ketchup bottles. He moved the napkin rack out of the way and beckoned Olivia over.

Olivia was completely star struck. She didn't know what to do or say, she didn't know where to look or what to think. She fidgeted, and her hands shook when she took his order and called it back to the kitchen. While his dinner was being prepared, they struck up a polite conversation; when his order was up, she brought it to him, and he patted the seat next to him and asked her to join him. He said he liked her company.

She opened the swing top counter and walked around the bar and sat on the round, red stool next to him. They sat and chatted for a good long while that night, he with his burger, fries, and Pepsi, and Olivia with a 7Up with a cherry. Talking to Elvis was easy enough. He was good natured, happy, and he put her at ease. He was nothing like the creepy men that would not leave her alone. He was a gentleman, he was funny and smart, and, oh God! how handsome. Eighteen-year-old Olivia couldn't take her eyes off him.

When he'd finished his dinner, Elvis smiled at her, a smile that lit up her world. He asked if she would like to have coffee with him sometime, and she said yes. She wrote her phone number for him on a napkin, and when he left the diner she fully expected to never hear from him again.

To her surprise, he called the next day.

Grandpa was watching golf on his big screen television, and it was like being right in the middle of the action. He was sitting in the massage chair that Beth had bought him for his birthday. The deep brown leather chair had cup holders and a place for the remote—this chair had every-thing but dancing girls. Grandpa was as happy as he'd ever been in his life, and it felt great. He was retired, his health was good, his friends and family were close, and Elaine was in a merry mood, off cleaning something she proba-bly cleaned ten times this week. She'd always said cleaning relaxed her, so, clean to your heart's content, Elaine. You do you.

Grandpa heard her humming in the kitchen. Despite all their sniping at one another, they really, truly did love each other. It made him smile. They'd even cuddled a bunch last night, and now she was singing Sinatra tunes. It had done them both good, and he just may cuddle her again tonight.

Grandpa sighed happily as she breezed by, her bucket of bathroom cleaning utensils in her hand. She ruffled his hair as she passed, wiggled her butt at him, and headed through their bedroom toward the master bath. She'd scrubbed it yesterday; he wasn't really *that* messy, was he?

The sound of a crash and Grandma's scream pierced the air, and Grandpa bolted from the massage chair, leaving shiatsu mode running. Cleaning supplies lay scattered on the bathroom floor, the bucket still rolling.

Grandpa came to a screeching halt. "What is it, Elaine?"

Grandma pointed to the bathroom mirror. All the items from the medicine cabinet were in the sink, standing perfectly aligned like little pill bottle soldiers. Across the mirror, scrawled in Grandma's Seductive Pink lipstick, the color she'd worn since she was a teenager, were the words, "I'm Watching You."

Grandpa gathered a weeping Grandma into his arms.

"We have ghosts, Albert," she said, holding tight to him. "We have ghosts and they want us out. I think they're poltergeists." Grandma sobbed into his shoulder, her body shaking in fear and her fingers clutched tight to his shirt.

"Poltergeists?" said Grandpa, "I don't care what nationality they are, baby, they will *never* hurt my wife! You will *not* touch this woman, am I 100 percent fucking perfectly clear!" he bellowed, and punched the wall. Grandpa could be very protective, and his Army days had made him a force to be reckoned with.

Grandma looked around the bathroom floor for her tube of lipstick. "It's not here, Albert, my tube of lipstick's not here…"

"We'll get you another," he said gently, and patted her hand. "I'll clean this mess up, honey, why don't you go sit in my massage chair and relax?"

"I'm too afraid to be alone," said Grandma.

Grandpa nodded and kissed her cheek. Together, they went about cleaning and setting the bathroom right.

Chapter Fourteen

Weird Cartoon Pigs

Glen Becknor sat handcuffed in the interview room of the Patton police department. He'd come staggering home from his bowling night and his home had been a red and blue light show and a cacophony of sirens and cops with bullhorns. He'd stumbled into this cop party not knowing what was happening and just wanting to get to bed. Before you could say doughnuts, he was on the ground in handcuffs, being read his rights. His bowling bag had split open, and his green ball was zipping down the gutter like it wanted as far away from this shit-show as possible. Glen had sobered up pretty darn fast.

From what he could gather, his son had seen Elvis leave Dan's Used Furniture and Supreme Meats the night of Manny and Bobby's murder. Elvis. Maybe he wasn't sober enough to process this.

Andy and Barney had called the woman from the Colorado Bureau of Investigation who was there the day after the murders, and she came into the holding room, pulled out a chair, and took a seat. Her hair was drawn back in a severe black bun, and she must have stood only five feet two and looked to be all business. She placed a cup of coffee in front of him, introduced herself as Special Officer Diana Baine of the CBI, and sat back and stared at him. She didn't say a word, just sat there looking at him with those piercing black eyes. Glen squirmed in his seat, feeling as if she could see right through him.

"I don't know why I'm here," he finally blurted out.

"Mr. Becknor, where were you on the night Manuel and Robert Ruiz were murdered?"

"I don't know," he answered, "probably watching TV and drinking beer."

"Was anyone with you at this time?"

"Yeah, my kid. He was in his room playing video games, I think."

"What time that evening did you last speak to your son?"

"I dunno, maybe seven?" answered Glen. "After dinner, he always locks himself up in his room and plays games or whatever kids do online together. He puts on headphones and it's like he's in another world."

Special Officer Baine made a note. "So, for all practical purposes you didn't hear or see your son from the time of seven P.M. till the following morning?"

Glen nodded. "Where is the kid?" he asked.

"He's in the other room, Mr. Becknor," she said, without expression. "One or the other of you—maybe both of you—has some explaining to do." She closed the folder in front of her, and stood. "Your wife is on the way. Enjoy your coffee, sir. I need to have a few words with your stepson."

Trevor was parked in Andy's office going over the events of this evening, playing them over and over in his mind. The sequins, the coat, the silver pistol. He knew that his stepdad wasn't a murderer, he didn't have it in him. His mom, on the other hand—she had a temper as hot as a cast iron pan. She'd shot his real dad in the street and hadn't batted an eye.

Things were so blown up about that night. Mom had found out about his dad's affair with Juanita down at the post office. He'd come home late that night, and mom had been waiting for him. She'd hit him on the side of the face with a coffee mug, and dad had pushed her away. That's when Helen went for the shotgun. The two of them were terrible to each other, and to him. Trevor had suffered at both their hands, and had a couple of scars to show for it. His stepdad, however, wasn't like them. He'd get drunk, and instead of being mean and belligerent he'd just fall asleep on the couch in his underpants. Glen wasn't the smartest or the best dad, but Trevor got the feeling most times that his stepdad liked him more than he liked his wife. Mom was hot-headed and sometimes unhinged— and here she was, walking in the door with Andy.

"What the hell, Trevor?" she yelled at him, "What the fuck did you do this time?" She shook him by the shoulders; Andy motioned her to the other chair in the room, where she sat with a huff and dropped her purse on the floor. "Useless pain in my ass," she muttered.

Andy looked at her and then at Trevor, who had shrunk smaller in his chair. "Start from the beginning, son. Tell me everything."

Trevor took a deep breath, and he told Andy every-thing.

Trevor explained to the CBI agent exactly what had hap-pened that night and the night of the double murder. She raised an eyebrow when he mentioned seeing Elvis leave the building about 11:15 P.M. and looked at him as if he were telling her a story about fairies and unicorns.

As his account of this evening's business unfolded, and he talked about the kids' trip to Manny and Bobby's apart-ment, the evidence they'd found, and then the hunt for pizza money, her eyebrows lowered a bit at a time and her face turned serious.

After two hours of questioning Trevor and his mother, they released him to her custody. Trevor's mom was quiet, and that was never a good sign. It was four A.M. by the time he opened the car door and slid into Mom's old Chevy.

She turned to him and slapped him hard across the face. "Never snoop in my room," she snarled, and looked at him. "Goddamnit, Trevor, mind your business, just once mind your own business." She was seething. "Do you have any idea how much this is going to cost us?" She slapped the steering wheel hard, glared at him, then drove home in silence.

Trevor rested his head against the window and stared out as his mom jerked the wheel and took them toward the exit. He couldn't blame BJ for going to the police—some-one had in fact murdered his dad and grandpa.

Trevor sighed as they turned out of the parking lot, leav-ing Glen Becknor behind bars in the Patton, Colorado jail.

Beth was stretched out on the couch in the living room, wine glass in hand, while Bobo watched cartoons. She didn't let him have too much screen time, but today she needed a break from what seemed to be the never-ending sexual exploits of Alejandra and Javier. Beth was lost in thought, the drone of some weird cartoon with pigs in it filling the background of her thoughts like white noise.

The ghostly occurrences were happening more frequently, and although she had never believed in such things, she was coming to the point where she was doubting those lifelong beliefs. Stairs creaked, doors slammed, things were out of place and lost—only to be found the next day in exactly the spot they should have been. Jack had changed the locks on the doors and had added extra protection on the windows. They'd added a home security system, installed by professionals, and it had been tested for accuracy. No one could break into their house without a barrage of alarms going off and the police being notified. Still, the strange ghostly incidents continued.

Maybe Walter Patton was unhappy with their noisy brood clattering through his once elegant home. An oval photo of him had hung over the fireplace in the parlor. She'd taken it down and replaced it with a family portrait, but yesterday she re-hung the antique photograph in hopes of appeasing his possibly angry spirit. That night it fell off the mantle with a crash loud enough to bring the whole family running. They found Walter Patton's glass-encased photo had toppled off the shelf and ended up perfectly upside-down, but not broken.

Beth was at a loss for explanations, but she'd be damned if anything would chase her out of the home she loved. It would just have to get used to them, and they'd just have to learn to live with whatever it was that was causing the ghostly hijinks. She looked over at the photo of Walter Patton, now leaning upright against the side of the fireplace, and slowly threw him the finger.

Maybe it wasn't Walter at all, but instead the ghost of Olivia Sharette who walked amongst them. Grandma had said that people who suffer violent deaths sometimes don't know they're dead, and, confused and angry, wander the place where they were the most comfortable. That made more sense.

Wait. None of it made sense. Maybe they needed a priest, or a bunch of ghost hunters.

Bobo walked over to the couch, clearly tired of the pigs on TV, and ran his hand over her calf.

"Mommy," Bobo said, a dead serious look on his face, "you have about a million splinters".

She laughed, gathered him up, and swore to herself to remember to shave her legs tonight.

"You know, Beth," said Grandma, "I watch this show on TV called GhostFinders. It's a bunch of people that come into your home with a ton of equipment like EVP recorders and ghost boxes and infrared cameras."

"An executive vice president recorder?"

"No, you silly goose," grandma said to her, "an electronic voice phenomenon recorder." Grandma rolled her eyes. "Everyone knows that."

Beth stared at her mother, dumbfounded.

"They come into your house and set up their equipment, and then they tell you exactly who's haunting you and how to get rid of your spooks."

"How in the world do you know about all of this?" Beth felt as if she were talking to someone from another planet.

"I pay attention," Grandma answered, tapping her head. "I think we should at least get in a medium to talk with our ghosts and tell them we want them to skedaddle right on out of here." She picked up her address book. "Cindy at the library has a friend," Grandma said, leafing through the pages that probably had phone numbers in them from the sixties. "Her name is Egypt December." She flipped through more pages, licking her fingertip with each turn. "Isn't that the greatest name for a medium?"

"You can't be serious, Mother," Beth said, not quite believing her ears.

"Darn tootin' I'm serious." Her finger jabbed the page. "Here she is. I'm making an appointment and you're coming with me."

Beth let out an exasperated sigh, "Okay, at this point, what could it possibly hurt?"

"Great. I'm calling GhostFinders next. I bet I'd make a fantastic GhostFinder. Maybe I'll join their team and get my own TV show."

Beth turned and walked toward the kitchen. "I need wine."

Chapter Fifteen

We're Screwed

Egypt December lived in a small two-bedroom, one-bathroom bungalow right off Main Street.

As always of a morning, she walked to the front window, flipped on the 'Psychic Readings' sign, then walked to the kitchen to make tea. Using a halfmoon shaped tortoise shell clip, she pinned up her long gray braid into a bun at the nape of her neck, sending the silver bangles on her wrists jangling. Taking her tea to the table by her front window, she sat down to enjoy it, her old bones creaking under her multicolored skirt.

Egypt stared at her phone that sat next to her teacup.

"Who is it?" she asked, and three seconds later the phone rang.

At 3:00 P.M. sharp, Grandma and Beth walked up Egypt's front path. It was lined with splashes of color from various perennials, pots of flowers, and too many windchimes to count. Grandma led the way, clutching her black purse to her chest and wearing her favorite pink stretchy pants. Her red, tightly permed bubble hairdo sparkled under layers of hairspray.

"I can't believe I let you talk me into this," muttered Beth.

Grandma rang the doorbell. "We're going to get to the bottom of this one way or another," she said, her foot tapping impatiently. "Sylvia Mejia swears by her." Grandma rang the bell again. "Said she helped her find her lost TV remote one time."

The door opened and Egypt smiled brightly. She was approximately Grandma's age, but her skin was unlined and tight. She was small, almost tiny, and by the size of the bun at the nape of her neck, her gray hair must have reached her waistline.

Egypt gestured them in, and Beth followed Grandma into the house, taking in the surroundings.

Egypt's house was a blaze of color. Teal walls, a mustard yellow couch, colorful art and plants everywhere.

"Welcome," said Egypt, leading them to the table by the window. "Please, have a seat and make yourselves at home." She turned to her small kitchen and brought out tea and cookies on a tray.

"What's that smell?" asked Grandma.

"Mom!" Beth said, color rising in her cheeks.

"It's incense," said Egypt. "I burn it when I do my Tarot readings.

"Oh thank God," said Grandma. "I thought it was pot. Not that I'd know what pot smells like…" She took a cookie and placed her black purse on the floor.

Beth spoke up before things could get worse. "Thank you so much for fitting us in today," she said, changing the subject. "We appreciate it."

"Absolutely," said Egypt, reaching for her Tarot deck. "Let's see if we can answer some of your questions." As she shuffled the colorful cards she asked, "I hear your house may have restless spirits?"

Beth filled her in on some of the ongoing activity disrupting her home. Egypt nodded as Beth spoke, continued shuffling, and finally laid out nine cards on the table.

"Are we screwed?" asked Grandma. Beth gave her a nudge under the table.

Egypt shook her head and pointed at one of the cards. "Something is lost in your house," she said.

"Probably Grandpa," Grandma said. "Sometimes he wanders."

"No, no. An object."

"An object?" Beth asked.

"Yes, it's lodged between the bathroom vanity and the wall."

"My Seductive Pink lipstick?" said Grandma.

"I believe so," said Egypt. "That'll be seventy-five dollars."

Beth and Grandma sat in the car in front of Egypt's house, seventy-five dollars in the red.

"She finds…things?" Beth asked, her voice lifting.

"She found Sylvia's remote." Grandma searched her purse and brought out a bottle of perfume. "I don't want to smell like pot when I get home."

The car instantly smelled of roses.

"Mom…"

"I'll call GhostFinders tonight."

Beth banged her head on the steering wheel, making the horn honk.

The GhostFinders had an unexpected opening. Though it wasn't the GhostFinders crew Grandma saw on TV, but a local branch made up of three young men.

"I think I have underpants older than these guys," said Grandma, when Beth showed them in.

The pimply-faced, red-headed GhostFinder set down a large silver case in the entryway and extended his hand. "Hello ladies, my name is Damon, and I'm the Denver area branch of GhostFinder's lead team member.

Beth snorted. "Your name is *Damon*? *Damon* the GhostFinder?"

"Yes ma'am. This is my teammate Damien," Damon motioned to the dark-haired, overweight twenty-something.

Beth laughed out loud. "I can't believe I'm doing this." She extended a hand to Damien and shook it.

"And who's this guy," said Grandma, "Beelzebub?"

The blonde man with the crew cut shook Grandma's hand and then Beth's.

"That's Kyle," said Damon.

Grandma led the team to the kitchen where they unpacked their gear. The rest of the house was quiet; Jack and Grandpa had taken the boys to the movies, which was a good thing because the Demon Brothers would have sent Grandpa into a spin.

Damon explained the function of the tools on the table. An EVP reader to capture ghostly voices; an EMF reader to register electromagnetic field readings; fishing line, night vision goggles, and a big bag of flour.

"What's the flour for," asked Grandma, "are we making the ghosts cookies?"

"We sprinkle it on the floor in the active rooms to check for ghostly footprints."

"Oh, hell no," she said, grabbing the bag. "You're not messing up my floors, I just washed them."

"Mother…"

Damien assured her that they'd clean everything up to her expectations after the session.

Grandma peeked into the case and saw a small hand-held vacuum. "Is that a Dyson? Dyson makes the best vacuums, I have a big one downstairs."

"Yes ma'am it is," said Damon, "it's my grandmother's."

"Smart woman."

Grandma seemed appeased, and the hunt began.

Beth and Grandma pointed out the most active spots in the house. The kitchen, the basement bathroom, the Beer Joint, Sam's room, and the attic and upstairs hall.

"That's a great bar," said Damien.

"If you get rid of our spooks we'll all have a drink," said Grandma.

The three GhostFinders nodded.

"Does that one talk?" Grandma asked, pointing at Kyle.

"Not usually," answered Damon. "He's the brains of the operation and the camera guy."

Grandma looked Kyle up and down. "We're screwed."

Beth took her mother by the hand, "We'll let you guys get to work." She began pulling Grandma up the stairs and out the back door. "We'll be here on the back porch if you need us."

"Don't break anything!" yelled Grandma as the door slammed behind her.

Two hours later, Damon came out the back door and walked up to Beth and Grandma. "We think you have a demon."

Beth burst out laughing. She hadn't laughed so hard since the monkey incident at Sam's school. "I can't…" she wheezed.

"What makes you think we have a demon, Damon?" asked Grandma.

"Well," said Damon, as Damien and Kyle joined him on the patio, "we couldn't find anything, and usually that means demons."

Beth bent over in her chair with her head between her knees. She could barely breathe. "Is it an 'Omen,' Damien?" she managed at last.

The corners of Grandma's mouth twitched upwards for a heartbeat, and a tiny snort escaped her. Beth almost peed herself.

"I don't think this episode will make it to TV," said Damien, setting down their packed case.

"I hope you numbskulls cleaned up after yourselves," Grandma said.

"Yes ma'am," said Damon, "We did."

"It was a pleasure working with you," said Damien, picking up the case.

"Bye," said Kyle.

Sam set the phone down after talking with BJ for at least an hour and a half. The police had questioned BJ, the Clarks, and Hank, after which they had finally come to the conclusion that Trevor had nothing to do with the double homicide, and they let them all go home. The police did not consider their escapades from last night B&E, since BJ had keys and it was, for all practical purposes, his mother's property now. She'd taken him home and read him the riot act, but she was glad he was safe, and knowing someone was in custody for the murders was a great relief. He, however, was grounded for a week.

Sam couldn't understand why Trevor's father would dress up as Elvis to commit a murder. He must have been completely hammered, which made him even dumber than he usually was.

Sam's parents had sat him down as well, and he was banished to his room until dinner. It was clear they didn't really know what to make of it. Having their oldest son questioned regarding a double murder was brand spanking new to them.

BJ had told Sam that he held no ill feelings toward Trevor. BJ didn't care if he ever saw him again, but he knew this was his father's doing, not Trevor himself. BJ had seen Trevor leaving the police station in the company of his mom at the same time he did; Trevor's mother had fire in her eyes, and her son seemed to shrink in size when she spoke to him. On the other hand, BJ's mom was clinging to him like she thought he'd float away if she let go. He told Sam that being grounded for a week was way better than what was in store for Trevor at the hand of Helen Becknor.

After the phone conversation, Sam lay back on his bed. They'd just solved a murder, and his house was haunted. Great.

A Red Pen of Shame dropped from above onto his pillow, bounced, and hit the floor. He gasped and looked up slowly, fear almost paralyzing him.

"I forgive you. Stay." was written in perfect, flowing red penmanship on the white ceiling. Sam sprang from his bed, did exactly the opposite and dashed out the door.

Jack was finally getting around to checking out the locked garage in the backyard. When they'd moved into the Patton House, there'd been so much work to do—remodeling, sifting through antiques, and making sure Grandma and Grandpa had the apartment just the way they wanted it. Grandma made him a little crazy sometimes, but Grandpa more than made up for it. That old man was a damn rock star.

Jack peered through the original glass-paned windows, all of them murky and smudged with age. Miss Sharette's old black Caddy was parked inside, a large, ominous, black panther of a car; the headlights stared at him through the opaque glass. The garage door on the other side of the building had been glued shut with Liquid Nails. Much to Jack's puzzlement, it was clearly a job which had been purposefully executed. He knew that if he tried to force the door from the outside it would not shear, and most likely splinter the wood instead, leaving all the garage contents exposed and possibly scratching the Caddy's paint. Jack had tried almost every key on the keyring he received at closing, and so far nothing fit. The keyring was old, large, and tarnished, the keys of varying ages and metals. Some were intricate and small, some large and heavy, some seemed newer and unused. Jack figured most of them were orphans for sure, but kept plugging away, one unique key at a time. When the last key proved to be useless, he headed to the tool shed for the bolt cutters. He hated to cut the antique lock, but it was a last resort and he'd run out of options.

He jogged across the yard toward the shed that butted up to the fence he shared with their neighbor, Mr. Frank. Mr. Frank was once again mowing his grass into submission with that backbreaking push mower. Jack had more than once seen him clean the blades after he mowed, taking care with each one and sharpening them as he went. Jack shrugged off this eccentricity, and supposed it was good exercise. Mr. Frank must have had his reasons for keeping the dinosaur of a mower, even though a cheap gas mower would be so much easier and they weren't that expensive.

Curious, Jack peeked through the slats on the fence. A big orange tabby cat looked back at him, its eyes the color of honey. Mr. Frank was heading directly toward it with the push mower. The look on the man's face said everything Jack needed to know—he was going to run over the chubby orange feline, and it was going to be ugly, bloody and horrific. Mr. Frank showed no signs of stopping, the spinning blades of the mower a deadly silver blur.

Jack jumped up, looked over the pickets, and yelled at his neighbor, "Frank! Stop! What the hell do you think you're doing?"

The startled cat looked over its shoulder and quickly clawed its way over the fence and into Jack's backyard.

He would have run right over it, Jack thought to himself, his heart beating double time. He had been aiming at it with obvious intent, what kind of maniac does that?

"Mind your business," Mr. Frank shot back, his eyes slitted, his face angry. Mr. Frank pulled the ball cap he was wearing farther down over his eyes, turned the mower, and headed in the other direction.

Jack watched him go, the lines in the grass made by the mower purposeful and straight. Jack looked down at the orange tabby who was staring up at him. Jack had no idea if he'd have really mown over the cat that now calmly sat at his feet, one leg in the air and licking its backside. What a shitty, inhuman thing to do, he thought, unclenching hands which had been balled into fists. He made a mental note to keep a keen eye on Mr. Frank, and on Mr. Tinkles, his wiener dog. No one messes with a man's wiener dog.

Jack got back to business and retrieved the bolt cutters from the pegboard inside the shed, the orange tabby tagging along behind him.

"You owe me," Jack said, looking down into its big amber eyes. He'd speak with Beth about this later; what he'd just witnessed was not something a normal person would do. She needed to be alerted, and they both needed to keep an eye on their kids and Mr. T.

Jack attached the keys to a loop on his belt and set about cutting through the lock. The process of cutting through a solid metal lock does not happen like it does in the movies. It took him about half an hour to chink away at the hasp until it finally fell to the ground with a thud. When he flipped open the shackle and turned the doorknob, he could tell that the door hadn't been opened in ages. Dust rained down onto his head, and he brushed it away with both hands. Miss Sharette must have pulled into the old garage, closed the rolling garage door, and entered the house via the gate in back.

He flipped on the light switch and a bare overhead bulb flickered to life. The walls were filled with shelves of old paint, tools that looked as if they'd been there since Walter Patton the first owned the place, and various un-used and very ancient-looking bits and bobs.

Then there was the car. Minus a fine layer of dust that covered the body and which Jack was sure had not been there the last time Miss Sharette parked it, the sleek black monster looked as if it had just rolled off the lot. Olivia Sharette had no known relatives, and when they purchased the house, it came with everything that was in it, including the vintage caddy. Some things had been donated to charity, some of the antiques that had be-longed to the first Mayor Patton had been given to the Patton Historical Society, and the rest they had kept and proudly displayed or stored with care. This car though—what a beauty.

"I promise to polish this baby up and keep it in perfect order," Jack said in a hushed whisper, as if he were in a room filled with sacred religious artifacts.

Something fell and skittered behind him and he turned with a jump, the incident with Mr. Frank and his murderous mower still fresh in his mind. Jack saw nothing amiss, but if he'd have looked a bit closer, if he had peeked behind the rear bumper, he'd have seen a red pen bounce its way under the body of the car.

Chapter Sixteen

Mr. Tinkles Has the Right Idea

ELVIS NEEDED SOME FEMALE COMPANY and decided it was
the right time to call Priscilla. He'd been putting it off.
Yes, she was beautiful, but she was filled to the brim with
drama, unlike his beloved Olivia. Olivia however, was
dead and buried, killed by that pair of beaners with the
cow truck, who also, by his hand, were dead and buried.
They had it coming. He still seethed, thinking of how she
was ripped from his life.

Elvis shrugged. He however, was still a living, breathing hot-blooded man in his prime.

He gave Priscilla a call. She bitched and moaned for
a while because she hadn't heard from him in weeks, but
finally softened and agreed to meet him.

"Wear that pretty white lace thing I like so much," he
told her. She agreed and hung up the phone.

He'd never get completely over his beloved Olivia and
had hammered down vengeance on anyone who had dared

harm her during her days with the living, but tonight was Vegas night with Priscilla. Vegas, baby.

It was a hot day in July, and Glen Becknor stretched out in the bunk in his cell at the Patton Police department. Glen's belly growled. What he'd give for a cheeseburger and fries.

He must have told the police the story of finding the coat baby a thousand times. He told them how he'd found the pistol wrapped in the white leather coat behind the dumpster, how he'd taken it home and hidden it from his wife. Oh, how that coat baby had come back to bite him in the ass! The police had come at him from so many directions, trying to blast holes in his story, but he'd come right back at them with the truth. Over and over again. His lawyer was trying to get bail posted, insisting Glen wasn't smart enough to be a flight risk.

He'd asked Helen about using the house as collateral, but she didn't seem too keen on that idea; he was all but certain that she'd prefer him behind bars and out of her hair. He'd know soon enough if that was a possibility. Jesus, he'd never kill anybody, why didn't they believe him?

The coat baby haunted his dreams, and sometimes he'd wake up screaming. Last night he dreamed he had retrieved the coat from under the dumpster, opened it, and inside was an actual baby pointing the gun right at him. He was losing his mind.

Trevor was allowed to see him once, as long as his mother was with him. His son believed he was innocent and said so; his wife on the other hand, just glared holes into him and looked at her watch every two minutes. He was fucked.

Sam, Hank, BJ, Trevor, and the Clarks sprawled out in Sam's backyard under the big cottonwood tree. BJ and Trevor had come to a private understanding about Trevor's dad's arrest. Trevor understood why BJ went to the police, and BJ felt horrible for Trevor, knowing his only quasi-stable parent sat in a jail cell and might have killed his family. Big emphasis on *might*. From everything Trevor said about Glen, he had a hard time tying his own shoes, let alone plotting and carrying out a complex crime.

Sam shared stories about the strange happenings at his home, and how the paranormal activities continued and had even escalated lately.

"I think our ghost has a split personality," said Sam. "It doesn't fit a pattern. One day I get the feeling it wants us here, and the next day something happens that definitely feels like it wants us out."

Jenny sat up, reached for her enormous backpack, and began eagerly digging through its contents. "I brought sage!" she said, and held up a light green bundle of herbs that looked like a fat cigar. She dug deeper. "And this!" Jaimie pulled out a Ouija board that took up a good portion the pack. "We're going to sage your house and have a séance and chase out the bad spirits like they do on that show on TV, Ghostbangers, or whatever it's called."

She handed the sage to Hank and he sniffed it. Sam took the Ouija board and examined it carefully, turning it over in his hands.

"What if we open a portal to hell or some shit?" he asked.

"It's perfectly safe," Jaimie answered. "We used it at my slumber party a few months ago and it said that John Marshall is my soulmate, and he talked to me three times in the next two weeks."

Hank took the sage bundle and brought it to his nose. "This smells like Thanksgiving," he said, sniffing it again. "Are you sure a bunch of turkey seasonings are gonna make ghosts leave a haunted house?"

"I'm not sure of anything," said Jaimie, "and it's called a smudge stick, but what harm could it do?" She shrugged her shoulders and snatched the smudge stick from his hands, then wrestled the Ouija board back into her pack. "Now, somebody go find me some matches."

"I'm on it." Sam said, and hurried into the back door followed by the others.

Sam found matches in the kitchen junk drawer. "Where do we start?"

It was a rare day that no one was home at the Patton House, but Grandma and Grandpa were at the botanic gardens in Denver for the day, Sam's mom was out with Bobo at her friend Ashley's baby shower, Dad was at work, and who knew where Ben was—he had so many friends, he could be anywhere. It was a stroke of luck, a sign from the universe, and it made for perfect ghost hunting.

The six of them and Mr. T decided that starting in the basement made sense. Since smoke rises, they'd clear the ghosts from bottom to top and hopefully they would travel, along with the smoke, up and out the highest point of the attic. Sam hoped that the scent of smoldering herbs would dissipate before Grandma came home. Not that he thought his grandmother would know what pot smells like, but he did not want to explain what they were up to, or hear a long lecture about saying no to drugs, and what would her friends think if she had to visit him in prison.

Led by Mr. Tinkles, they started in the back of the basement, where Grandpa's bar shone a rich mahogany brown and smelled of lemon oil. Behind the bar was the locked wine cellar.

"That's a big-ass lock," said Jaimie.

"I know the code," Sam grinned, "Grandpa's not too creative." Sam spun the four-digit lock until it read Grandma's birthday, 1102. The door clicked open.

"My dad would love this place," said Trevor.

"Your dad would clean this place out," BJ said back at him and gave him a punch in the arm. They'd obviously buried the hatchet, and thankfully not in each other's heads, because murder was a mighty big proverbial hatchet.

They gathered close together in the ten-by-ten-foot room, and Jaimie lit the tip of the smudge stick; a small flame caught on the second try. She allowed it to burn for a few seconds, the tied bunch of kindling sending out fragrant smoke when she puffed out the fire, leaving the smudge stick smoldering. She lifted the smudge stick and twirled it around the room.

"We're supposed to get all the corners," she said, the smoke gliding gracefully after her.

Her sister Jenny coughed as the smoke made its way lazily into the nooks and crannies of the wine cellar, swirling around the tequila bottles.

"It smells like that time my aunt Doris burned the Thanksgiving turkey," Hank whispered, his voice wavering. It was obvious he was more than a bit freaked out by all the supernatural paraphernalia. And no wonder he was nervous, his granddad was a preacher. Hank's eyes were so huge, they looked as if they just might jump out of his head, grow little legs, and make a screaming run for it.

Jenny giggled.

Jaimie hushed them. "This is some serious, big-time ghostbusting shit about to go down." She closed her eyes and held the smudge stick up with one arm, waving the smoke to disperse it with the other hand. "Patton House ghosts!" Jaimie said, her tone serious. "I'm demanding you vacate this home now!"

She looked so serious that Sam had to bite his lip until he tasted blood to keep from laughing.

Mr. Tinkles was sniffing around the back wall of the room. Hank noticed that the back shelf of the wine cellar stood away from the wall a couple of inches, and he pushed it back into place. Mr. Tinkles growled deep in his throat. Unfortunately, a growling wiener dog can't look vicious, no matter how hard he tries.

"Jesus Hank, don't touch anything!" Sam said. "My grandpa is so obsessed with his bar I bet he dusts for fingerprints. He's getting a couple of pinball games, and you don't want to be on the banned list!"

Hank jerked his hand back, and they left the wine cellar and spun the lock closed.

Walking slowly and deliberately through the basement apartment, Jaimie let the sage smoke waft into the corners, room by room, leaving a pungent, but not unpleasant fragrance behind that made Sam's mouth water and crave breakfast sausage.

After climbing the back staircase, they made their way through the first floor of the Patton House; Jaimie smudged each corner of every room and commanded that all ghosts be gone from the property. The parlor door stood open, and Sam noticed that Walter Patton's oval portrait was no longer above the fireplace, but propped against the wall. Smoke hung in the air, and the old photograph stood silent and immobile, Walter Patton III's eyes dark, serious, and following them as they went.

Treading up the stairs to the second floor with the bedrooms, they walked through each one, relighting the smudge stick when needed. The last stop was Sam's parents' room and up the spiral staircase to Beth's office. Sam had to carry Mr. Tinkles, who didn't like the open metal staircase one bit.

"Don't touch anything!" Sam warned, "my mom will notice if one Post-it note is out of place."

Hank paid no attention. He wiggled the mouse on Beth's computer and it sprang to life.

"Who's Alejandra?" he asked, pointing at a folder on the desktop. It was named, *Alejandra Gets Busy.*

"My mom writes books she won't let me read," said Sam, and shrugged. He had read bits and pieces, and it totally grossed him out thinking that his own mother had written this stuff.

Sam pried Hank away from the computer and opened the gate to the playroom. It was bright and cheery and speckled with star stickers and rainbows. There was a TV on one wall, and toddler toys were everywhere. Somehow, Bobo had gotten his hands on a black marker, and the back wall was covered in black scribbles that looked as if they were written in some alien language. The floor was a killing field of scattered Legos. Two new skylights lit the attic from above. It was bright and happy, and there was no place for Bobo to escape, unless Beth purposefully opened the gate. Jaimie led the way through the playroom, moving blocks and a huge stuffed panda out of the way in order to smudge the corners.

Toward the back of the playroom was a door with a sliding latch placed high enough that the baby could not reach it. Sam stood on tiptoe, unlatched the door, pushed it open, and peeked inside. He'd only been in the storage portion of the attic once, when they had moved in and it was filled with things that needed to be kept but not used. He switched the light on; it burned a weak yellow, and the bulb fluttered a few times. The weak glow of the single light didn't do much to illuminate the attic, and since the room had no windows, the largest portion of light came from the cracks and spaces above them in the rafters. The area was packed with boxes and crates, old clothes, bikes, Christmas decorations, and carefully covered antique furniture whose dust cloths had seen better days. Dust motes swirled and danced as they passed, particles stirred into motion by their footfalls and breath.

"If I were a fucking ghost, this is exactly where I'd live," Trevor whispered.

Jaimie waved the smudge stick and began her walk of the room, lifting and lowering the bundle of sage until the room was filled with haze. The fragrant fog swirled, oozed, and twisted its way to the ceiling, and in a sudden shift the smoke became darker. A heavy, menacing feeling took over the space, and the air felt thick.

All eyes were on the black vapor as it churned into a vague, human shape with smoky gray limbs, long tendrils of fingers, and the illusion of a misshapen, elongated head. A cold breeze filled the room; drawn-out fingers of smoke dipped and lifted Sam's dark hair, then let it flutter back down. A sliver of ice ran down Sam's back as the black figure roiled and billowed its way across the rafters to the back of the room, ducked and skimmed under and through the wall in the corner by a stack of old paint and books. Hank covered his face with his hands, and Jenny screamed. Trevor looked as if he might faint, the color draining from his face to leave him pale and stunned. Hank backed toward the door.

Sam touched his hair and it still felt cold, the breath trapped deep in his constricted lungs, finally giving way to a soft exhale. The air smelled vaguely of smoke and perfume.

"What's happening?" Sam whispered.

"This, ladies and gentlemen," said Jaimie in a hush, gesturing toward the back wall, "this is where we have our seance—just to make sure whatever that was is gone for good."

"How the hell can you be so calm!" Hank whispered to her.

"I'm a professional."

Sam shook the fog from his brain, still trying to make sense of what they had all just witnessed. Needing to actively find answers and *do* something, he desperately blurted out, "We'll need candles for this!"

He jogged down the stairs, past the second floor and into the kitchen, Mr. Tinkles hot on his heels—the fat little dachshund had made it down the spiral stairs under his own energy. Sam rummaged through the kitchen pantry, gathering up some of his mom's stinky candles that she'd bought at a friend's candle party. Mr. Tinkles flew out the dog door into the back yard. Sam watched him whiz by as fast as an overweight wiener dog can whiz, and concluded that the dachshund had the right idea and was probably smarter than all of them combined. He trotted back up the stairs, two at a time, arms filled with flowery candles and flashlights, his wiener dog nowhere in sight.

Jaimie had set a drop cloth on the floor. It had covered an old armoire for God-knew-how-long, and dust spun in the air. Jaimie had turned off the overhead bulb, and the room was lit only by renegade sunlight from the rafters.

"We're all in this together?" she asked them.

Everyone bobbed their heads—even Hank.

Sam looked from friend to friend. "You guys, listen. This is my house and my problem, and if any of you want to leave, I'll be okay with it."

"You've been here for me through all of my shit, Sam," BJ said. "I'm not backing out on you now."

Hank made a strangled sound, and attention turned toward him.

"It's okay if you want to go home, Hank," said Sam, "It's really okay, no hard feelings."

Hank squared his shoulders, sat up straight, and somehow gathered a bucketful of courage, "I'm in. Let's do it. Ghosts can't hurt the living." It was obvious he was talking to himself and swallowing his fear.

Jenny took Trevor's hand in hers and they nodded in agreement. "You're a brave man, Hank," Trevor said, clapping him on the shoulder. Hank took in a deep, steadying breath.

Jaimie removed the Ouija board from her pack and set it with a flourish on the paint-splattered drop cloth. Dust puffed up in a cloud at even this small movement, and Jenny coughed. Jaimie set the planchette pointing upward in the center of the board, *Yes* to the left, *No* to the right.

"We're in business," she whispered. "Let's see if someone has something to say to us."

Mr. T sat in the center of the backyard. "Fuck this shit," thought Mr. Tinkles.

Chapter Seventeen

A Bucketful of Ghosts

Many years ago

OLIVIA SHARETTE lay across her bed, her diary open in front of her.

Olivia saw Elvis four times the summer of her nineteenth birthday. She loved everything about him, but she was the type of smart, levelheaded young woman who knew she couldn't expect a far-fetched, fairytale ending. He was famous, rich and handsome. She was nineteen, worked in a diner, lived with her parents, and couldn't afford tuition for college.

By the end of the summer, she saw less of him; his schedule was busy and he was on the road most of the time. The visits became farther apart, the phone calls cooled to once a week, then every two weeks, and by the end of July had stopped for the most part. Early in August, she received a phone call from CU Boulder, in Boulder, Colorado. Her tuition had been pre-paid in full by someone who refused to be identified.

Olivia knew who did that for her. She'd spoken to him often of her dreams of becoming a teacher, and maybe someday moving out of Nashville and starting a life farther west.

The next day, a pale pink 1957 Cadillac sat in her driveway, along with a gift box and a note. Olivia opened the note first; it was from Elvis.

My darling Olivia,
May all of your dreams come true, I'll never forget you.
Happy Birthday,
E.

She smiled, squeezed her eyes closed, and refolded the note, tucking it safely back into its envelope. Inside the gift box inside was a long, beautiful brown mink coat.

Come September 1, she left Nashville and her diner job. Left her parents and her childhood friends and headed west in a flashy pink Cadillac, her belongings stowed neatly in the trunk, along with a very carefully packaged mink coat. She was officially following her dreams. After that, until his death, he called her every year on her birthday without fail, and after graduation and being hired as a teacher in Patton, Colorado, she received a congratulatory card—along with the deed to the Patton House tucked inside.

Priscilla sat on the edge of her bed and slipped a toe into the white lace stockings that Elvis loved so much—he had this thing about the purity of white underthings. It made her smirk and roll her eyes. She rolled the stocking up, smoothed it, and clipped it securely with a garter.

She'd met him two years ago at a community Christmas party her husband had dragged her to. They'd struck up a conversation, and he'd mentioned how a girl like her should be dripping in diamonds. That's all it took for him to get her attention—that, and she was four martinis into a half-dozen. He was nice enough looking for an older man, she supposed.

She shrugged, and began on the other stocking, sliding it up her long, toned leg. The first time they had been together alone was a bit of a shock to her, but quite the adventure, and she'd come home with a pricey gold-and-diamond tennis bracelet. Priscilla didn't like the fact that she played second fiddle to Olivia. She felt as if she was Olivia's understudy, and she didn't like it one bit. She didn't like that their relationship was a dirty little secret, either, but how could she complain about that? He was her secret as well. He was her good-time guy who kept her from losing her mind because of the boredom of her job and family life.

Tonight, though, her head still wasn't 100 percent into seeing him; she hadn't seen him in person since the accident involving the cow truck, and he hadn't been himself for weeks. She resented how hurt he was at the loss of the other woman. When she spoke to him today, he sounded a lot like his old self, joking and teasing, and even though she'd resented his grief, it was a bit unnerving how his mood had changed on a dime. Two weeks, and it was like the accident never happened. It made her uneasy, but she needed to get out of the house and breathe, and he usually had a gift waiting for her. She hoped he'd bought the wine she liked—God knew he had the money for the good stuff. They always ended up having a good time together, although his kinks were…interesting, to say the least…but for the most part she was fond of him, and what's a little dress up between fuckbuddies?

She smoothed her gartered stockings and slid into a short blue mini skirt, zipping it up the back. The white, low-cut blouse she wore was just deep enough to allow the lace from her lingerie to peek from the V neck. She left her heels off while she applied her makeup in the way he liked. Winged liner, light foundation, glossy pink lipstick. Priscilla brushed her long black hair past her shoulders; she picked three-inch sections at a time and back-combed it into a bouffant, giving her a good three extra inches of height. She slipped gloves over her pale manicure, stepped into her heels, and took a long look in the mirror, turning to admire herself from behind. Yep, this was worth at least a gold necklace, or that emerald ring she'd been hinting about.

Priscilla opened the door to the bedroom, grabbed her purse and headed to the front door.

"Where are you going, Mom?"

"I'm going out, I probably won't be home tonight." She turned and looked at the boy. "There's leftover Chinese in the fridge, and for God's sake, Trevor, stay out of my bedroom and out of my stuff."

Sam lit the candles, his eyes straying every few seconds to the place the smoke had mysteriously disappeared under the wall. He touched his hair where the ghostly fingers had lifted it. The contact had been almost a caress, without any sense of hostility or malice. It was, however, crystal clear that the ghostly apparition had singled him out. What he was feeling wasn't terror or threat, it was more puzzlement and wonder. He had a deep-seated need to know, and he eagerly went forward with the seance, arranging the sweet-smelling candles as Jaimie directed. He took a deep, calming breath and took his seat on the floor with the rest of his friends, with the hope of finding answers and truth.

"Put two fingers of each hand on the planchette," Jaimie instructed, "like this." She demonstrated with her own fingers. "And remember, this is some serious shit, no one better even think about moving this on their own."

There was an all-inclusive nod, and each of them placed their fingers on the little rolling board.

"We need answers to who is haunting Sam's house," Jaimie whispered. "Are you still here?"

The indicator vibrated but didn't move.

"Are you still here?" she asked again.

The smell of smoke and perfume filled the room, and there was a collective gasp when the planchette jerked to the left.

Yes

Sam saw a trickle of sweat run down the side of Hank's neck, Jenny's eyes were wide, and anxiety filled the room like heavy steam. But no one dared move.

"Are you female?" Jaimie asked.

Yes

The planchette zipped to the other side of the board.

No

Jaimie's eyes met Sam's and Sam whispered, "Are there more than one of you?"

Yes

"Are you Miss Sharette? Sam's English teacher?"

Yes

The triangular disk jerked, moved and spelled out,

WP3

"Walter Patton III is here?" she asked.

Yes

"Tell her I'm sorry, Jaimie." Sam said quietly.

"Miss Sharette, Sam says he's sorry."

The disk wiggled and jerked from letter to letter.

Forgiven

It skipped wildly around the board.

Help her

Sam whispered into the dim room, "Help who?"

Find her

The kids looked from one to the other: no one knew who it was that needed finding.

Jaimie cleared her throat and went in a different direction. "Mr. Patton, what do you want, why do you stay here?" The planchette dashed around the board, and the room reeked of smoke and flowers.

Find her help her

"Who, Mr. Patton? Who do you want us to find?"

Alice

Help

Alice

The board bounced as if punched, dust rained down from the rafters, the candles blew out, and the planchette flew across the room, hitting the spot where the smoky entity had disappeared.

"Christ on a stick!" whispered Jaimie. They quickly gathered their candles, and Sam shook Hank out of a terrified stupor.

The storeroom door slammed against the wall as they ran out of the attic.

Alice…

Chapter Eighteen

It's Beer Joint Time!

THAT EVENING, AFTER BEING SCARED half shitless, Sam told his parents everything.

Jack stared at his son and repeated, "Miss Sharette dropped the winning lotto ticket."

"I should have told you, I just couldn't. Everyone was so excited about the new house." Sam looked at Grandpa. "And the new beer joint."

"The kid has a point," Grandpa said.

Grandma lightly punched his arm. "Stay out of this, Albert."

Beth was pacing the room, holding Bobo; Ben was watching TV and not at all interested in the conversation.

"I should never have picked it up, I should never have put it in my pocket." Sam looked at his mother, his face drawn and pale. "I wish we still lived in our old house."

"Sam," said Jack quietly, "no crime was committed, and there was no way that you could know what would happen. If you hadn't picked it up, she still would have been crossing the street coming back for it, right?"

Sam had never thought of it that way. Jack put a hand on his shoulder. "I think the only way to proceed from here is to do something that Miss Sharette would have approved of with part of the winnings. I think we need to honor her in some way."

Everyone nodded in agreement, and the weight of the world seemed to ease a bit from Sam's shoulders. They decided to all think about what they could do in her memory, and always respect her home and her spirit.

"Thank you, Miss Sharette," Sam whispered under his breath.

"What?" Said Grandma. "I can't hear a blasted thing over all the barking in the backyard."

Mr. Tinkles still refused to come back into the house.

"And Jesus Christ, Beth, something smells like a burning turkey. I bet it's that damn old stove."

Trevor sat at the desk in his room, and the big orange tabby which had been in Sam's back yard sat upon his lap.

Sam's dad had found the cat and said he was a stray; he said that he'd take him to a shelter in the morning, and being that he was awfully friendly, he would surely find a good home. If not for the fact that Sam's dachshund hated him, and barked as if there was a monster in the yard, they might have kept him. When Trevor asked if he could take him home, everyone readily agreed. Trevor's mother said that he could keep him, as long as he kept him out of her room, fed him, and cleaned up after him.

Trevor named him Tang. He stroked his new feline friend's ears, put on his headphones to listen to music, and fired up his computer to read articles about his stepdad's arrest. It had become an obsession for him. It was unthinkable to Trevor that Glen Becknor could commit this level of heinous crime—it just didn't make any sense. While his biological father, Mike, had been cunning and angry, Mike's brother Glen was more the lazy, good-natured type. They couldn't have been more different. Mike had stood over six foot and lean, with a head full of dark hair; his brother Glen was a head shorter, and had auburn hair and a red beard.

Trevor was only seven years old when his mother shot his dad in the street, but he remembered it vividly. The screaming and arguing, the slaps, the sound of the door slamming, the shotgun being racked.

He doesn't remember much of his childhood before that awful evening; all but a few fragments seem lost in a fog, almost as if it happened to someone else and he is only an observer looking in from above. He remembers he was alone a lot; he remembers the sound of arguments…but not what they were about. He remembers his mom bringing home a puppy once, and how excited he was when the dog slept next to him on his pillow. He remembers being miserable the next morning when it had somehow "run away" in the middle of the night. He remembers his older stepsister left home the minute she was of age to do so. He remembers being hit and told he was worthless.

He remembers enough.

Trevor removed his headphones, sat Tang down gently on the chair, and walked to the window. Across the street was Dan's Used Furniture and Supreme Meats, windows shuttered and a "For Sale" sign tacked to the brick wall. The streetlight glowed yellow, as it had the night of the murders, the same missing dog poster taped to the pole hung in ragged tatters, the ends lifted gently by the wind.

Trevor picked up the cat, placed him on the bed, and crawled in next to him. Tang purred, kneaded the pillow with his paws, turned a circle, and positioned himself in the same spot that Trevor remembered his puppy had all those years ago.

"You better be here when I wake up," Trevor whispered.

He was.

The day Beth Hamlin decided to do some research into the home she now occupied started with an enormous clatter—miraculously, one that did not involve Bobo—in the attic storage space.

The bang came unexpectedly as she sat at her desk finishing up a scene involving Javier, Alejandra, Javier's Yacht, and a missing cache of Russian diamonds. Beth jumped from her chair and ran to check on the baby. He was sound asleep in his toddler bed in the playroom. She laid her hand protectively on his back, felt his breath deep and peaceful. She quietly made her way to the storage room door and placed her ear against it. Was that…crying? Beth did a quick spin and hurried back over to Bobo's bed. The boy was fast asleep, his mouth open and his lips moving, his hands flexing—busy, even in slumber.

Beth cocked her head and followed the sound back to the storage room door. She had certainly heard weeping, soft and faint. If it was not coming from her sleeping baby…she touched the door, the sound of a child crying tearing at her heart, but also filling her with dark curiosity.

Beth remembered the half drained glass of Pinot that sat on her desk and wondered if that might be the cause of the phantom sound, but no, it wasn't the wine, she wasn't imagining this. Where was it coming from?

She slid the door latch open and peeked inside. Nothing looked amiss, and nothing seemed to have fallen with a force that could make such a loud sound it brought her out of her office in the first place.

The sound, definitely a young child weeping, stopped abruptly; Beth stood very still in the center of the room, listening carefully for other out-of-place noises as the crying sounds echoed away into the darkness. All was quiet and still.

Beth noticed the tarp that covered the antique dresser in the far corner was askew, and she gathered the courage to creep over to inspect it. Ripping off the tarp in a flurry of dust, she saw that the mirror which had once been attached to it had fallen behind the dresser, the glass in pieces on the floor. In one of the open spaces of wallboard there was an old newspaper, and Beth reached behind the dresser and retrieved it, paying close attention to avoid the jagged shards of mirrored glass. It was an old copy of the Patton Gazette from 1964, with a headline which ran, "Walter Patton Builds Bomb Shelter Behind Mansion."

The remaining pieces of mirror surrendered their grip on their fractured frame and fell to the ground behind the dresser with a clatter so loud Beth shrieked and ran for the door, taking the old newspaper and still-sleeping Bobo with her.

Downstairs, Beth spread the paper over the kitchen table, its pages fragile and yellow with age. She could hear Bobo, now wide awake, bumping down the back stairs to visit with his grandparents. She heard him yell for his grandpa, "Grandpa! It's beer joint time!" Then, "Grandma! Stay in the kitchen, no girls allowed!"

The Gazette was labeled July 3rd, 1964. The construction of the bomb shelter had made front page news. Small towns reported everything. The paper revealed that Mayor Patton had gone along with the American cold war trend of backyard fallout shelters, and had a crew of five men working in the southwest corner of his property building a shelter that would house a family of six along with enough supplies and provisions to last nine months. The structure would contain bunks, a pantry, cooking area, wash and bathroom facility, and a state-of-the-art water purifying system. There was a photo of the property that showed the back of the Patton house along with the garage. None of the details seemed to have changed much over the course of all those years, except for one major difference: Mr. Frank's house was not in the photograph. Instead, the land on which his house now stood was a part of the Patton property, and in the exact location where the five-man crew was working on constructing Walter Patton's bunker.

Beth decided it was time for a trip to the Patton Library to learn a little more about the house in which she now lived.

PART II

Chapter Nineteen

I like Cats, Don't @ Me

MAYOR WALTER PATTON had everything a man could ever dream of wanting, and much more than he would ever need. Vast wealth, power, a beautiful home, a wife who loved him, and three children who were the lights of his life. "And of course, you too, Callan," he said to his smoke gray Siamese cat, then gave him a scratch between the ears and took a puff of his pipe.

Mr. Patton smiled to himself; his brood would soon grow to four children. Along with little Alice and his twelve-year-old twins, May and Glenda, his nephew, fourteen years of age, would soon be coming to live with them. Mr. Patton's sister had recently passed away, leaving the young man without a family, and in Mr. Patton's eyes this simply would not do. A young boy on the brink of adulthood needed a stable home with steadfast rules and discipline, and since the boy's father was long gone, he had made the decision to take the boy in and be the solid, male presence that he needed.

Unfortunately, Mr. Patton hadn't seen much of his sister in the past fifteen years; life and distance had gotten in the way, and it saddened him since they had been close as children. He hoped by taking in the child he would make it up to her in a small way. He'd guide the young man as he had been guided, and raise him as he had raised his girls—with fairness, an open mind, and discipline when needed. Sometimes that meant a good swat on the backside, but Mr. Patton believed unequivocally that words and actions worked far better than any form of physical punishment. He was confident in his and his wife's parenting abilities, and he was sure he could handle any disciplinary issues that would certainly pop up, given the boy's age, hormones, and circumstance.

Mr. Patton glanced out of the window, watching his girls play in the back yard; he could hear their laughter through the closed window. The welfare of his family worried him. With the state the world was in, the threat of war was high on everyone's mind. He'd thought about a safety shelter for a while now, but the idea of being responsible for four children solidified the idea. He would begin tomorrow on plans.

He stroked Callan's soft fur and watched his gleeful daughters, all ruffles and ribbons, chase one another across the expanse of green grass behind the house, and he let his usually busy mind daydream a bit about having a son at last.

Ten days later, Mayor Patton stood on the platform of the train station, wearing his best suit and holding his youngest in his arms. His wife, Maria, stood next to him in a yellow sundress and white cardigan, her black hair tucked back in a chignon. His three daughters, all dressed in their Sunday clothes, wiggled eagerly. The twins, May and Glenda, were bouncing on the tips of their black shoes. Meeting the boy that would now, for all that made sense, be their brother, was an exciting event, and the children had been up bright and early, eager for the day to proceed.

"Will he be here soon, Daddy?" Alice asked impatiently, clutching her yellow-haired doll, Bridget, to her chest.

Mr. Patton looked at his watch. "Shouldn't be long now, baby girl." He tapped the tip of her nose. One of her brown pigtails, fancy with purple ribbons, had come undone, and Maria reached over to tie it. She smiled happily.

Mr. Patton glowed. Oh, how he loved the precious women in his life. He kissed his wife's cheek and pointed down the tracks. "Here it comes now. Look, ladies!" Mr. Patton removed his hat and held it to his chest so that it would not blow away in the blustery aftermath of the train. The girls squealed excitedly.

The train was on the way to Denver, and not many people exited at the Patton stop; only two women in their fifties stepped off, followed by a very thin and very tall teenage boy.

Alice wiggled from Mr. Patton's arms, and his three daughters dashed over to greet their new brother. He looked incredibly surprised as the trio of girls hugged him, and he smiled. Alice thrust her blond baby doll at him for him to hold. Disengaging himself from their grip, and holding Alice by one hand and her doll by the other, he walked straight and tall over to Walter and Maria Patton and extended his hand. "Hello, Sir," he said politely; then, turning to Maria, "Ma'am." He smiled. "I'm Franklin."

The following day, Mr. Patton stood in his yard and watched the construction workers. He was content. Yesterday afternoon Franklin had settled into the guest room and was told to make it his own, and to please let Maria know if he wanted to paint or rearrange things to his liking. The boy insisted that everything was perfect as it was, and promised to let her know if he changed his mind. After washing up, they had a roast chicken dinner together as a family, and the girls had hung on every word their new brother said, particularly interested in his train ride and the things that he'd seen on his way from California. Mr. Patton smiled to himself; it had gone very well indeed.

Mr. Patton walked closer to the dig site, dodging equipment and tools to survey the progress of the fallout shelter. The earth was turned, and the men were beginning to pour concrete. It was a sweltering day, and he'd left his suit jacket in the house. He had his sleeves rolled up to right below the elbow, and he tugged at his collar and undid the top button. All but one of the men working were Mexican nationals. He had so much respect for their work ethic and culture, and oh! how he ached to get into the action of building and get his hands dirty. He knew quite a bit of

Spanish which he'd learned from his wife of fourteen years, Maria. He had met her on a business trip to New Mexico, and in Mr. Patton's mind it was love at first sight. Her long black hair, her sharp features, her dark, almond-shaped eyes, and her ever-present grace and poise had swept his heart away. Unfortunately, love at first sight wasn't something that Maria believed in, and it took almost two years for her heart to catch up to his. But when it did, and she agreed to be his wife, Mr. Patton was overjoyed, and things moved along quickly. They married in her hometown of Taos, had a quick honeymoon in Angel Fire (he promised her a more exotic trip the following year), and he brought her home to Colorado. Maria always said that Colorado was so much like New Mexico, except for the fact that New Mexicans would give you the shirt off their back— and Coloradans would sell it to you. It made Mr. Patton laugh, since being a businessman from Colorado was how he had made his fortune.

Mr. Patton walked over to the workers, who were now deep in the swimming pool-shaped hole in the yard.

"¡Hola amigos! ¿Quieren que mi mujer te haga limonada?"

They agreed happily, obviously surprised that the gringo in a suit could speak Spanish.

"!Eso seria maravilloso, señor Patton!" answered the only Caucasian man in the hole.

Everyone laughed.

Mr. Patton strode quickly back across the wide yard of grass and went up the cement stairs leading to the kitchen. Franklin sat at the kitchen table holding Callan, Mr. Patton's Siamese cat. The young man smiled up at him; Callan jumped down from his lap, screeched, and with wide eyes and looking spooked, dashed out the back door.

"Is everything alright in here, son?" Mr. Patton asked.

"Yes of course, *father*." Franklin said politely.

Something was just off about this situation, Mr. Patton thought. "Good, then. Please find Maria and ask her to make lemonade for the workers."

Franklin rose from his seat and headed to the hall. "Yes, Sir."

It was the first time Mr. Patton had a peculiar feeling regarding the boy. It would not be the last.

By the end of June, the fallout shelter was completed. A tunnel led from the outer corner of the basement, across the back yard, and into a sturdy concrete building which sat six feet underground. A ladder led down into the structure, giving the thirty-by-twenty-foot rectangular safe place two points of entry. Inside was everything that the family would need for nine months of confinement, including three sets of bunk beds, a fully stocked pantry, toilet area, a kitchen area, a generator and water processing equipment, a notable library filled with books for all ages–and a safe.

Mr. Patton did not fully trust banks. Yes, he had a savings account and a checking account, any businessman needed these things, but he'd lie awake at night, worrying about their security. He planned on taking half his fortune and placing it somewhere secure, where he could keep an eye on things—in a safe, deep underground in his own backyard. He'd alerted the bank about the upcoming withdrawal, and of course they tried to change his mind, declaring how his money was supremely safe, tucked away in their institution, but Mr. Patton had heard of too many banks failing; and with the threat of nuclear war hanging over their heads, there was no way in hell he was keeping his money all in one place. He would leave his accounts open at the bank with a notable sum to deal with business and finance, but the rest of his money was going into the underground safe. The money that his family would need to live on, in case some type of catastrophe occurred that left the banks useless, would be locked carefully away.

Mr. Patton felt good about his decision, and laid a hand on the heavy, antique safe which needed a combination as well as a key to open. It was cemented into the wall of the fallout shelter, its walls almost a foot thick of solid steel. Mr. Patton was confident it could withstand any kind of onslaught—foreign, domestic, or act of God—which could be thrown at it. He gave it a pat, placed the key in his pocket, and memorized the combination which he would only share with Maria. He headed back down the tunnel to the main house, his sense of security regarding his family and his assets guaranteed—protected by earth, concrete, and a safe that would remain intact no matter what type of adversity were to come.

Mr. Patton's Siamese cat had gone missing. He'd had Callan since he was a tiny ball of smoke-colored fluff, and with the approaching dusk, Mr. Patton began to worry. To his knowledge, this particular cat had never missed a meal, and the fact that he was still missing two hours past his supper time gave Mr. Patton pause. He supposed that Callan could be out doing normal cat things; prowling, stalking, exploring and hunting…but overall, it was strange.

Mr. Patton went to the back door and shook the box of cat food, thinking it may remind the puss that it was dinner time, and he was late for it.

He left the back door open a notch and went back to his office to finish the work he had missed today while helping Maria decorate for Alice's fourth birthday tomorrow. He left the office door open a crack as well, hoping that before nightfall he'd hear Callan come home, meowing loudly and demanding his dinner.

By the time Mr. Patton stopped work for the night, folded his papers, and straightened his desk, Callan was still not home. He sighed, stopped by the kitchen, filled the cat's food bowl and took his chances, against his better judgment, to leave the back door open a bit—just for that night.

The next day began bright and clear, the emerald green of the back lawn awash in sunlight and interlaced with shadow from the big cottonwoods. Maria's roses were in full bloom on that late August day, and even though the yard was decorated for Alice's birthday, with princess-pink streamers and balloons, the roses added a bold touch of red and yellow for balance.

Alice was as bright as the day, her dark hair in pigtails tied with pink ribbons, her dress a lavender clutter of lace, satin, and sparkles. Mae and Glenda were dressed in identical white sundresses with bright blue ties; it was unusual for the twins to dress identically, but it was Alice's fourth birthday and she had made the request. The grill was filled with charcoal, the cooler filled with beer for the adults, and a large punch bowl filled to the brim with ice and a cherry-red concoction of Hawaiian Punch and pineapple juice. The guests would be arriving soon, and Mr. Patton and Maria sat in lawn chairs under the shade tree watching Franklin chase the three girls to their delighted squeals.

"Maria," Mr. Patton asked his wife, "Have you seen the cat today?"

She lifted her face to his and raised her eyebrows, "He didn't come home last night?"

"No, I haven't seen him since yesterday morning."

"I'm sure he's alright," she said, laying her hand over his; she knew how much he loved that silly kitten. "He probably found something interesting to do–more interesting than us."

He smiled at her and squeezed her hand in his.

"I'm sure you're right, my love."

The first guests began to arrive, and Maria rose from her seat to greet them. Mr. Patton continued to watch his girls romp in the yard, chased by a boy who was a total stranger. The knot in his gut tightened and rolled; he shrugged it off. "Give the kid a chance," he whispered under his breath, then stood, smoothed his trousers, and went to help his wife greet their friends and neighbors.

After the presents were opened and the cake eaten, Alice went missing.

The last anyone had seen of her was right before a game of hide and seek. She went off to hide, and an hour later she was still unaccounted for. The joviality of the day turned to anxious tension as the guests scoured the surrounding area, which included the open space behind the house and the thatch of cottonwoods that ran beside a small brook.

An hour and a half later, Mr. Patton went to get his gun. As the day sweltered on, the police were notified and turned out in force to join in the search for the mayor's youngest daughter.

Two hours later, after Alice had been missing for most of the late afternoon and evening, the sun began to set, and anxiety turned to full-on panic. Maria could be heard in the distance wailing and calling out for her youngest daughter. Well into dusk, one of the searchers found Mr. Patton's cat, Callan, dead and hung by the neck from one of the cottonwood trees.

Maria was completely hysterical as Mr. Patton gathered her in his arms and asked her to take the twins back to the house. He swore to her that he and the group of neighbors and the police would continue searching through the night.

"We'll find her, Maria," he said to her gently, "I promise you; we will find her." Mr. Patton's fingers tightened on the grip of the shotgun he had thrown over his shoulder. "We'll find her."

Morning came, and four-year-old Alice was still missing. It was as if she had vanished into thin air, no trace of her to be found. The area surrounding the Patton house had been searched multiple times to no avail. The creek had been searched thoroughly, five miles downstream. The house itself had been all but ransacked, no single inch of the home left untouched; even the bomb shelter was scoured.

An exhausted and disheveled Mr. Patton walked up the back steps to his house and sat at the kitchen table, his head in his hands. It took him a while to gather his wits, his mind whirling in a million directions at once. Suddenly he calmed, stood, grabbed his shotgun and walked up the back stairway to Franklin's room.

Mr. Patton threw the door open with force, and entered, the gun propped against his shoulder. The boy was still fast asleep. Mr. Patton kicked the sleeping boy's bed with his heavy work boots.

Franklin sat up with a jolt, rubbing the sleep from his eyes. "Sir?"

"Where is she?" Mr. Patton asked in a hushed tone, dead serious and dangerous.

"What?" asked Franklin, swinging his legs over the side of the bed.

"Don't move," said Mr. Patton, pointing the gun directly at the boy's chest. "What did you do with Alice, you son of a bitch, where is she!"

Fear washed over Franklin's face as he fully took in the shotgun pointed straight at him, held by his uncle, who at this moment looked like a crazed wild man.

"You killed the cat."

"I don't know what you're talking about!"

"I know you killed Callan." Mr. Patton swallowed hard. "Where the FUCK is my daughter, Franklin?"

"I don't like cats," his nephew whispered.

Mr. Patton jabbed the shotgun into the boy's chest with force enough to almost send him sprawling. "Get up."

Maria and the twins were now up and at the doorway watching. Maria, having heard everything, ran to Franklin and slapped him hard across the face, her cheeks flaming and her eyes deadly.

"What have you done with my baby!" Maria screamed, spittle flying from her lips, tears streaming down her pale face. Mae and Glenda, still in their night clothes, stood in the hallway sobbing and hugging each other.

Mr. Patton turned the boy around and marched him down the stairs. "Maria," he ordered, "Get the sheriff. Get him now, before I handle this my own way and regret it."

The police questioned Franklin for hours; it turned out he had a valid alibi, which was acknowledged by several of the party guests and Mayor Patton's twins. Franklin had been sitting with Mr. Patton's other girls and a pair of neighbors during the younger children's game of hide and seek. He was allowed to return home that afternoon and Mr. Patton was waiting for him with his suitcase packed on the front step. Mr. Patton shoved a wad of bills into the boy's hand.

"Taxi fare and train fare." Mr. Patton said to him. "Get out." He swallowed hard, his face ashen from lack of sleep, worry, and grief. "Get out, now."

Franklin took the money, picked up his suitcase, and headed to the waiting taxi. He looked back at his uncle as he opened the door to the car while the taxi driver stowed his suitcase in the trunk and slammed it shut. Then Franklin got in, closed the door, and was whisked off to the train station, with a secret hidden deep in his pants pocket.

The summer passed with no sign of Alice. Searches were called off, and the consensus was that she had either been abducted, the chaos during the child's birthday party giving ample opportunity, or the nearby creek had washed her body farther off than previously thought, leaving the possibility of coyotes and other predators.

Mr. Patton and Maria were overcome by grief. Mr. Patton threw himself into his work, not arriving home till much after dark, and Maria barely left their house. The twins had started school again, but the family was broken, silent and distraught, changed forever in an instant. Changed forever by a dark, sinister, and unknown act which would not be discovered for many years to come.

Chapter Twenty

I'll Take That Wine Now

Trevor Becknor stared at his phone. The grainy photograph of Elvis that he had taken the night of Manny and Bobby's murders glowed in his hand. He glanced out the window toward Dan's Used Furniture and Supreme Meats, then back at his phone.

"Well, shit…"

Trevor dialed the sheriff's department and asked for Andy.

"Why didn't you show us this before, son?" Jimmy Cruz asked Trevor. They were sitting at Trevor's kitchen table, and he'd never seen Andy—Sheriff Cruz—look so serious in his life.

"I was afraid," Trevor said, his voice muted, "I thought it would make it look like I was in on it." Trevor looked down at his hands, which were folded on the dining room table. "Or worse, make it look like my stepdad was 100 percent guilty, and I knew he wasn't." Trevor looked up at Andy. "I knew he wasn't, he doesn't have it in him."

The photo from his phone clearly showed Elvis walking past the light pole with the poster of the missing dog still in the same spot. It also showed a beardless person that looked a good foot taller than where the poster was attached to the pole.

"My dad has had a beard as long as I can remember and he's not near that tall! That ain't my dad, Andy! Just look at this!"

Andy pointed to the time stamp, "I think you're onto something here, son."

Two days later, Glen Becknor was a free man, and the case of who had murdered Manny and Bobby Ruiz was once again officially open and unsolved.

Beth grabbed her purse, asked Grandpa to watch Bobo, and promised she'd take over Grandma's evening cooking duties tomorrow. She hopped into her car and headed to the Patton public library, the old newspaper clutched under her arm.

Beth had only been in the library once, when they donated some of the antique items from the Patton house; as she opened the door, she saw that the grandfather clock, which had belonged to Walter Patton I, sat proudly displayed in the entryway.

The woman behind the desk, Cindy Mendoza, was the same person she'd spoken with when they'd made their donations. Cindy smiled and stood as Beth came in the door. The woman had an honest, open look on her face, and Beth could tell she was genuinely happy to see her.

"Beth!" Cindy said, "It's so nice to see you again!"

Cindy stood all of about four feet nine, with salt-and-pepper hair in a shoulder length bob, her wrists and neck embellished with turquoise and silver jewelry. She walked around her desk and gave Beth a hug.

"What can I do for you today?" she said happily. "May I get you some coffee? Tea?"

Beth hugged her back. "No thanks, Cindy. I'm actually here to search for documents regarding the Patton house." Beth sat the newspaper on the desk, "I found this in our attic this morning, and it made me really curious."

Cindy leaned in and examined the date on the paper. "Is this the approximate time frame you want to search?"

"No," said Beth, "I want to start at the beginning. When the house was being built."

"Follow me." Cindy led Beth to a back room filled with boxes, shelves of chronologically ordered microfilm, and row upon row of filing cabinets and storage racks. The librarian explained to Beth how to use the microfilm reader and showed her how to search the Patton Gazette reels. "We have every newspaper printed in Patton, all the way back to 1887," she explained, then chuckled. "You may be here awhile!"

Beth took a deep breath, totally overwhelmed. "Maybe I'll take that coffee now, Cindy."

Cindy laughed and gestured with her hand. "Follow me, I'll show you where I keep the pot."

Walter Patton I was mentioned many times in the history of Patton, Colorado, the first time being the first edition of the Patton Gazette in 1887.

June 1st, 1887
Walter Patton breaks ground on Patton, Colorado Courthouse!

July 4th, 1892
Gold Money Paints Town Red! Walter Patton Sponsors Huge Independence Day Pic-nic on Main Street Square!

Beth smiled. Old newspapers were so much more flowery by today's standards.

November 2, 1897
Walter Patton Elected Mayor!

The Gazette went on to document the first Walter's life, his marriage to Bridget Swanson from Oklahoma City in 1895, the construction of the Patton Manor in 1896, the birth of their only son, Walter II, in 1898, Bridget's death, Walter I's death, Walter II's marriage, and the birth of Walter III in 1920.

Beth read through small town events, marriages, church gatherings, the openings of stores and restaurants—all interesting but uneventful. She decided to zero in on Walter III's life, since before that all that was documented was small town everyday life, and the paper she had found was from 1964—*that* was the period of time she was looking for.

Walter III was born on December 15th, 1920.

Walter had traveled the southwestern US and made a hefty fortune in oil. He married Maria Alonzo from Taos, New Mexico, in the fall of 1952, and that marriage resulted in three children—twin girls, Glenda and Mae, and their youngest daughter, Alice.

Beth rubbed her eyes, took a long drink of her now-cold coffee, then forwarded the microfilm reader to the year 1964 and finally came across the issue with the same date as the newspaper she had found in her basement that morning, July 3rd, 1964, with the story detailing the building of Mayor Patton's fallout shelter.

The layout of what was now her backyard was on full display. Beth checked the directional arrows on the property lines. She checked them again and nodded. She'd been right: the bomb shelter was built squarely below what was now Mr. Frank's home.

She almost stopped there, excited about her new find and feeling the need to tell Jack this news, but curiosity got the best of her, and she continued scrolling.

For the next few weeks, minus the Fourth of July Parade, it seemed Patton, CO was lulled into a quiet spell; the pastor's wife had a baby, and a couple named Julia and Stephen White opened a restaurant which still was open to this day, and still was called Julia's Diner.

Beth took a break and went to make another pot of coffee. "How's snooping going?" Cindy asked her, looking up from a pile of books she was stacking on a cart to be returned to their shelf.

Beth grinned. "Fairly well, actually. I've found the edition that matched the paper in my attic, and more in-depth photos of my back yard." Beth leaned against the counter as the coffee perked. "Did you know that part of the original land where my house sits was annexed out, and another house was built on it? The house where my neighbor Mr. Frank lives."

Cindy thought for a moment and set down a stack of books she was examining, "I remember hearing something about that, but it was a long time ago; after the tragedy that struck the Patton family."

Beth almost spilled the coffee creamer she was holding and juggled it back into an upright position. "Tragedy?"

Cindy nodded, "Keep scrolling, you're almost there, you can't miss it."

Beth grabbed her mug and a napkin and hurried back to the microfilm reader. She anxiously pulled out her chair, causing it to screech against the tile floor; she set her mug on the desk, rubbed her eyes, and went back to the important work at hand—snooping.

Nothing much through the end of July and August, until the August 29th edition popped up.

August 29, 1964

Mayor Walter Patton's Youngest Daughter Disappears from Birthday Celebration.

Beth gasped and covered her mouth with her hand, "Oh my God."

Mayor Walter Patton's youngest daughter, Alice, went missing from her fourth birthday celebration in the early afternoon of August 27th. The party, which included fifty-seven guests and the Patton family, was held on the grounds of the Patton estate. Alice was last seen around 2:00 P.M. by her parents, Walter and Maria Patton, and numerous guests. The police were informed and an in-depth search began late afternoon and continued through the night.

Saddened by the thought of what her parents must have gone through, Beth felt an overwhelming need to hug her children. Not long ago, she'd lost Bobo in Target for about ten minutes and thought she'd lose her mind. He'd been hiding in a round rack of ladies' dresses when she saw his smiling little face peeking out at her. She didn't know whether to strangle him or plant kisses all over his face.

Beth continued reading that several of the party guests were questioned, along with Walter Patton's nephew, Franklin, who had come to live with the Patton family earlier that summer. All those questioned had been cleared by the police.

As of publication, Alice Patton remains missing.

Beth gulped the last of her coffee from the mug, promised herself to replace it with a wine glass when she got home, said thank you to Cindy, and proceeded to hurry home to hug her kids. Snooping had just turned into some serious business.

The beer joint was hopping when Beth arrived home. The enormous TV was on mute, playing last Sunday's game.

Bobo, sitting atop the polished mahogany bar and wearing Richard Miller's garrison cap, was making an empty shot glass pyramid—the glasses engraved with Al's Beer Joint. Jack and Ben were deep into a game of pool, and Grandpa was making Grandma another old fashioned; by the looks of her, she was a few old fashioneds into tipsyland. Grandpa had recently purchased two vintage pinball games, and Sam, BJ, Trevor, and Hank were whooping up a storm, the music and bells and flappers singing nostalgic music to a new generation of delighted ears. The Clarks were playing poker at the poker table with Stumpy Joe and Shorty, and by the look of the stack of chips, Jenny was kicking some ass.

Grandma batted her eyelashes at Richard Miller and took a sip of her old fashioned. "Beth!" Grandma chimed in over the clatter, "now the whole fam-damily is here!" Grandma was a lot of fun when she'd been drinking. "Have Grandpa pour you a glass of wine and join the party!"

"No, thank you," Beth answered.

The party noises screeched to a halt and all eyes turned to her.

"What?" asked Jack, "No wine?" He was looking at her like she'd grown two heads.

"I found some interesting information about our house at the library today," she said, walking toward one of the bar tables and setting down the old Patton Gazette. One last pinball clanged its way home.

Everyone gathered around as she spread the yellowed newspaper out on the tabletop. Even Bobo left his carefully constructed shot glass tower, clambered down onto a bar stool, and jumped to the floor.

"I wanna see," he said, and lifted his arms to his dad to be picked up. Jack scooped him up and they all bent over the table as Beth explained today's findings.

"Our house used to have more land," she said, pointing to the news photograph of the adjacent lot.

"Mr. Frank's house, or rather the property it sits on, used to be part of the Patton property—it was divided into two lots in the seventies."

Beth pointed to the headline regarding the bomb shelter.

"There was a fallout shelter under Mr. Frank's house and a tunnel that ran between point A—" Beth pointed to the shelter itself— "and point B." She pointed to their home.

Grandma let out a gasp and spilled half of her old fashioned down her sweater. One of the booze-soaked maraschino cherries bounced from her lap toward the floor, where Mr. Tinkles gobbled it up before it hit the ground.

Beth continued, "It seems Walter Patton III had bit into all of the Cold War hysteria and built what the article states could be 'the biggest bomb shelter west of the Mississippi.'"

"My uncle had one of those," said Shorty, "it filled with water after a while and was deemed a safety hazard. They finally filled it in and cemented it over." Shorty paused, "As a kid I remember looking down those dark stairs and seeing half-submerged bunks and a wall filled with rusty old cans."

"The door to the tunnel was in our house?" Sam asked, his eyes wide.

"Yes," Beth answered, "but I have no idea where that might be," she said, deep in thought. "Some place in the basement, or a hatch next to the house, I suppose."

Grandma made a choking sound and downed the rest of her old fashioned in one gulp, then held the empty glass out to Grandpa. He hurried to the bar to pour her another from the shaker.

"It gets even more strange," said Beth. "Walter Patton's four-year-old daughter went missing a few months later that summer," Beth continued, "and as far as I can tell, she was never seen again."

"I bet she's in that old bomb shelter!" Ben exclaimed.

Sam's mom interrupted him. "No, the entire grounds and miles of countryside were searched after her disappearance—including the bomb shelter."

"How awful," Grandma whispered, looking down into the drink Grandpa had just handed her. "That poor family."

Sam looked into the faces of his friends. "Mom?" Sam asked cautiously, "what was her name? The missing girl? What was her name?"

"Alice," Beth answered, "her name was Alice Patton."

The kids gasped and stared one at another. Sam looked at BJ and whispered, "Alice?"

"I'll take that wine now, Dad," Beth said to Grandpa.

Chapter Twenty-One

Espionage and BEES

"We gotta find it," Sam told his friends, as they lay back on the lazily spinning kid launcher in the park. "We'll check every inch of the basement." He drew a roughly house-shaped square in the dust on the metal base of the merry-go-round. "We'll search every inch of the perimeter for a hidden hatch."

"I feel like we're in a spy movie," Hank said, hanging on every word. He pointed to the house diagram on the metal platform. "If we start here—" his finger hovered over what would be the front porch— "and then Sam, Ben, and the Clarks head this direction—" he dragged his finger through the dust in a southerly direction— "and me and BJ and Trevor head this way—" he circled to the north— "we'll meet up in the backyard, approximately... here!" Hank stabbed his finger in the area that would be the back door stairs.

"That means that you and BJ and Trevor will be taking the side of the house closer to Mr. Frank's place," Jenny said. "Wouldn't it make more sense that the entrance would be in that area?"

BJ shook his head. "Not really, it could open up from any part of the foundation." He turned to her. "The cold war had people terrified. My grandpa said, and I quote, 'Those Commie bastards were sneaky fuckers.'"

They all nodded in agreement and agreed on a plan: first, load up with drinks and snacks from Mark's Market, then head over to Sam's house and start their investigation into finding the Commie bastard hidey hole in full force.

Armed with two six-packs of soda, three bags of chips, and a dozen candy bars, they headed back to the Patton House.

Trevor opened the squeaky front gate. "When's somebody gonna oil this thing?" he mumbled.

After the snacks and soda had been stowed safely in the house, the seven of them gathered on the porch. Sam had hedge clippers in hand in case they came across a barrier of shrubbery, and his brother had a hammer. BJ had on work gloves and held a can of bug spray. He hated spiders.

"Can't we just get your dad's chainsaw?" Hank asked Sam, looking down at the puny shears in his own hands.

"Don't be an idiot, Hank," Jaimie said, raising her protective eyewear and peering at him. "This is a covert operation, and that means we need to be quiet. Basic OPSEC." She rolled her eyes. "You'd suck at being a spy."

Jaimie lowered the safety glasses back over her eyes. "Let's do this."

Jenny nodded her affirmation, adjusted her backpack, and saluted.

They split into two groups, confident their mission would provide ample results and the mystery would be solved.

Ten minutes later they were sitting on the back stoop, discouraged, empty-handed and minus any kind of evidence of an entrance to a bomb shelter.

"Nada," said Sam.

"Nothing on our side, either," agreed Trevor, shaking his head and scratching Mr. Tinkles between the ears.

Hank had been stung on the wrist by a wasp and was acting as if he should get a purple heart. "I didn't know you'd have *bees,*" he whined, examining the sting closely. A small red welt had appeared.

"Jesus, Hank," Jaimie said, "weren't you the one that wanted to use a *chainsaw?*"

Hank huffed at her and hid his arm behind his back.

"We'll have better luck inside," Sam said confidently and opened the back door, letting his friends go in first. Grandma and Grandpa were out shopping, so the basement would be still and empty. Grandma wouldn't be a fan of seven kids snooping in her kitchen. Grandma wouldn't be a fan of seven kids, period.

Sam unlatched the inside door that led down the stairs to his grandparents' apartment, gestured Ben through, and clicked on the light. "Let's start in the kitchen."

They opened every cabinet door, checked and knocked on all the walls, made their way through the front room, carefully examining baseboards and looking for any discrepancies in the drywall without success, and finally found themselves in front of Grandpa's beer joint.

"I stinkin' love this place," whispered Jenny.

Sam entered the code to the wine cellar, and they shimmied their way into the small, earthen, bricked-in space. They checked behind the bottles and barrels and rummaged through the shelves.

"Nothing," said Jaimie, "nothing but a shit-ton of booze. Jesus, Sam, who's going to drink all this?"

"Have you met my mom?" Ben said.

"I can't believe we came up empty handed," said Hank, still rubbing his wrist absentmindedly. "Maybe they just bricked it all over and filled it with cement, because there'd have to be some kind of…"

Something tinkled down from the ceiling to the floor. They all jumped in surprise. Sticking out of the dirt floor in front of the cabernet was a red pen of shame, its point embedded into the ground.

Jenny screeched. Trevor dropped his flashlight. Hank began to hyperventilate, the war wound on his wrist totally forgotten.

"Jesus on a stick!" yelled Sam, but then bent down to examine where this obvious sign was aiming. "Let's move these bottles and see what's behind the shelf! Damn, Grandpa's gonna kill us."

Sam and Ben began to move wine bottles, beginning with the bottle closest to the red-pen arrow. Sam tugged on a bottle of cabernet, and it stuck tight three-quarters of the way out. The back shelves creaked and pulled away from the wall a few inches, taking all the wine bottles and the false, lightweight, but realistic-looking brick wall behind it along with it.

"Mother…"

"…Fucker," finished Jenny.

The wall was a false front, and as one end swiveled in and the other swiveled out, the kids could see that all that lay behind the metal, brick, and dark glass bottles was a rough-edged, gaping, five-foot-tall cavern, as black and bottomless as a yawning, toothless mouth.

Trevor bent to pick up the flashlight, his eyes never leaving the tunnel they'd just uncovered; his hand brushed the red pen and he yelped as if burned. Grasping the flashlight in both shaking hands, he flicked the on switch. It took three tries before he got it to light.

Trevor aimed the beam into the blackness. Beyond the entrance, the dirt floor of the cave sloped down, flanked by concrete walls. Twelve feet or so in was a metal door. A newer-looking keypad blinked red in the darkness.

"This lock is not from the sixties," said BJ. "It looks state-of-the-art, like the keypad that locks in your grandpa's booze."

Sam nodded in agreement, "Guys," he said, his voice turning serious, "it's time to bring in the big guns." He turned and looked at them, "I'm telling my grandpa the whole story, and he can call in the Army."

There were high fives all around: the cavalry was on its way. God bless our troops.

Javier kissed Alejandra, his tongue deep and probing; her breath tasted of lavender and honeycomb.

"Yes," she said, tears sliding down her cheeks in salty rivulets of happiness.

He wiped them away with the pad of his thumb.

"Yes, Javier," Alejandra said again, her moist eyes spar-kling in the waning light of sunset, "of course I'll marry you."

The End

Beth let out a whoop, stood, and with an overly dramatic flourish, hit Save. She grabbed Bobo, spun him around, and kissed his nose. "Mama said moist!"

Mr. Tinkles barked happily.

"Moist!" squealed Bobo.

"Ice cream for everyone!" Beth gave Mr. T a pat on the head. "You too, little man."

When Beth, Bobo and Mr. T walked into the kitchen, Sam and his friends were sitting around the kitchen table.

"I finished my book!" Sam's mom exclaimed. "I'm taking these two—" she gestured toward the baby and the dog— "out for ice cream." She smiled brightly, seeming not to notice the somber cloud that hung over the room. "I'll bring enough home for everybody."

Beth grabbed her car keys from the hook by the back door. "Be home in a bit!" She danced out the back door, and Sam could hear her shout a greeting to Grandma and Grandpa, who were just now coming home.

"Great timing," said BJ.

Grandma and Grandpa came in the back door, and Grandma waved. "Hi kids," she said, heading down the stairs to their apartment. "Don't eat the ham, it's for dinner."

Grandpa waited until Grandma was out of earshot, walked on over, and put his hat on Sam's head.

"So!" Grandpa said, clapping his hands, "Who wants ham sandwiches?" He looked from one gloomy face to the next.

"What's the matter with you kids?" he asked them. Grandpa knew that if pre-teens didn't jump on the offer of food, something mighty big was up. He crossed his arms over his chest. "Who broke what?"

"Grandpa?" Sam said, laying his hands on the table. "We need your help."

Grandpa's gaze went from one glum expression to the next, their serious faces telling him all he needed to know. "This is gonna be one of those, 'don't tell Grandma' kind of things, I can tell," he groaned. "Right?" He took the last empty kitchen chair, spun it around, and sat, straddling it.

"Tell me everything."

Chapter Twenty-two

Bumbling Dumbasses

ELVIS AND PRISCILLA had a huge whopper of a fight. The kind of fight that rattled the rafters.

He had bought her a small but exquisite opal and gold pendant, and she'd been livid and ungrateful. Supposedly, opals were bad luck—unless they were massive, and enormously expensive opals. She'd told him in no uncertain terms that she was worth much more than what he had bought her, and had thrown his gift on the dining room table without giving it a second look.

As the evening continued to sour, Priscilla brought up subjects that he thought were long buried. The subject of Olivia came up again. Priscilla whined on and on about how she felt second to her, always his second choice, and her relentless temper and out-of-control jealousy stabbed at him like a red-hot poker.

He'd had enough. Yeah, she was one good looking woman, but nothing was worth all this insane drama. He reminded her that Olivia was now dead as a stump, and still that hadn't quelled her green-eyed wrath. The evening had ended with two broken champagne glasses, a shattered mirror, and words so heated he was surprised the place didn't catch fire. Elvis could hold onto his anger, and had long ago learned to control it unless it served a purpose, but the last straw came when she'd gotten into his face and called him crazy and phony, and an old has-been wannabe.

No one called him crazy. Ever.

He'd snapped. His hand shot out fast as a snake and grabbed Priscilla by the neck. The dangerous look in his eyes must have told her that he was no longer playing her emotional games, and she went silent, her haughty temper tantrum dissolving instantly.

Elvis knew his eyes went black with psychotic excitement when he was almost at the point of no turning back, and she must have smelled it. She dug her nails into the flesh of his hand, pushed him away, grabbed her handbag, and went to the door, slamming it with a force great enough to shake the plates in the cupboard. He could hear her scream angrily through the closed door as she gave it a kick. "Fuck you, old man," she yelled drunkenly, and kicked the door again. "You crazy son of a bitch!"

He calmly watched her out of the window, and with black amusement saw her teeter off on her heels, drop her purse, pick it up, stomp her feet like a child, kick a tire, and open the driver's side door of her car. Under the dome light he could see her throw him the finger before slamming the door and peeling out in a squealing fit of rage. What a piece of work.

He hoped this would be the last he'd hear from her, and he planned to never see her again, no matter how much she begged—and he knew she would. He knew she saw him because of his money, and she'd been fun, but he was done with her. And when Elvis made up his mind, it was rock solid.

Elvis was enraged. Everyone he loved betrayed him, and everyone who betrayed him paid for it. It didn't bother him in the slightest that Manny Ruiz was dead, the dupe had gotten in the way, but Bobby…Bobby had it coming. The goddamn fool had taken something that had belonged to him, and his dad was collateral damage.

Even Olivia, who for a brief moment he'd thought he loved, betrayed him. It took him a while to understand it was her *house* that he loved, not her. Olivia in her flat shoes and conservative clothes. He shrugged it off: that was just the way things happened sometimes. A messy means to an end. Adios, Bobby and Manny. Toodle-oo, Olivia. Don't let the door hit you in the ass, Priscilla. The plan was to ghost Priscilla completely, because he knew a second round of this type of anger would end… messily.

Elvis stripped out of his white pants and took off the red shirt, a few sequins falling to the floor as he did so.

"I'll never need these again," he muttered. Elvis was now purged from his life.

He opened the safe, moved the contents carefully to the side, wadded up the shirt and pants, and tossed them onto the top shelf. He spun the lock, slammed the door, and closed that chapter of his life along with it.

Unfortunately for Elvis, karma sometimes wiggles its sneaky way between the best-laid plans.

Years ago

Olivia Sharette opened the squeaky iron gate that led to the Patton House. She'd need to remember to oil it, but first things first.

She picked up the two suitcases filled with her belongings and climbed the steps to the porch, set the suitcases down, found the right key from the ring, and opened the front door.

Her front door.

The house was stuffy and a bit musty, so she left her suitcases by the entryway. She opened curtains and windows, letting in fresh air and sunshine, and when she opened the kitchen windows, the cross breeze blew through the house, bringing with it a whole new atmosphere.

Olivia smiled and retrieved her suitcases from the foyer, carefully bumping them up the stairs to the second floor. She stood before the master bedroom taking in its circular turret and antique furniture. She pulled open the shades and sunlight flooded the room; a large glass prism hung by the window, and sunbeams splashed rainbow colors over the walls.

She threw herself over the bed and kicked off her shoes, watching the colorful lights spread magic through her new bedroom. Tears fell from her eyes and slid into her ears, tickling them. She wiped them away and mouthed a quiet "thank you" to the man who had made this possible. All that he had done for her went above and beyond anything she could have imagined just four short years ago. Granted, her heart held a bit of guilt for accepting so much help these past few years, but she hoped that the love she felt in her heart, the honest, pure love, made up for it.

She smiled, wiped away the last of her tears, and stood, walking to the smaller suitcase. Opening it, she retrieved a framed 8x10 photograph which a waitress at a bar had taken of them. They were sitting in a jazz club, their faces happy, laughing into each other's eyes, two beer bottles on the table. She remembered the joke they'd shared at that moment. He'd told her that he knew that all her future pupils would have wild crushes on her, and how he was already jealous of a bunch of twelve-year-olds. It was a spontaneous photograph that said so much about how she was feeling. She'd cherish it forever.

She removed a small painting of a landscape from the wall and replaced it with the photograph she was holding. She straightened the bottom and smiled. She felt no resentment or regret. How could she?

Olivia slipped back into her shoes and explored the rest of the mansion one room at a time, each one a happy surprise of antique furniture and carefully cared-for treasures. She danced down the back stairs and opened the door leading to the large expanse of the backyard. The size of the property shocked her. It stretched out in a beautifully manicured stretch of green.

This is so much more than I need, she thought as she walked slowly from one end to the other. The roses were in bloom in a wash of red and yellow and pink; it was stunning.

She stopped a few feet from her back stoop. An excited grin spread over her face as an idea came to her. She'd sell half of this property and donate the proceeds to St. Jude's Hospital for Children in Memphis, since it was one of Elvis's favorite charities. The pangs of guilt she felt dissolved as she made this decision, and she dashed back into the house to unpack. Tomorrow, bright and early, she'd head to Patton Elementary school to begin to decorate her classroom for incoming pupils, and on the way home she'd stop at the courthouse to file the paperwork to divide the property.

Olivia Sharette had never in her life felt more content and certain about the future. Life was good.

Grandpa listened as the seven children shared their experiences of the last few days, the supernatural occurrences, the seance, the smoky, dark shadow that filled the attic, culminating with them finding the entrance to the tunnel that led to the fallout shelter.

Grandpa drummed his fingers on the table. "It was that easy to guess the code to the wine cellar?"

This made Sam laugh.

"You'll help us?" BJ asked.

"Damn skippy," said Grandpa, pointing at him, "I'll call the troops tonight after your grandma goes to bed." His eyes narrowed. "Do not try to go on your own—" he made them promise that— "and don't tell anyone."

He pointed at them. "I mean it."

They all nodded.

"No police, the bumbling dumbasses. I want to handle this little issue on my own." Grandpa stopped and thought for a moment. "Getting through that second door isn't going to be easy." He paused. "Although you all got through my door easily enough."

Jaimie's eyes got bright and she held up a finger. "The code was Grandma's birthday, right?" she said, looking from one face to the next.

Grandpa rolled his eyes and huffed. "Yep, I should have known better."

Jaimie lowered her voice, her eyes filled with excitement. "Miss Sharette," she whispered, "when is Miss Sharette's birthday?"

Chapter Twenty-three

A House Filled with Secrets

Years earlier

BEFORE THE INK WAS DRY on the paperwork that split the Patton property into two halves, someone named Miles Frank purchased the property. It was early in the summer of 1972, and within weeks construction began on a small bungalow.

After taxes and fees were paid, Olivia Sharette donated the remainder of the profit to charity. She felt good about it, her guilt had vanished, and she was anxious to meet her new neighbor.

A week into construction her doorbell rang, and when she opened it there was a man standing on her stoop. He looked to be about her age, and he introduced himself as Miles Frank, her soon-to-be neighbor.

"Call me Frank," he told her, and handed her a box of fancy chocolates. "Housewarming gift." He smiled.

Olivia accepted them and smiled back. "Frank?" she said to him, "I haven't had lunch, and breakfast was just a piece of toast, so I'm famished, and these," she said pointing to the chocolate and vanilla treats, "look delicious. Would you like to come in for a cup of coffee and a cupcake?"

Frank removed his hat and entered the foyer, "Amazing," Frank said, "It hasn't changed a bit."

"You've been here before?" asked Olivia, her curiosity piqued.

"Just once, when I was a boy," he said curtly, brushing off the question. "Coffee sounds great." He gave her his best charming smile.

Even that day, she knew something was off about him. Olivia couldn't pinpoint what exactly, but her ability to read people's character was exemplary and she trusted her instincts. She'd keep a close eye on her new neighbor.

Frank followed her into the kitchen, and she prepared coffee the only way she ever had, in an old Mr. Coffee machine from her college days. She reached to the window ledge to turn the radio down, and as chance would have it, Love Me Tender was playing. "I love Elvis," said Frank with a smile, "no need to turn it down."

"I do too," said Olivia, "my goodness, I do too." She laughed and turned the volume up a notch.

Frank smiled at her and took the cup of coffee from her hands. He already knew that, of course. Miles Frank did his homework.

Mr. Frank was never a fan of Elvis's music. He'd laid it on thick for Olivia, and at first that seemed to work out damn fine. They had music in common, something to talk about, stories to share, albeit his were mostly fabricated. She shared with him a bit about her past life, but never came right out and told him what he already knew—that Elvis Presley had bought the Patton house…right out from under his nose. Mr. Frank seethed at the thought of it. How could he have missed out? How did the King of rock and roll snatch it up right under his nose? A property in Colorado? Elvis had no ties to Colorado. It made him feel jilted.

Miles Frank would do anything to get his hands on the deed to that property, because he knew its secrets, he heard it speak to him, he knew what lay under it, what drifted through it, and in his mind he was its rightful heir. The boy he'd met on the train ten years ago, the real Franklin, Walter Patton's nephew, never knew what hit him when Miles followed him to the back of the train on the pretense of showing him some rodeo memorabilia. He didn't know what hit him when the Bemis & Call monkey wrench crashed down on his fourteen-year-old skull, splitting it open like a ripe Rocky Ford melon; nor did he know when Miles dragged Franklin to the back of the train and tossed his body off right around Reno.

Miles had had enough time to find out a lot of details from young Franklin that day, and oh, how Walter Patton's nephew had talked. He talked nonstop all the way from California. He'd explained how his mother had passed away, and how he was on his way to live with his aunt and uncle in Patton, Colorado and how they were filthy stinking rich. Miles also knew that they'd never met their nephew, so there'd be no questions when he walked off the train in Colorado and ran into the loving arms of his new guardians and foster siblings.

Miles Frank chuckled: he hadn't even had a legitimate train ticket. He stole a ticket from a young mom when she was busy dealing with her two unruly children, and no one was the wiser. Before disposing of the body, he'd emptied Franklin's pockets, found his suitcases, memorized his lines and all the details he'd pulled out of the sad, needy, and talkative Franklin.

Everything had gone off without a hitch, but Walter Patton seemed to smell the deceit on him almost from day one. And then there was Alice. The dumb, squealing little bitch. He'd only wanted to hold her on his lap, she was just so beautiful. She wiggled off his lap swearing to tell her parents that she didn't like the way he touched her, and he made her promise not to tell—she wouldn't want to get her *brother* in trouble, would she? The next day she found him in Mr. and Mrs. Patton's bedroom, rummaging through dresser drawers. He picked her up and hugged her, told her he loved her, and again made her promise not to tell her parents. She didn't seem so sure this time, so he promised her a big surprise during the birthday party, and that seemed to appease her.

Mr. Frank let out a sigh; if ever in his life he'd loved anyone, it had been Alice, and she'd threatened to undermine him.

Yeah, the women in his life made him crazy. He tried hard to impress Olivia and it only made her back away from him. Did he love her? He thought maybe he did. He imagined moving into the Patton House with her, living the good life, being the new bigshot in town with all that money. But did he love her? He thought about this; probably not. He wanted to own her, to be her, to live the life she had, to be closer to the secrets. That house was filled with secrets. Miles Frank loved the secrets.

Mr. Frank took a long, deep breath. Why the hell did he kill Manny and Bobby? Not because he loved her, but because they had taken his property. No one steals from Miles Frank—well, no one steals from Thomas Gleason. He'd been Thomas Gleason before the train ride that changed his life. Poor dead, buried, long-forgotten Thomas Gleason whose body had been half eaten by coyotes was found just outside of Reno carrying his wallet with his ID. Thomas Gleason was dead, and Miles Frank was very much alive.

He'd end up owning the Patton House again sometime soon, all it would take was a little patience and a whole lot of smarts. Mr. Frank, formerly known as Elvis, formerly known as Thomas Gleason, was a lot of things, and smart was right on top of that list. The Hamlin family had to go.

Grandpa gathered the Army buddies at Julia's Diner for an impromptu breakfast. Lydia brought them all coffee, and Stumpy Joe an orange juice. They thanked her, asked her about her mother, who'd been sick and in the hospital, and then politely waited for her to drift back to behind the pancake bar.

"Okay," said Richard Miller, "where's the fire?" He took a sip of his coffee, grimaced, and reached for another sugar packet. "Bottom of the pot, right there," he said, stirring his mug, the spoon clinking on the sides. "You sounded damn serious when you called this meeting, Sarge," he said. "You're never serious, what's up?" He took another sip of his coffee, seemed satisfied, and set it back down.

"Well," said Grandpa, "first off, my damn house is haunted." Three sets of bushy, gray, ex-Army eyebrows lifted in unison. Grandpa sipped his own coffee and said, "Secondly, I think we have an…intruder."

"A living intruder?"

"Yep," said Grandpa, "flesh and blood and breathing." He looked from one buddy to the next. "I want to catch the sumbitch red handed."

"I ain't afraid of no ghosts," Stumpy Joe said, making air quotes with his fingers. "It's the live ones that'll getcha."

Lydia brought their food, each plate filled with some of the greatest heart attack breakfast chow you could get in the whole state.

Not even Stumpy Joe began to eat: all their attention was on Grandpa and his mission. None of them questioned his story; they knew that when Sarge was serious, he was dead serious and it was time to snap to it, pull up your pants, and pay attention.

"Since we moved into the Patton House, we've been having some very odd things happen," Grandpa went on. "Doors open and close on their own, cupboards open and slam, shit drops from the ceiling," he said, thinking of the red pens.

"Literal shit?" asked Shorty, as his bushy gray eyebrows shot up like electrocuted caterpillars.

"No, dummy, not literal shit—pens. Red pens come out of nowhere."

Grandpa took a bite of his eggs. "Sammy's late English teacher used red pens."

"Okay…" said Shorty, "that's better than literal shit— by a long shot." Shorty nodded and motioned for him to continue.

"As you all know, we bought our house with the lottery money we won," Grandpa said. "The ticket itself was found by Sammy." All eyes were on Grandpa as he slathered butter on his toast and continued. "The ticket was purchased by Olivia Sharette, Sam's English teacher, who just happened to own the house before us. Minutes after he found the ticket, she met her maker, when Dan's Used Furniture and Supreme Meats truck smashed her in the street in front of Mark's Market."

"So," said Stumpy Joe, "you're living in a house that for all practical purposes you bought from a woman with her own money."

"Yep," said Grandpa, "didn't know it at the time though."

"Do you think whatever it is is dangerous?" asked Richard Miller. "The supernatural part, I mean."

"You know, Rich, I don't think so." The activity that feels like it comes from Olivia seems…" Grandpa struggled for a word, "…benign. Almost…helpful." He filled them in about the red pens of shame, seeming to drop from nowhere. "All of that seems to be centered around Sam." Grandpa sipped his coffee. "And the kid says he never feels threatened."

The Army buddies nodded.

"However," Grandpa said, "there are other things. My dumbass grandson and his friends decided it would be a good idea to have a séance in the attic." Grandpa saw Lydia looking over, smiled, and pointed at his coffee cup. She hurried over, pot in hand and filled all of their mugs. They nodded their thanks.

"Stuff happened in that attic that scared the kids shitless. The dog, too. Took a whole boxful of treats to coax him back into the house. Poor fella still won't go upstairs." Grandpa told them about the Ouija board incident and how the board had spelled out "Alice."

He picked up his fork and stabbed at his scrambled eggs, which were smothered in green chili. Everything in Patton was smothered in green chili. You could even buy green chili beer from a craft brewery in Fort Collins. "Turns out," Grandpa said through a mouthful of eggs, "that Walter Patton the III, the guy that was Mayor in the 60's—remember him?" They all nodded. "He had a daughter named Alice who went missing in '64 and was never found."

Their eyes went wide.

"No shit," said Shorty.

"No shit," said Grandpa.

Grandpa filled the guys in on how Beth had found the newspaper from that summer in question and had done some research which proved that Alice had indeed gone missing.

"There's something else in our house though, I can feel it."

"The squatter?" asked Richard Miller.

"There's that, and I'll get to it, but something else too." Grandpa thought for a moment, "Something that feels…I wouldn't say threatening, more like…trying urgently to get our attention."

The guys hung on every word.

"As for the intruder," Grandpa went on, "during Beth's research at the library, she also found out that the property where we now live used to be larger; it encompassed the property next door, and old man Patton had a bomb shelter built back in the sixties…right about under where my neighbor's house sits."

Grandpa banged a fist on the table. "I know how he gets in, and I'm pretty sure I know who it is!"

The buddies waited for him to continue. Stumpy Joe's fork, filled with eggs, poised halfway between his plate and his mouth. This was a sure sign of a serious issue; Stumpy Joe always inhaled his food.

Grandpa pointed at Stumpy Joe with his own fork. "Remember a few weeks ago when you found those gold sunglasses in the wine cellar?"

Stumpy Joe nodded, the eggs on his fork dripping green chili.

"Did you notice anything else when you were back there?"

Stumpy Joe thought for a minute. "Well," he said, "Now that you mention it…the back wall seemed a little off kilter, and I pushed it back into place."

Grandpa nodded. "Bingo," he said, as the buddies took it all in. "That's where the tunnel to the bomb shelter comes out of our house. The same bomb shelter that Beth found out about in her research in the library. The same damn bomb shelter that sits under our neighbor's house. This is why I called you together today. We need to plan a reconnaissance mission and do this right." Grandpa lifted his coffee cup. "We're gonna catch this bastard and call him out!"

His Army buddies lifted their cups in solidarity.

"Who ya gonna call?" asked Shorty.

"Ghostbusters!" the buddies said in unison, then toasted on it. Java splashed on the red checked tablecloth.

"Hey Lydia," yelled Stumpy Joe, "can I get some more hash browns and another plate of bacon?"

They all looked at him.

"What?" He said. "An army travels on its stomach."

"Tomorrow night," Grandpa said, "Twenty hundred hours."

Stumpy Joe saluted with his fork, a glob of green chili falling onto his lap.

It was like old times.

Chapter Twenty-four

Don't You Idiots Scratch the Paint

In 1966, Maria Patton finally learned how to drive.

Walter was no longer mayor, and was now doing research work for an oil company. In his sorrow he'd thrown himself into his work—and into a bottomless bottle of whiskey. He wasn't home much, and Maria needed to be able to get her twins to events, doctor's appointments, and school activities without relying on him. Glenda and Mae were now thirteen years old and busy, active teenagers.

Walter's personality had changed so much since Alice's disappearance. It was hard to get him out of the house other than to work, and he was sullen and angry a lot of the time…not to mention his drinking. He drank a lot, and was the kind of drunk who distanced himself from situations to avoid pain. When he was home, he wasn't really present. Maria knew he carried a lot of unwarranted guilt on his shoulders; "I should have, I could have, I would have" started most of his sentences, especially when he'd been drinking. Maria never in a million years thought her life would have turned out the way it did, but she had two growing girls to tend to, and now that she was driving things might be easier.

Maria kept her driving duties close to home. The school, the grocery store, doctor and dentist appointments…but after having her license for three months, she felt confident enough to pack up the girls and take a trip to New Mexico to visit her parents. The children were on spring break, and the thought of having the freedom to get out of the house for a week without Walter, even though she loved him dearly, was appealing.

She had the girls pack a couple of bags, kissed her husband goodbye, and headed south to Taos for a much needed break and change of scenery.

The drive down was glorious; the cottonwoods were just beginning to leaf out, that tender green that only comes in springtime. The weather was clear and warm, and it filled her with a feeling of peace—something she hadn't felt for quite some time.

The twins, whom Maria adored, were at that complicated age between being a child and being an adult. Sometimes it was challenging to deal with their budding teenage drama, but Maria had expected it. And when things got a bit tense, she always reminded herself that this was normal and thought about what she'd been like at that age. She smiled to herself; she'd been a handful!

Pulling into the driveway at her parents' house filled her with happiness, the home she'd grown up in looking every bit the same as it had when she was a child. Her mother was on the front porch waiting for them, and the girls dashed from the car into their nana's arms. Maria smiled, sat behind the wheel of the car, and watched the scene unfold. It was bittersweet. Alice should be here, running to greet her grandmother along with her sisters. Maria missed her so much. She missed her every day, but this trip was about happiness and reunions, and Maria believed with all her heart that someday she'd be reunited with Alice. She shook the momentary sadness away, stepped from the car, and just as the twins had done, she ran into her mother's arms.

The week in Taos passed quickly, every minute taken up by some sort of family activity. Dinners were made that took all day to cook, but with three extra pairs of hands the job was fun and filled with laughter. Music filled the house, cousins came and went, Maria's crazy uncle Guillermo visited and brought along his guitar and two lady friends. The twins explored every bit of the twenty-plus acres her parents owned, most of it on horseback. They visited the family's well-tended graveyard—twice, her father laying fresh flowers on the graves and telling stories about each of the relatives whose markers showed their resting-places.

"Your uncle Marvin would still be here if he hadn't fallen on his head," her father said. "He was so drunk when he fell out of the back of that truck, I don't think he even knew he'd fallen out." Maria's father whispered, "He was never the same after falling on his head. Took him three years to finally die." Her father gave a small chuckle as he laid yellow carnations on his grave. "*Sonso*," he muttered, calling his brother a dummy, which happened every time they passed his headstone.

The night before Maria and the girls were scheduled to leave, the house was packed full of people for a goodbye party—cousins and uncles and aunts and friends of the family. Some she remembered from her childhood; they were older, but still exactly as she remembered, just with more gray hair and quite a few more wrinkles. Plastic tablecloths were laid over folding tables, and guests brought chairs and food. Lots of food. The house was noisy and happy and filled with cheerful laughter, and plenty of hugs and kisses. For most of the evening the twins and their cousins were in the backyard by the small barn. The family dog had had puppies a few days earlier, and the children were enthralled.

Glenda came in through the back door and told her grandmother that it was beginning to snow. She was worried about the puppies being out in the cold for the night, and her grandmother asked her granddad to bring the dog and her puppies into the back room and set up a bed next to the coats and boots.

As the night went on, the weather became colder and light snow continued to fall, but Uncle Guillermo had read that there wasn't going to be much of an accumulation, which was good, since Maria didn't like the idea of driving all the way home in the snow.

By morning the snow had stopped, but the air was chill. Maria had the twins bundle up in winter coats and hats, and they wore the mittens their grandmother had made them. Goodbyes were said, tears were shed, promises made to visit more often. Maria stowed their suitcases into the trunk of her Ford Falcon, slammed the trunk, got behind the wheel, and backed slowly out of the driveway to a chorus of "Drive safe! Call us when you get in! Love you!"

Maria and the girls drove straight through to Pueblo, Colorado before stopping for gas and food. The twins dashed around the convenience store, grabbing handfuls of snacks as Maria paid for gas.

Snow began to fall as they walked back to the car, and Maria's brow creased in worry. They still had four hours of driving, and she swore to herself she'd drive slowly and carefully, no matter who was behind her, or who got impatient with her cautious driving.

It took two hours to get from Pueblo to Colorado Springs, and with the slow traffic it was obvious she'd be adding a few extra hours to her journey.

The car crept through The Springs and made its way to a precarious portion of I-25 called Monument Hill, some fifty miles from Denver. Snow blanketed the countryside and the wind blew loud and fierce, with the Falcon's windshield wipers slapping back and forth trying to catch up with the accumulating snow. Traffic was all but stalled, and Maria hoped it would stay that way, creeping along until she got to Denver. "We'll stay the night in a motel," she told the girls.

They didn't see, nor did they hear the semi-truck barreling toward them, its brakes burned out, its trailer fishtailing.

It was in that instant that Walter Patton, home alone, asleep on the sofa beside a half empty bottle of expensive bourbon, became a widower.

Grandpa and Jack struggled getting the butcher block island down the stairs. It had been in the kitchen before the remodel, and Jack had kept it in the tool shed thinking that someday he might use it for something. He probably would end up throwing it out in five years, but hey, you never knew, right?

The former kitchen island was a solid, heavy-as-hell, well-worn chunk of oak. Its surface was marred from years of being the heart of the old kitchen.

"A little to the right," Grandpa said, while Jack bumped the dolly down the stairs, "you're getting close to the handrail."

"Don't you idiots scratch the paint!" Grandma ordered from the bottom of the stairs.

After a lot of struggling, a bunch of cursing, and one smashed thumb, the big behemoth of solid wood was downstairs sitting next to the bar.

"They sure don't make them like this anymore," Grandpa said, giving it a kick with his boot.

"Where do you want it?" asked Jack, wiping the sweat from his forehead with the back of his arm. "Better question, *why* do you want it?"

Grandpa entered the code to the wine cellar. "I, um, we want to make a fancy wine tasting table out of it, for those times when me and the guys are feeling…elegant." Grandpa shrugged. "Or we're out of beer."

Jack laughed. He loved the crazy old bastard.

Grandpa swung the door open and directed Jack in. "Right there, next to the back wall."

Jack dropped the island from the dolly, then wrestled it forward, inch by inch, until it butted up against the wall. "About here?"

"Yep. Looks good."

"You and the guys enjoy your fancy-ass wine tasting parties. Make sure Beth gets invited sometimes."

"Sure will," said Grandpa, hustling him out. "Thanks again!"

"You bet," said Jack. "Anything else you need while I'm down here?"

"No, no." Grandpa put a hand on his back and guided Jack toward the stairs. "All's good, thanks!"

Jack knew when he was being dismissed. "Maybe you can buy some of those fancy wine charms with zodiac signs on them, and an *elegant* chandelier, and some cute little napkins, and…"

Grandpa shut the door. He could hear Jack laughing and heading up the stairs. He patted the kitchen island, its surface scratched and sliced from years of food prep. "No one's getting past this 300-pound baby."

Grandma was calling for him, "Albert! I think you dummies nicked the wall!"

He chuckled and headed out to grab the touch-up paint. "Yes, dear," Grandpa said, hiding his bruised thumb in his pocket; she'd want to call an ambulance if she saw it.

He took one last look at his new little room divider and closed the wine cellar door.

Jack paid the man who installed the new garage door, thanked him, and watched him drive off down the alleyway. The repairman had agreed that the door had been purposefully glued closed, but hadn't asked too many questions; just as well—Jack didn't have many answers.

He walked into the garage, flipping on the light. He'd replaced the bulb with an updated light that turned on when the garage door opened. With the door open and the light on, it was much easier for Jack to inspect the items in his garage without having to juggle a flashlight and dodge spiders. Old tools with wooden handles hung from the walls and amber glass jugs were piled to one side, making him wonder if someone, sometime, had bottled their own liquor. A red Radio Flyer wagon hung from the rafters, along with a rusty-looking bike with fat, flat tires, various pulleys, an ancient, two-man crosscut saw, and what looked to be a Christmas tree in a box, one silver branch extending from the end. It reminded Jack of his grandmother's house.

He dug the keys to the caddy from his pocket, opened the driver's side door, pushed the seat back, and slid in behind the wheel.

"I'm buying fuzzy dice," he murmured to himself.

He slipped the key into the ignition and gave it a turn.

"Incredible," Jack said, as the engine roared to life. He'd expected that after three months the battery would be dead as dirt.

He put the car in reverse and backed out of the garage, turning down the alley; he gave the garage door opener a click, and the door slid shut behind him.

His first stop would be Grandpa's friend Stumpy Joe's auto shop. Jack was taking no chances with this old beauty. He'd have it fully inspected, the oil changed, and every-thing completely checked out before driving farther than Stumpy Joe's shop. Jack straightened his arms at two and ten, leaned back, and grinned.

"This is gonna be great!"

Mr. Frank watched the scene unfold from his upstairs bedroom window, his hands clenched into fists, his jaw tight.

"This is gonna be ugly."

Walter Patton III had the false wall built in front of the bomb shelter entrance that led from his basement to the underground chamber. He'd asked for it to be heavy enough for only an adult to be able to open, though he was pretty sure that his girls wouldn't be investigating the basement much; they'd made it clear they thought it was creepy and full of spiders, ghosts, and maybe even rats. Still, Patton had a practical outlook on life, and better safe than sorry was a very good motto to follow. Especially with his background in the oilfields. Safety first. Always.

The hatch in the back yard was also completely child-proof. The heavy, circular trapdoor was flush to the ground and it took a crowbar to open it. Keeping his family safe was his first priority in life.

And now, all of them were gone. Patton took a long drink from the whiskey glass in front of him. His hands shook and he hung his head. He was so tired.

He didn't buy the expensive whiskey any longer—it seemed a joke to waste his money when he could coast through a full bottle a day. Yes, Patton prided himself in being safe, but also in being thrifty. He took the bottle and walked down the back stairs to the basement. It was dark and filled with relics of the past; ghostly memories from a time when he was happy and his family was *safe*.

Safety was a word he thought about a lot lately. It was 1972, and his heart still hurt as much as it had the day the pounding of police fists on his door had woken him as he lay passed-out-drunk on the couch. His world had changed in that instant: all the breath had left him, and his soul became a dark, black thing which inhabited his body but was frozen and dead. For all intents and purposes, Patton stopped living that day.

He walked to the fallout shelter's false front door and laid a hand on it. This had been built to keep his family safe—there was that word again, it haunted him. Patton hadn't been inside the shelter since the day it was searched by the police…the day Alice went missing. The police had scoured it top to bottom, and he had too, his gun still slung over his shoulder.

When Alice went missing.

That was the day his mind finally grasped that he was a fraud. He was a pumped-up farce of a man who, through self-assurance and conviction, had convinced himself he could keep his family *safe.*

He slid down the wall onto his backside, partially in grief and mainly because the room was spinning in whiskey-drenched circles. His shoulders hitched as he sobbed into his hands. Oh, Maria, he thought. He should have been with them.

Maria. She'd always been the solid one. He was all bluster. A shell. A counterfeit man. He'd give everything he owned for just one minute with her.

Patton staggered to his feet, the whiskey bottle tipped on its side, forgotten. Bracing himself with one hand, he took down his old shotgun, the one he'd used the evening of Alice's disappearance, the one he'd pointed at his nephew before he marched him to the police station. He slung it over one shoulder, floundering on the stairs a few times, his gait unsteady.

Filled with liquid courage and grief, Walter Patton III stumbled his way to the attic, feeling safe and sure for the first time in eight years.

Chapter Twenty-five

You Look Beautiful When You're Sleeping

OLIVIA STRUCK UP A FRIENDSHIP with her neighbor, Mr. Miles Frank. He was a nice enough man, but there had always been a niggling itch in the back of her mind about him, a little voice telling her that something was…askew. It wasn't anything he did, specifically, it was only a gut feeling that came and went, like the shadow of a hawk; you never saw the bird, but the shadow proved the existence of its talons. One minute she felt tense around him, the next moment he'd wash that feeling away with his charm and humor. Truth be told, Olivia didn't know what to make of him. He was great fun to be with, but her gut told her to be cautious, so she kept things platonic.

The two of them ended up spending quite a bit of time together, and he remained always the gentleman. They'd taken day trips together. One trip was a fun day at the Denver Zoo followed by a great lunch downtown. They'd taken a drive to Estes Park, through Rocky Mountain National Park, up and over Trail Ridge Road, and taken the scenic (but very long) drive back home through Granby and Winter Park.

He'd taken her to dinner a few times, each time insisting on paying without letting her see the check. It made her uncomfortable and she had told him so, but he'd brushed it off, insisting he could afford it. Olivia was working full time by then, and their fun dates were a welcome relief from a class filled with thirty very noisy sixth graders. He occasionally bought her small gifts, which she at first refused; later, on her birthday, and out of courtesy, she accepted a bracelet on the condition that he never buy her another lavish gift.

One evening Miles made her dinner at his home. They'd drunk a lot of exceptional, and probably expensive wine, and the lasagna he made was actually very good. They'd laughed about his cooking abilities.

It felt good to have a friend who lived right next door—one she could call on if something in the house needed fixing, or to have a cup of coffee with on the patio.

That night, after her third glass of wine, Olivia's head was spinning a bit and her tongue was loose, and she told him details about her summer with Elvis. She told him how they'd met, how he put her through school, how he purchased the Patton House as a graduation gift. She sighed, telling him about it all, and the look on her face must have given it away. Mr. Frank knew Elvis had purchased the Patton House, but he had no idea of the depth of their relationship.

"You were in love with him," he said, his tone flat.

"Yes," she answered, "I always will be." She shrugged. "I'm content with the memories, Miles," she said, taking another sip of wine, "I have to be."

She paused as her mind wandered in a haze of Chianti, the wine making her head fuzzy and her heart open. "No one will ever measure up to what I had that summer. I've come to terms with that." Olivia swirled the red liquid in her glass. "It was a short period of time with Elvis, and I'll be forever grateful. My heart was filled with love," she chuckled, "unrequited love. Although I know he cared for me."

She shrugged again, a soft smile on her lips. "But that's really okay, I'm a reasonable woman." She set the glass down, feeling as if she'd had enough alcohol for one night. "The memories comfort me."

She looked at Miles and saw that his eyes had darkened and his brow had furrowed. She patted his hand. "That doesn't mean I can't have wonderful, close friendships."

He nodded, his eyes never leaving hers. She stood then, smoothing her skirt, "I best be going," she said, giving him a short hug. The mood in the room had changed, and it was making her uncomfortable, even through the cloudiness of expensive alcohol. He walked her to the door, and they said their goodnights before Olivia carefully made her way home.

After some time, and many dates, Miles kissed her on the front porch of her house. She placed a hand on his chest and pushed him away. Not a hard push, just enough to let him know she was uncomfortable with the situation. She knew that soon she'd have to have an awkward talk with him about boundaries, and how she didn't have romantic feelings for him—the way he obviously had for her. Trying to kiss her had solidified her suspicion that Mr. Frank was looking for more than a platonic friend to spend time with.

The end of the relationship came on a Tuesday morning, when Mr. Miles Frank was in the parking lot of the elementary school waiting for her.

"Yesterday I saw you walking out with the vice principal," he said. "There's something shifty about him, Olivia, and I'll be here every day from now on to make sure it doesn't happen again."

Olivia was so shocked that she was unable to speak for a moment.

"I need you to be cautious, Olivia," he said. "Sometimes you do very reckless things." He looked at her, his face serious and his body posture tense. "How do you think that makes me feel?"

Her eyebrows raised and she glared at him. "You've been…stalking me?" she asked, her voice lifting an octave.

"I just want you to be careful," he repeated, and added, "and, Olivia, you're not going out with him this Friday night, it's just not right."

Olivia couldn't believe what she was hearing. "How on Earth did you know we're going out for dinner?" she asked him. "Not that it's any of your business, but a few of the teachers are going with us as well."

She thought for a moment, totally perplexed. "How do you know all this, Miles?"

He stared into her eyes, his pupils expanding slightly. "I have ways of knowing just about everything, Olivia. I have *ways*."

She backed up toward her car, her keys in hand. Her gut feeling from the first time she'd met him was resurfacing and proving itself true.

"I think this," she said, gesturing from him to herself, "has gone just about as far as it can go, Miles." She slid behind the wheel of her caddy. "I don't think we should see each other again." Her hands were shaking as she thrust the key into the ignition. She missed and tried again.

His hands grasped the open window, "I love you, Olivia," he said.

"You don't even know me," she replied, and drove away. In her rearview mirror, she could see him standing in the parking lot, fist clenched and boring holes into the back of her head with those dark, empty eyes.

That evening, Olivia retrieved her diary from under a loose floorboard in the corner of her bedroom, lay across her bed, and detailed the events.

Some time passed, and Olivia kept her distance from Mr. Frank. She was cordial and would always say hello to him; she figured it was easier that way, since he lived right next door. She wanted no more trouble and kept her conversations with him short—usually one-word answers. If she needed anything around her home fixed, she'd call a handyman.

Eventually, with time, she put the uncomfortable incident in the parking lot at Patton Elementary School behind her. She didn't forget it, but she refused to dwell on it and let it run her life. She was beginning to make friends in Patton, and she was not going to let Miles Frank keep her from having a social life. As far as Olivia could tell from his words and actions, he'd also put it into the past, but who knew what was going on in his mind. He kept his distance for the most part, was cordial and cool, and Olivia fell back into a routine of work, gardening, reading, and cooking, and taking advantage of every opportunity to enjoy peace and solitude. Not loneliness, but the kind of solitude she knew was good for her and put her in touch with her feelings and with nature. Writing in her diary helped as well.

She had a spiral staircase built off her bedroom that went up to the turret of the house. She painted the turret room sage green and decorated it with plants and book-cases, a comfortable reading chair, and a small television set. Olivia had a few silly TV shows she just couldn't bring herself to miss. The space was safe and cozy, her escape from the world at large.

She was standing at the turret window taking in the view of the lights of Patton twinkling on for the evening and thinking about hot chocolate when the phone rang, and to her surprise, it was Miles Frank. He asked her to come over, as there was something very important he needed to show her, He promised it would only take a minute. He sounded happy and excited, and it had been months since the un-comfortable incident in the school parking lot. So, against her better judgment, Olivia put on her shoes, grabbed a car-digan and headed across the yard to his front door.

The door was open when she got there, but she knocked anyway. Three small raps. "Miles?" she said, "are you in there? Is everything okay?"

It took a second for him to answer. "Yes," he said, "ev-erything is just fine! Come in Olivia, I have a big surprise for you that I've been working on for weeks."

She opened the door and stepped into his living room, her keys grasped tight in her hand.

The house was dark except for some well-placed candles. Red roses in at least a dozen vases filled the room with a sick, sweet, almost unnatural scent: it reminded her of the air freshener her mother had kept in their bathroom.

"In the kitchen," he called out, "I'm in the kitchen."

Olivia slowly walked to the kitchen, the hairs on her arms rising in a sudden rash of goosebumps. Everything was very quiet until she heard the unmistakable sound of a needle touching a spinning record, and Love me Tender began to play.

Olivia stopped and stared. She couldn't believe what she was seeing.

There, next to the avocado green Frigidaire, stood Miles Frank dressed as Elvis. From the black wig to the overdone gold sunglasses, to the gaudy white bell bottoms with sequins and fringe. He wore white, well-shined loafers and a large silver belt. Olivia had never seen her Elvis in anything but black pants and a shirt. She backed up a step, shocked.

"I love you Olivia," Miles said, opening his arms as if he thought she'd run into them. "Jesus, woman, I've loved you since the first day I saw you! Remember the chocolates? Remember how we laughed when we'd eaten all of them?"

"Miles, what do you think you're doing?"

"I did all of this for you, Olivia! Everything I do is for you. I need you to love me." He took a step closer. "I want us to get married someday, I want to move into your home and make it our own, I want to be the best husband and father." He paused. "I want you to be mine, and I'll do whatever it takes," he said, gesturing with both hands at his clothes, "even this."

Olivia stepped back, overwhelmed by what she was seeing and hearing. "My God, Miles!" she screamed at him, tears welling in her eyes. "Are you out of your mind?"

Miles Frank removed the gold-rimmed glasses and looked at her, his eyes narrowed as he took a step forward. "Don't you ever," he hissed, "*ever* say those words to me again."

Olivia gasped; the anger seeping from him filled the air like poisonous smoke. She gripped her keys tighter.

"I want you to be mine, I *need* you to be mine," he repeated, "and, Olivia? I get everything I want. I always, *always* get everything I want."

Olivia shrieked as he took a step toward her, and she ran to the front door. She felt him close behind her, his fingers clutching the back of her cardigan, fastening onto it for an instant. She screamed and swung her keys at him, slicing his face. He lost his grip on her cardigan and she pulled herself free, leaving the garment dangling in his hands. Olivia tore through the living room and flew out of the door, letting the screen slap back into place, and sprinted back across the yard to the safety of her own home. She could hear him bellowing in the background. She slammed her door shut, locked it, stared down the darkness of the hallway, and flipped on the lights. Adrenaline was making her heart pound so hard it felt as if it wanted to claw its way out of her chest.

She slept in the parlor that evening, the shotgun she had found in the basement sprawled across her lap. The next day she had all the locks on the windows and doors changed. She never spoke to Miles Frank again. Ever.

The night after the locksmiths had left and all was quiet, after Olivia brushed her teeth and fed her goldfish,

Bonnie and Clyde, she slipped into bed, unsure if she could sleep. Two hours later, Miles Frank stood at her bedroom doorway with a white bandage on his cheek. He watched the soft rise and fall of her chest against her blue floral nightgown.

He stood there for hours, watching her sleep.

"Well," said Stumpy Joe, "the caddy is in great shape, for the most part. I changed the oil and gave her a once over." He headed toward the rear of the car. "Follow me, I found something really interesting.

Jack followed him around the car, and Stumpy popped the trunk.

"Look at this."

Jack bent closer to look at the spot where Stumpy was pointing. "It used to be pink?"

"Yep. There weren't too many of these back then."

"Did it belong to some lady that sold make-up?" Jack asked, "I know they gave out pink caddies."

"Can't be," said Stumpy, "those make-up lady pink caddies came out in 1970." Stumpy ran a finger over the pink paint spots. "There were a few of these back in the mid- to-late fifties. Elvis was famous for having one and giving a whole lot of them away."

"You don't think…"

"You never know," Stumpy said, "but if I were you, I'd do some research."

Chapter Twenty-six

A Potato is an Apple

Years before

Fourteen-year-old Thomas Gleason, who someday would be known as Miles Frank, had stolen a train ticket from a young woman with two very upset and rowdy children. He pocketed the ticket while the woman was distracted with the younger child's temper tantrum, then went directly to the train and made sure that he was in a position to enter before the woman knew it was gone.

Once settled on the train, he began to daydream about which city would be his final destination. Maybe a podunk town in Nowhere, Nebraska, or maybe he'd ride the train all the way to Chicago and disappear among the crowds of people. He had plenty of time to decide. Thomas closed his eyes and let out a breath; even with no knowledge of where the future would lead him, he was happy to be able to escape the prison his mother had placed him in.

Thomas had never known his father. His mother referred to him as Mr. Satan. Thomas had no idea what his dad's real name was, or how to possibly start looking for him.

Thomas and his mother lived on the outskirts of Sacramento, in a small house with a postage-stamp yard filled with weeds, mainly those angry little sticker weeds that had a mind of their own, and he swore they would jump at him and become tangled in his socks and skin.

His mother was the kind of woman who couldn't throw anything away. Their house was filled from floor to ceiling with boxes and bags of trash. The house reeked of infrequently cleaned cat litter. It was his job to clean it, and it made him sick just thinking about it. Thomas couldn't bring himself to change it very often, so most of the time he would hold his breath and scoop the solids into the old litter bags, and when they were full, he'd push them to the back of a closet.

Thomas sat back in his train seat and let some of the weight of the world lift off his shoulders. He was getting out.

Thomas's mother had a gray tabby with an ugly stump of a tail and an attitude to match. She had mustered up every ounce of her creativity and named the cat Felix. One evening, Felix didn't make it home by dinner time, and she'd wandered the neighborhood in her pajamas and robe looking for him. He didn't make it home the next night, nor the next, and his mother finished an entire liter of vodka, heartbroken and sure that Felix had been taken by a coyote or run over on the highway.

Later that evening Thomas stood over her, listening to her snoring, blacked-out drunk on the couch, surrounded by trash, papers, and liquor bottles. He reached down and pinched her nose closed, his other hand firmly over her open mouth. He held her that way until she started to struggle. In her drunken state, her hands flailed, and Thomas held on until she began to still.

It would have been so damn easy, he thought, and let go. She sucked in a phlegmy breath and rolled onto her back, her chapped lips smacking and little half moons of white showing beneath her closed eyelids.

Thomas went to her bedroom and found his mom's purse lying on her bed amidst more papers and old mail. He shook out the contents, took forty-seven dollars from her wallet, and pocketed it.

He left the bedroom and went to the basement, where he retrieved Felix from his hiding spot behind the hot water heater. He took the cat's lifeless body upstairs and left him on the dining room table. He picked up the cat litter box, dumped it on his unconscious mother's chest, packed a small suitcase and headed out to the train station, wishing he had held her nose and mouth shut for a few minutes longer.

And now here he was in seat 35B, traveling east with forty-seven dollars in his pocket and no plan for the future, and feeling totally fine about it.

As the train filled with passengers, another young man boarded and took the seat next to Thomas. He was also traveling alone, and on his way to live with his rich uncle (he must have said "rich" one hundred times) in Patton, Colorado. The boy was chatty and talked nonstop, telling Thomas his story, with so many personal details that Thomas thought his head might explode from the intake of so much information; but about halfway through Walter Patton's nephew's monologue, a plan formed in Thomas's mind. He let the boy talk and talk, storing away little tidbits of information, until Walter Patton's nephew Franklin made an unpleasant, and impromptu stop outside of Reno—face first off the back of the train.

It was Beth's night to cook, and after a long day working on the second draft of her book, it was going to be breakfast-for-dinner-night. Easy peasy. Her brain was still reeling after reading and editing the first four chapters of Javier and Alejandra's romp-fest, and she'd found a few doozies in the error department. She'd spelled it 'pencil' instead of penis. *"Alejandra stroked Javier's thick, erect pencil."* Just thinking about it made her cackle.

"You okay over there?" asked Grandma. "It sounds like you're going to cough up a hairball right into the French toast."

Beth brought her mind back to the business of cooking, and flipped a piece of half-burned French toast. With the table set, and everyone gathered around, she set a bowl of melon on the table alongside a large spinach salad.

"Salad with French toast is just wrong," Sam said, and Beth shot him a look that said, *I cook. You eat.*

"You need to eat something other than candy and soda, Sammy," Beth said, passing him the melon and giving the salad a toss. Sam took an ample serving of honeydew. He passed the melon on to his father, and Beth handed him the salad bowl. He wrinkled his nose.

"Take some vegetables," Grandma ordered.

Sam tried to pass the bowl on its way around the table, and pointed to his melon. "Fruit is a vegetable."

"And a potato is an apple," Ben muttered.

Jack coughed and took the bowl from his son's hands. Beth rolled her eyes, took a piece of French toast and began to cut it into pieces for Bobo. She reached over to set it on Bobo's empty highchair tray.

"Shit," she said, "I forgot the baby." No one else had noticed him missing, and all eyes were on the highchair—minus Bobo. Beth sighed. She'd left him asleep in the playroom.

Sam seized on this as the perfect excuse to get out of the vegetable ordeal. "I'll go get him, Mom." He stood, scraping the chair legs against the floor, then plowed up the back stairs before anyone had a chance to intervene.

"The kid's quick," Grandma said, gesturing toward the stairs with her fork.

"The kid's smart." said Grandpa, passing on the bowl of spinach without taking any.

Sam hurried up the spiral stairs, through his mom's office, and into the playroom. Bobo was fast asleep in his toddler bed, his thumb halfway in and halfway out of his mouth, a tiny puddle of drool forming on the mattress. Sam laid a hand on his back. Bobo didn't move, he was out for the count. Sam debated whether to wake his baby brother or let him sleep. If Sam picked him up and took him downstairs, he'd just scream and not eat anyway; if he left him sleeping, they'd *probably* hear him if he woke up. Either way he's gonna cry.

There was a crash behind the storage room door, and Sam whipped around. He hadn't been in the storage room since the day of the séance, and the place creeped him out, but he crept closer and placed his ear against the door.

A hard thump shook the door as if a fist had hit it from the other side. Sam fell back and stared at the latch at the top of the door. It wiggled from the impact, then slowly lifted on its own, fell free from its hook, and the door squeaked open about three inches.

Sam crawled over and peeked in; all was dark and still.

He stood and reached in to turn on the light, sure that a slimy, dark *something* would grab his wrist, pull him into its storeroom lair, and eat him like a nacho. The bulb flickered to life, casting the familiar sallow glow over the sheet-covered furniture and boxes. The slats in the rafters stood out like bright hatchet marks against the dark roof.

Sam stood just inside the doorway, checking the corners for shadows, ghosts, uninvited intruders, and—hell—maybe even monsters.

Another loud bang came from across the room, shaking the far wall and sending dust motes dancing across the still air.

Sam jumped and covered his ears. "It's gonna break the front window," he whispered, and then stopped dead.

The half-moon window. Where was the half-moon window? The half-moon window that was so predominantly placed on the attic when you looked up from the front yard? The window that made Sam think of a bad horror movie when he first saw it that day they'd moved in. *That* window!

He moved closer to the wall that would be the front of the house. He peeked behind an old dresser. Still no window, but there was the faint outline of a door. A door all of about three feet tall and held securely closed with a padlock. From this angle, Sam noticed that there were scratches in the floor from where the dresser had obviously been moved away from the wall and then back again. "What the actual hell," he whispered, giving the door a sharp rap with his knuckles to check if it was indeed hollow behind.

The sound of an empty space beyond the door rang through the attic.

Something knocked back.

Sam gasped, fell back and knocked his head on the dresser. Scrambling to his knees, he leaned in, "Hello?"

A diminutive voice answered, "Daddy?"

Chapter Twenty-seven

A Special Place for a Special Girl

Years before

MILES FRANK would enter Olivia Sharette's home every day after she left to teach her twelve-year-olds at Patton Elementary and spend his time wandering the house, boiling with angry thoughts. This was *his* home. He should have inherited this home. If Olivia would have given in to his advances, it would be his, right this minute. One way or another he would live here—where he belonged.

Miles lay on Olivia's bed and stared at the ceiling. His eyes wandered over to the photograph on the far wall, the photo of Olivia Sharette and Elvis. The bitch. He'd humiliated himself, dressing up as Elvis and thinking she'd fall at his feet.

Miles stood, walked to the photo, picked it up, smashed it on the floor, then instantly regretted it. He'd have to clean this up. Perhaps there was a broom in the storage room.

Opening the storage room door, he saw that much of the furniture from three generations of Pattons was stored here. He walked through the attic, reminiscing each time he came across an object he recalled from his short stay.

A large white tarp covered a cluster of furniture on the south side of the room, and he yanked it off. Dust rained down on him, and he rubbed his eyes and face in disbelief. He had stumbled upon the bedroom set that at one time belonged to the youngest Patton, Alice. A white bed, white dresser and nightstand, a lamp shaped like a cartoon mouse, and boxes of toys. There were curtains, bedding, and all the pictures that had hung on her bedroom walls. He picked up a blonde rubber doll from the crate of toys, and it brought back flashes of memory from when life had been happy. It was an absolute miracle, that's what it was. He picked up the yellow-haired doll Alice had called Bridget and tucked it under his arm.

That was the day he decided Alice needed to come home.

Miles's visits to the Patton house now had purpose. He hauled lumber up the front stairs, all the way up to the attic. As far as he knew, Olivia had never set foot in the attic, having gone so far as to express her distaste for the unfinished, cobweb-infested area. Which meant she knew nothing of his clandestine visits there.

He set down the last of the lumber and took a step back, surveying his progress. Alice's bed had been freshly painted white; the sheets and blankets and a frilly yellow bedspread were crisp and clean and returned to their place. He'd also painted the dresser and nightstand white, and the cartoon mouse lamp sat proudly atop the bedside table. Alice's toy box was filled with her stored toys, and he'd washed and dried some of the plush animals in Olivia's washing machine and dryer in the basement. Pictures hung on the walls, and a jewelry box with a tiny, but bent, ballerina sat on a doily on the dresser. Miles gave the jewelry box key a spin, and the tinkle of Für Elise filled the room.

He had painted three of the boards black the previous day; he picked them up and nailed them carefully over the half-moon-shaped window, and only then did he dare turn on the lights and inspect his work. He stood back, crossed his arms over his chest.

Perfect.

He set Alice's blonde doll between the bed pillows and smiled. Falling to his hands and knees, he slipped from the small door that was now the entrance to her new bedroom. He closed it behind himself and locked it securely.

All it needed now was sweet Alice.

For the next thirty years, Miles Frank, formerly known as Thomas Gleason, and then for a brief period as Walter Patton's nephew, Franklin, had a job to do.

His short time with the Pattons had given him the only taste, however brief, of a normal, functioning family life he'd ever known. In those short weeks living as Mr. Patton's nephew, he had a mother and father and three siblings. There were no fights, no yelling, no slapping, no mess, no *cats.* He'd had family dinners, picnics, and game nights, and although he never felt as if he truly fitted in, there were those fleeting moments when he would forget he was an outsider and bask in the normality of it all. It was like a television show, the story of an everyday family—but not his family. It felt as if he were participating from behind a glass screen. He was in attendance, he was *there*…but separated by the slightest partition which kept him from fully being present, a divider that kept their love, devotion, and happiness to one side, and his anger and resentment on the other. It was as if Patton could smell the secrets on him.

He'd taken a shine to Alice, so small and delicate, almost doll-like with her long dark hair and thick eyelashes. He didn't want anything from her but for her to love him; but she was her daddy's princess, and when Mayor Patton doted on her, no one else existed. Her father would pick her up and spin her around, her ribbons would fly and she would laugh and hug him. It gave Thomas jolts of jealousy. He wanted her to run to him that way, to jump into his arms and tell him he was the best big brother ever. He wanted Patton to look at him as if he were proud and dote on him too, instead of regarding him with suspicion.

Alice never did look at him that way. Instead, she eyed him warily, and at one point—when Thomas had grabbed her and spun her around in the way her daddy did—she'd screamed and kicked at him. He dropped her then, and she scooted away from him, running into her bedroom and slamming the door.

Alice kept her distance as much as possible after that; up until the day of her birthday party, when he told her how sorry he was that he had frightened her and promised to make it up to her by day's end.

He knew that Patton didn't trust him, it was all in the way he looked at him. The way Patton screamed at him when he'd caught him holding Callan the cat just a wee bit too tight. Thomas had lived on instinct and wit for as long as he could remember, and he knew that his days of being in a functional family, with actual siblings and parents, were numbered. He could feel it deep in his gut, and his gut never steered him wrong.

Alice and Mayor Patton. His *uncle* was going to ruin everything and had to be stopped—and the best way to do that was through Alice.

Sam thundered down the back steps. His family was still eating breakfast for dinner, and as far as he could tell, the spinach salad was untouched.

"Grandpa!" he shouted as he took the last three steps with a jump, "Do you have a sledgehammer?"

Grandpa scooted his chair back from the table, "Coming right up!"

"Wait!" Jack said, his voice filled with alarm, "Aren't you even going to ask him what for?"

"Nope," said Grandpa, heading toward the back door and toward the tool shed, "all I have to hear is, 'sledgehammer,' and I'm in."

"Jack, you better go with them," Beth said to him, nudging him to follow.

"Fine, fine, fine. Jesus." Jack got up and followed them out the door.

"Sam! Where's the baby?" Beth yelled.

"Pass the syrup, please," said Grandma.

Chapter Twenty-eight

I'll Be Doing the Sledging

FOR THIRTY YEARS, until the day his basement entrance to the Patton house was blocked by the butcher box island, Miles Frank had taken Alice from her hiding place, made his way through the tunnel that connected the houses, crept up the stairs, and laid Alice in her attic bed to sleep. He'd sit by her bed, lay her blond dolly, Bridget, next to her, turn on the cartoon mouse, and read her stories from one of her many books. Miles had heard Maria reading *The Wind in the Willows* to her at one point in his childhood, and he knew that was her favorite. He would smooth her hair down (or what was left of it), and kiss her on the forehead, tucking her curled body under the bright yellow bedspread.

"I'll see you in the morning, princess," he'd say as he turned off her lamp, before creeping out of her room in the attic—the room that looked exactly as he remembered her childhood bedroom to be. He'd close the door and silently slip down the stairs, avoiding the ones that creaked, and check on the sleeping Hamlin family. He'd always linger at Bobo's door, sometimes actually going so far as walking to his crib and pulling up the blankets.

Miles Frank was fond of toddlers.

"You watch way too many scary movies," Jack told his son, as he hoisted the sledgehammer over his shoulder and followed his wife and father-in-law up the stairs. Grandma had wanted no part of "these shenanigans," and offered to stay behind and do the dishes. Ben went to his room to play video games.

Beth lifted Bobo, who was now awake, from his toddler bed in the playroom and placed him on her hip. The door to the storage room was still open, the light was on, and the dresser was pulled away from the wall.

"See?" said Sam. "There's no window!"

"You're right," said Grandpa, "where the hell's the window?"

Jack and Grandpa pulled the dresser farther into the center of the room so they could get a better look.

Jack bent and examined the small, padlocked door. "Hand me the sledgehammer, Albert," he said to Grandpa, holding out his hand.

"Oh, no," said Grandpa, pushing him out of the way. "It's my sledgehammer, and I'll be doing the sledging." He lifted the hammer, and instead of aiming at the padlock, smashed the door right off its hinges, splintering a section of wall.

Beth stood back with Bobo, although she was dying to get a better look. Bobo had his arms outstretched and was crying. Snot poured down his face as he screamed, "I hit it!" over and over.

Bobo plus sledgehammer plus secret ghost room equaled a probable ambulance ride. Although Beth's curiosity was piqued, she figured that for safety's sake, she had best take the baby back downstairs.

As Beth called, "If you boys find anything, call me right away!" Bobo scrambled free from her arms and took off running toward the little open door.

"Bobo!" she yelled. She made a grab for the back of his t-shirt, but she lost her grip, and he zipped right through the small doorway.

"Oh my God, grab the baby!" Beth hollered to no one in particular, and Sam dropped to a crawl and followed him in.

"Fast little shit," said Grandpa, dropping the sledgehammer, "and brave too—maybe he'll be a Navy Seal someday."

Beth had a momentary vision of Javier the Navy Seal, from the Blaze Bolivar books, and shook it away.

A small click signaled that Bobo had found the light switch in the hidden room, and through the dim glow of a twenty-watt bulb Sam followed Bobo inside, crawling on hands and knees.

A very old lamp shaped like a cartoon mouse sat on a short, white table next to a small bed. The bed was covered in a bright yellow bedspread. Atop a white dresser sat a music box on a frilly lace doily. The air was stale and musty, and smelled of age-worn linens and freshly splintered wood.

Bobo stood next to an antique toy box filled with old toys; he settled onto the floor and began pulling out dolls and stuffed animals.

"I can't see shit," said Grandpa, pulling a claw hammer from his belt. He turned to the wall where the front window obviously should be and began to pull nails out of boards. The nails creaked and groaned, but gave way. As Grandpa set the boards on the floor, bright light streamed into the room through the murky glass of the front window, exposing what had apparently been a little girl's bedroom.

Beth walked to the bed and picked up a foot-long black hair from the pillowcase. "Someone slept here," she said. "It must have been a very long time ago."

"That girl is my friend," said Bobo.

"I heard someone in here," Sam said. "I heard a little girl's voice say 'Daddy?' I'm not making it up, we have to find her!" He fell to his knees and looked under the bed, and pulled out a small black shoe. He held it up.

Beth gasped. It looked to belong to a girl of about three or four.

Bobo reached deep into the toy box and pulled out its mate. "That's hers," he said, lifting it. His other hand grasped the hair of a blond baby doll.

Beth shrieked. Bobo dropped the shoe, and she pushed him and the yellow-haired doll through the door and into the storage space. Sam peeked out after them. His mother was dashing to the door clutching Bobo, who was clinging to the baby doll. The doll's bright blue, unblinking glass eyes stared back at him, its tiny lips turned up in a pink rubber smile.

The police left the Patton House later that evening, having combed over every inch of the attic area. They found no evidence of foul play, or that any kind of crime had been committed, and it was agreed that no matter how odd it was, it was most likely just a long-forgotten bedroom. Sam continued to insist he'd heard a voice, but there was nothing to indicate that the abandoned room had been occupied anytime in the last thirty years.

Sam whispered to Grandpa, "We really should tell them about the door in the basement."

Grandpa put his fingers to his lips, and Sam saluted.

Beth concluded that the bedroom furniture was Alice Patton's, the little girl that went missing in the sixties. "Maybe they stored her furniture up there," Beth said, her eyes wistful. "Maybe they just couldn't bear to part with it after she disappeared."

Beth shivered and looked around for her own toddler, who was quietly playing with the blond baby doll he found in the attic. Beth had washed its face and hair, and given the rubber doll back to Bobo. Beth smiled down at him. He smiled up at her.

"Hold Bridget, Mama." Bobo said, and handed her the rubber baby.

"Hello, Bridget," Beth said, then looked quizzically at her son. "That was random, why did you name her Bridget?"

"I didn't name her, Mama," he smiled, showing a mouthful of tiny baby teeth. "She told me."

Sam woke up thirsty. He just might be hungry too, and he knew just where Dad hid his cookies.

Walking into the hallway, he heard voices, which was odd, since it was just after one in the morning. He followed the voices down the hall and stopped in front of his baby brother's room. The voices were coming from inside.

Sam very carefully opened the door a crack and peeked in. Bobo was out of his bed and sitting amidst a pile of Legos which he had divided into two equal stacks. He sat in front of the blue and green Lego pile, and Alice's blonde baby doll, Bridget, sat across from him, a pile of red and yellow Legos at her rubber feet. Bobo was carrying on a serious conversation with the doll, its blue eyes half-closed and staring.

"I'm not supposed to go into the wine cellar," Bobo told her.

He waited for a beat.

"Because Grandpa said no."

Bobo pushed his pile of Legos toward Bridget. "Don't cry," he said, with a sad look on his face. "We'll find you and put you to bed."

It was then that Sam noticed that Bobo wasn't talking to Bridget at all. His attention was focused above and behind her.

Sam closed his brother's bedroom door and leaned against the wall. He heard high-pitched giggling from inside Bobo's room, and dashed back to his own room, forgetting all about being thirsty.

Chapter Twenty-nine

1215

MILES FRANK had been livid for weeks, and now the police were at the Hamlins' house, at *his* house, and he was sure they'd be knocking at his door next. He paced the living room, his mind racing and plotting. Maybe it was time to jump another train. No, he had to stop thinking that way. The Patton House was *his*. He would not be driven from his home by this intrusion of his privacy and his property, because what would become of Alice?

Why the hell hadn't Olivia Sharette fallen for him? He could be living there *right now*.

A few weeks ago, Miles had gathered Alice from her hiding place, wrapped her in his arms, and carried her to the tunnel entrance to take her from the basement to the attic and put her to bed. The door was jammed shut from the Hamlins' side, and Miles, being the cock-sure man that he was, was perfectly certain the old man next door had placed something heavy in front of the shelves, not knowing the portal was there. It had to be a stupid coincidence because Miles Frank never made mistakes.

He set Alice down, her body small and light, her skin stretched tight over fragile bones, and put his back into it, pushing against the door with all the strength he had. The door didn't budge.

Cursing and screaming with anger, Miles snatched up Alice's body and stormed back through the tunnel to the bomb shelter. He leaned against the safe and slid down hard to the floor, cradling his princess close. Damn Olivia! He picked up the photograph of her and Elvis—the one he'd broken into pieces and stolen from her house and then lovingly glued back together—and threw it to the ground, shattering it for the second time.

His poor Alice. After so many years of being moved and tousled, fragile bones finally gave way to their age; Alice's skull tilted crooked on her neck until, with a soft crunch, it broke at the neck and toppled to the floor.

Miles screamed and picked up the little skull, long black hairs still clinging to the leathery skin.

"I'm sorry," he whispered, tears choking his words, "I'm so sorry." Miles Frank, formerly known as Thomas Gleason, looked into Alice's mummified face, her eye sockets long-empty hollow black cavities. "They'll pay for this," he said, kissing the paper-thin skin on her cheek, "I promise you. We'll be home soon." His breath hitched and he kissed her other cheek. "Very soon."

Miles brought himself back to the present, walked to the window, and pulled back the drapes. The police were leaving the Hamlins' house, and he held his breath, waiting for them to make the turn to his front door. Surprisingly, they got into their patrol car, sat for five minutes, and pulled away. Mr. Frank let out a sigh of relief. He'd outsmarted them, of course he had. He needed to recount the evening's events to Alice, so he headed down to the bomb shelter with her body in his arms.

Thirty years ago Walter Patton's fraud of a nephew listened to a conversation between Walter and Maria. The couple were in their bedroom on the second floor and had not closed the door. Thomas Gleason, *aka* Miles Frank, listened from the hallway.

"The key will be here," Walter said, lifting the loose floorboard that would someday hold Olivia Sharette's diary. He put the board back seamlessly in place. "Maria, there's a four-digit code as well," he said, smoothing his hand over the wooden hiding place, seeming satisfied with its ability to blend with the rest of the floorboards.

Walter stood and placed his hands on his wife's shoulders, "I need you to remember this number, honey," he said to her, his tone hushed, "I'm not writing it down. It'll be up here," he said, tapping his head.

Maria nodded.

"1215."

"1215," she repeated.

He kissed his wife softly on the mouth.

Walter's nephew slipped quietly back down the hall toward his bedroom. Bridget, the blonde rubber doll, lay on the carpet near his door; he picked her up and slipped inside his room, closing the door behind him.

"1215," he repeated, and tapped Bridget's curly blonde head.

Beth was so preoccupied with the findings in the attic that the only way to clear her head and get back to her writing was to go back to the library for more research. She still had so many questions.

Cindy greeted her with a happy wave when she entered, and pointed to the coffee pot.

Beth laughed, made a fresh pot, and headed to the room with the microfilm. She started with public records, pulled up the title to the house and the history of its sale, and almost spilled hot coffee on her lap.

1971- Elvis Aaron Presley.

"That's impossible," Beth muttered to herself, "Miss Sharette bought it that year."

She continued to search. The deed from the cash purchase of the Patton House had been transferred from Elvis Aaron Presley to Olivia Jean Sharette in the summer of 1971.

"*The* Elvis Aaron Presley?"

Beth sat back in her chair. There had to be a simple explanation, she thought, her hands circling her coffee mug, its contents warming her fingers. Perhaps there were two Elvis Aaron Presleys and it was just a coincidence? Then she thought of something. The caddy in the garage that had belonged to Miss Sharette, how black paint covered the original pink.

"Son of a bitch," Beth said, setting the coffee mug down before her shaking hands dropped it. She gathered her printouts and hurried home.

Beth dropped her purse on the entry floor. "Elvis bought Sam's English teacher a house," she said to Jack. "Please, please tell me there's an open bottle of wine."

"Looks as if he bought her a car too," said Jack to Beth, after doing some research of his own. The VIN number of the Cadillac revealed that Mr. Elvis Presley had purchased it and turned the title over to Olivia Sharette.

"Another thing I found out was that Miss Sharette's college tuition and living expenses had also been funded by Elvis." Beth stared at him. "Miss Sharette and Elvis had a 'thing'?"

"What kind of thing?" asked Ben.

"A grownup thing," said Jack.

"Ew." Ben covered his hands with his ears and promptly got up and left the room.

Beth thought about the old woman who had sat across from her on parent-teacher conference nights. "Do you think they were sleeping together?"

"Ew," said Jack.

She looked at Jack and smirked. "You could dress up as Elvis for me and take me upstairs and I can pretend to be an English teacher and conjugate your verbs."

Jack laughed and took her hand. "How about you just 'thank me, thank me very much' afterward." Jack dropped her hand and abruptly stood, his eyes wide. "Beth…" He looked at her, his expression one of serious surprise. "The police are saying someone dressed as Elvis was seen leaving the scene of the Dan's Used Furniture and Supreme Meats murders."

Beth's mouth dropped open.

"And," Jack continued, walking across the kitchen to the junk drawer, "your father found these." he said, holding up a pair of gaudy gold retro aviator sunglasses, "in our basement."

Miles Frank looked down at the broken little body in his arms and wept. Alice had been his constant companion since he purchased the land upon which his house sat. His reason for everything. For living where he did, for trying to get Olivia to love him. For all of it.

Alice was the only one who loved him, he thought, stroking her fine hair. Olivia didn't love him, she'd made that abundantly clear. Helen? She only tolerated him by dressing up the way she thought he'd like. She used him for his money.

He used the key, the key he had hidden in his pocket the day he left the property when he was fourteen, and pressed in the code to the safe, 1215. It opened smoothly, revealing its contents.

Miles had always been a thrifty man, and the fact that the two million dollars neatly stacked on the top two shelves had barely been touched proved it. All the jewelry that he'd given Helen and Olivia had come from Maria's old jewelry box that was tucked neatly in one of the safe's corners. He'd snuck his way into the abandoned bomb shelter years ago and siphoned off a bit at a time for living expenses, and when the land on which his house stood had come up for sale he bought it for cash. But Olivia, and then the Hamlins had bought the Patton House before he even realized it was for sale. It made his blood boil. It was rightly his. *He* was the heir. It was his family home.

Alice lay light in his arms, her bones like those of a bird. A broken bird. As much as Miles Frank loved her, he did not like things to be untidy. He left the bomb shelter, went to the kitchen, and got a trash bag. Returning to the chamber, he gathered up what was left of Alice Patton—the strands of hair, the wisps of fabric that were once a frilly pink dress—shoved her unceremoniously into the bag, and threw it over his shoulder.

"I'll make a new friend," he whispered to her. Miles Frank smiled.

Beth stood at the kitchen window watching Bobo play in the yard with Mr. Tinkles. Bobo had got his hands on an entire bag of bacon dog treats and was running around the back yard holding one above his head, with Mr. T trotting along close on his heels with his tongue hanging out. Every few minutes Bobo would stop and give him a treat, dig out another, and continue running in circles around the yard, squealing and laughing as he went.

Beth dried her hands on a dishtowel and smiled. "Those two are going to nap all afternoon," she told herself. Bobo was a little terror of a toddler, but he was *her* terror and she loved him to pieces. Everyone who met him thought he was the cutest, most precocious little human they'd ever seen. Beth laughed. That was because they only spent a few minutes with him, she thought.

Across the yard she could see Mr. Frank taking out the trash. He opened the bin next to his back door, tossed in a black trash bag, and slammed it closed. On his way back to his house, he waved to Bobo. Bobo waved back.

Beth frowned and called him in for cookies. Mr. Frank gave Beth a bone-deep case of the creeps. Something was so off about him. She reached for the cookies that she kept hidden on top of the refrigerator, put two on a plate, and sat them, along with a glass of milk, in front of her very sweaty toddler.

"Can I have another plate, Mama?" He asked her.

"Sorry buddy, Mr. T can't have any cookies. He's had too many treats already. He'll explode!"

"Not for him, for my friend."

The hair on the back of Beth's arms stood up like little soldiers.

"What friend?"

"The little girl with the black hair," Bobo said, smiling through a bite of cookie.

Beth reluctantly set another small plate on the table and Bobo placed an oreo on it.

"I share nice, right, Mama?"

Beth nodded and kissed him on the forehead. "Yes you do, baby."

"I'm not a baby," Bobo said, laying his head onto his folded arms.

"You're right, honey," she said, stroking his hair. "You're a very sleepy big boy."

Bobo went out for the count. She carried her sleeping son to his bed and gently laid him on his dinosaur quilt.

Beth felt the need to stay close to him, so she went across the hall to her bedroom and grabbed a book. It was nice to read something just for the joy of it. Something completely different than what she wrote. She picked up the sci-fi thriller that she was halfway through and settled herself into one of the plump chairs by the circular window. Filtered light shined through the old glass, and the curtains gently billowed.

Beth took a deep, cleansing breath, the deep kind of breath that she'd learned in her short-lived yoga career. She'd gone to class three times before her body complained, and she was left with two hundred dollars of yoga gear—and the knowledge of the merit of deep, cleansing breaths. She filled her lungs and exhaled three times.

Feeling more settled, she thought about the incident in the kitchen. All kids had imaginary friends, right?

She cracked the book open and something slipped out onto the floor. Another red pen. She looked at it, alarmed, as it balanced on its end and drew a small circle. It continued to spin, the red lines becoming broader and broader. Beth held her breath and watched.

After a few seconds, the pen dropped and rolled under her chair. Beth stood, more intrigued than frightened, then fell to her knees, examining the circles of red ink, wanting to make sure she wasn't imagining things. Running her fingers over the floorboards, she found that one plank stood a little higher than its mates. It also felt loose. Beth lifted it with her fingernail, the board rising easily from its resting place.

Setting it aside, she reached into the space below and pulled out a journal. From the looks of it, and its obvious age, it appeared more of a diary than a journal. On the inside of the brown leather jacket was written, *Property of Olivia Jean Sharette*; and directly underneath, *According to Miles: lucky lotto numbers to use: 12+15.*

Chapter Thirty

Aliens, Guns and a Pajama Party

HELEN BECKNOR hadn't been out of the house for a good time in weeks—not since that bastard Miles Frank had all but thrown her out on her ass.

She looked across the living room at her husband, Glen, and son Trevor. They were playing video games and whooping it up. It set her teeth on edge. Her husband was a big child. A big, drunk child.

Helen felt her hands clench. Miles Frank wasn't perfect, but he *was* a good time, and dammit! on top of it all she was low on cash. He owed her—she'd dressed up as his plaything for years. She'd put her hair in a bouffant for him, for chrissakes, and a few times had to stop at the store on the way home, all dolled up like Priscilla fucking Presley. The stupid, selfish bastard.

Trevor and Glen cheered, as one or the other of the imbeciles she lived with blew up a virtual alien spaceship or whatever.

She had to get out.

Helen picked up her phone, stood from her chair, and headed to the bedroom slamming the door behind her.

"What's with her?" asked Trevor.

"No idea—watch it! To your left at eleven o'clock!"

Helen sat on the bed and dialed Miles Frank's number. He answered on the second ring.

"What?" he asked, his tone terse.

"I have on that green dress you like so much," she said, her voice oozing seduction. "How about I slip into some stockings and heels and come on over…"

"Absolutely not, Helen. I told you unequivocally that we're finished," he hissed, "and when I say something I damn well mean it."

"C'mon, Miles," she purred. "Your Priscilla is low on cash and high on horny."

"You're a pathetic whore," he spat, and hung up the phone.

Helen flung the phone to the floor and kicked it, went to the closet, picked out some heels and stockings, slipped into the green dress, did her hair and makeup, and headed toward the garage.

Trevor and Glen stared at her, shrugged, and went back to killing aliens.

Dressed to kill, Helen opened the driver's side door and threw her sparkly white purse, which housed the silver Colt .45, into the back seat. She grabbed the shotgun from where it hung on the wall and threw that in as well for good measure. She slipped behind the wheel and opened an extra button on her dress. "He's gonna fall at my feet," she said, opening still another button. "One way or an-other."

It was 8:30 P.M., and the day of the reconnaissance mission, along with Mr. Frank's bowling night, had arrived. "I don't want any of you kids—" Grandpa said, then turned his attention to his Army buddies, pointing to include them all— "that includes *you* dummies, to get your damn fool asses killed."

Grandpa turned and looked directly at Sam, bending to his eye level. "I'm supposed to be responsible for you," he said, "and if you so much as stub a toe, Grandma, your mom, and your dad will skin me alive—so we've got to do this smart, and we have to do this quick." He stood and jabbed Stumpy Joe in the chest. "And I don't want to have to save your ass…again."

"Shave my ass?" asked Stumpy, his voice raising an octave, "What the hell are you talking about, Sarge?"

"*Save!*" Grandpa whisper-yelled.

The whole group broke out in snorts and chuckles, and Richard pointed to Stumpy's ear, meaning, "Check your hearing aid."

"Oh," said Stumpy Joe, shaking his head, "you didn't really save me, you just hauled me out of a pit latrine."

"If you shave your ass, will you shave my initials into it?" Shorty asked him.

Stumpy punched him, not so gently, in the arm.

"You three," Grandpa said, gesturing to Ben, Jennie, and Jaimie, "will stand guard here in front of the wine cellar door." The twins stood a little taller. Grandpa looked at his watch. "If my wife happens to wake up and see you,

you're waiting for the rest of us. Tell her we went on a snack run and will be home soon." He turned his attention to Ben. "If Grandma doesn't buy it, tell her you have a bellyache and need a ginger ale. That gets her every time."

"You want me to lie to Grandma?"

"If it gets to the point where Grandma is asking questions, I promise you you'll have a bellyache anyway."

"Trevor and Hank, position yourself at the bottom of the stairs. Same story if Beth or Jack try to come down. Your job is to keep them out."

Trevor saluted and went to take his position, Hank following after him.

"Sam? BJ? You're with us," he said, motioning to include Richard, Stumpy Joe and Shorty. "You boys run faster than we do, and if things go south we'll need your legs. And come to think of it, we'll need your backs too." He pointed at the butcher block island that blocked the door. "Soldiers? Move that big-ass whatever-it-is."

Sam and BJ, with a little help from Richard, scooted the block into the center of the room. Sam wiped his forehead with the back of his arm. "I have the possible lock combinations, Grandpa," he said, holding up a piece of paper written in red ink. On it were scribbled birthdays and more possible combinations.

Grandpa nodded proudly. "We got this."

Stumpy Joe pulled the wine bottle from the bottom shelf, and with little effort the door slid open.

Sam dropped the piece of paper with the codes. The door to the bomb shelter already stood ajar.

An hour before the reconnaissance mission was to begin, Jack and Beth had gone to bed early and were huddled together reading Olivia Sharette's diary.

"This is incredible!" Jack whispered as Beth turned a page. "She really did know Elvis. He bought her this house, and put her through college." He looked at Beth. "I'm totally blown away. This is better than anything you've ever written."

She punched his arm playfully and peeked over at the baby monitor. Bobo was sound asleep on his back, clutching Bridget the baby doll. "I don't know why he's so attached to that creepy thing," she muttered, and went back to reading.

They read together for another hour, completely engrossed in Olivia Sharette's secret life and loves.

"Miles Frank is a serious asshole." said Beth, pointing out the entry about their encounter in the school parking lot, where he had first threatened Olivia. She flipped the page and skimmed through most of Olivia's musing over day-to-day activities in which she wrote about her garden, the birds she loved to feed, the books she was reading, her students and—full stop.

Jack read the entry. "Our neighbor, who we thought was harmless, accosted our son's English teacher and tried to win her love by putting on a cheap Elvis costume. That's the most terrifying thing I've ever read." Jack looked at his wife. "He has to be crazy!"

"Elvis costume," Beth repeated, thinking of the Dan's Used Furniture and Supreme Meats murders, and the connection between Elvis, Olivia and Miles Frank. "Jack, I think we have a motive…"

A squawk came from the baby monitor, jolting them back into the moment.

Bobo's bed was empty.

As Jack and Beth Hamlin began a frantic search for their missing toddler, Miles Frank had carried Bobo out their front door and into his house. He gave him another cookie. "We're going to be great pals, you and me," Miles said, tapping Bobo on the nose.

Bobo smiled, took the cookie into the hand that wasn't holding onto Bridget, and took a bite of it.

"But now," Miles said to him, "we have to go to sleep first."

"In my bed at home?"

"No, little friend. I have a special bed for you because we're having a sleepover."

"Does Mama know?"

"Of course," Miles told him. "She's the one that gave me the cookies for you."

This seemed to satisfy Bobo, and he wrapped an arm around Mr. Frank's neck.

Miles carried him down to the bomb shelter, and opened the door to the safe with the key and the code. "This is my favorite place for hide and seek," he told Bobo, setting him down. "Do you want to play hide and seek before bed?"

Bobo nodded enthusiastically. "Can I hide in the safe?"

"Of course you can. Sleepovers should be fun and you're my guest, so you get the best hiding spot."

Bobo took a handful of cookies and climbed inside. "Count to twenty, Mr. Frank!"

"Sure will, little buddy," Miles said, and closed the door.

Miles leaned against the metal door, his heart hammering and tears welling up in his eyes. He could hear the toddler inside, but the sound was muffled because of the thickness of its walls. There was perhaps half an hour of oxygen left, and then he'd not be alone again.

"So much for bowling night," Miles said aloud, a slow smile spreading across his face.

Helen pulled up in front of Miles's house and parked.

His living room light was on and she knew the bastard was home. Tuesday was bowling night in Miles Frank's life, and he'd stayed home—which meant he wanted her company, and her company wasn't cheap.

She adjusted her stockings, pulled the neckline of her dress a bit lower, grabbed her heavy purse, and headed to his door. She knocked, three rapid taps. Where was he? She knocked again and heard shuffling and footfalls.

Miles swung open the door. His face was flushed, and it looked as if he may have been crying. He said nothing, just stared at her dumbfounded.

She gave him a twirl, sending her skirt flying. "Oops. Dropped my purse." She bent slowly to pick it up, knowing she was giving him quite the show.

Helen stood, smoothed her skirt, and smiled at him, "I have something for you…Miles," she said, lowering her lashes and running her tongue over her pink lips.

Miles Frank said nothing, and closed the door.

She stood there for a second, her arms at her sides and her purse clutched tight in her hands. Fire rose hot to her cheeks, humiliating, searing anger rushing through her. She dropped her bag, marched back to her car, and grabbed the shotgun from the back seat.

"Yep," she said aloud, "I've got something *big* to show you." She racked the shotgun and threw it over her shoulder.

Chapter Thirty-one

Muthafucka

"Maybe Sam has him?" Jack said, after checking Sam's room and finding it empty.

"Sam was going to pal around tonight with Grandpa," Beth answered, wringing her hands. "I bet he climbed out—he's done it before, but he's always stayed in his room and played with his toys or come to find us." Beth looked at her husband. Her voice hitched and she clutched his arm. "Jack, something feels very wrong."

"We'll keep looking, we'll find him," Jack said. "Let's check the kitchen. Maybe he wanted more cookies or a drink of water."

Grandpa pushed open the bomb shelter door and surveyed the scene. Shelves filled with old mason jars of what used to be pickled vegetables, and dry goods with labels straight out of the sixties, filled an entire wall. Bunks with faded linens lined another.

"You could survive a nuclear blast and live for thirty years down here," whispered Shorty, ducking his head as he entered the large cement room.

Stumpy Joe picked up a jar of thirty-year old pickles that floated like some kind of science experiment in black brine. "Yeah, but would you want to?"

Grandpa examined the safe on the left side of the room. "They don't make them like this anymore," he said, giving the combination a spin. "I'm not sure you could cut through this with an industrial metal saw."

He surveyed the room. "That bastard has been traveling back and forth between our houses without us knowing."

There was a ladder to the far right side of the room that ended in a hatch in the ceiling. Sam stood under it and pointed up. "This probably leads straight into Mr. Frank's house."

Grandpa walked over to take a closer look and slipped on something small on the floor, catching himself on the handle of the safe mid-fall. He bent and picked up the small blue piece of fabric. "Isn't this Bobo's sock?"

That's when they heard the gunshot.

Helen Becknor was done with Miles Frank's shit. She kicked the front door open, losing a heel in the process; she punted its mate across the room, knocking over a lamp, and stood in her stockinged feet, staring the bastard down. She aimed the shotgun square at his chest.

"I want you to open that safe right now and fill my bag with money." She pointed at the sequined bag that laid on the floor. "We could have had a good time, you know, but you ruin *everything*, Miles, you crazy bastard."

Miles ignored her request, turned his back on her, and headed toward the back door.

"Don't you dare turn your back on me, you son of a bitch!" she shouted after him. "You owe me, goddamnit. Say something! Miles!"

Miles walked out the back door, reached into the trash can, and picked up the black trash bag that held Alice's corpse. He upended it, and let the bones scatter on the patio.

"She's the only one that ever loved me," he said, spreading his arms as if accepting his fate. "And you, Helen, are a manipulative, pitiful whore."

Helen shot him right in the face, and he fell back amongst the tiny bones.

Many years ago

The day of Alice's fourth birthday, Walter Patton's nephew called the birthday girl over and she reluctantly sat next to him on the grass.

"I have a surprise for you," he said.

"A birthday present?" she asked, her eyes twinkling, and gave him the first genuine smile he'd seen from her in weeks.

"Kind of," he answered. "I'm going to make sure you win at hide and seek." He took her hand and placed a key in it.

"You know how to get into the bomb shelter, right, Alice?" he whispered to her, and her eyes brightened. She nodded and leaned in closer to him, and it made him feel as if he was her partner in crime. They shared a secret.

Thomas Gleason took her hand and whispered into her ear, "I've opened the safe down there, all you need to do is climb in and pull the door closed after you."

Alice hugged him, a genuine, happy hug, and ran off to ask her mother to lead them in a game of hide and seek. Mayor Walter Patton, the pompous ass, looked on from across the green expanse of the yard.

"Bobo!" Beth screamed, running down the basement stairs, and was startled when she saw Ben, Trevor, and the Clarks standing there. "Have you seen Bobo?" she asked Trevor, grabbing him by the shoulders, her voice in a panic.

The kids could tell Beth was not to be messed with and forgot all about the fib they were to tell about a snack run.

"No," Jenny told her. "We haven't seen him all night."

Beth grabbed Ben's hand, dragging her middle son with her. She shot past Jenny and Trevor and into the basement.

Grandma was standing in the hall in her nightgown, robe and curlers. "What the holy hell's happening?" she said.

"Mom, we can't find Bobo!" Beth was in tears now. "I can't find my baby."

Grandma walked up to her and took her hands. "We'll find him."

Sometimes Grandma really stepped up to the plate.

Jack was in the back yard calling for his son. The night was quiet until Miles Frank's back door flew open and a figure with a bouffant hairdo followed him out. A shotgun blast shredded the stillness, and an owl flew off to the west from one of the cottonwoods.

After a shocked instant, Jack jumped the fence and took off at a sprint toward Miles Frank's patio, leaving Mr. T howling in the yard.

"Shit, *I* even heard that!" said Stumpy Joe as the gunshot shook the house.

"You kids stay here," Grandpa said, as Richard Miller opened the hatch that led up to what would be Mr. Frank's home. Grandpa, Stumpy Joe, and Shorty followed him up the ladder and into Miles Frank's dark bedroom.

Trevor, Ben, and the Clarks led Beth and Grandma into the wine cellar and past the open wine rack. They looked at each other, stunned.

"Has this been here since we moved in?" said Grandma.

Jenny nodded, "It's how Mr. Frank would get into your house."

"It wasn't ghosts? It was Miles?"

"Some of it, I think," said Jaimie, and pushed open the second barrier that led to the bomb shelter.

"Holy shit on a stick," said Grandma, taking in the magnitude of the underground chamber.

"Bobo!" screamed Beth, "Bobo, where are you? You're scaring Mommy!"

Grandpa and his buddies, followed by Jack, came sliding back down the ladder.

"Cops are on the way," Jack said.

"Miles Frank is dead in the yard," Grandpa said.

"Some woman with big hair shot him right in his ugly mug," Stumpy said, bending with his hands on his knees and trying to catch his breath.

Beth started up the ladder, "Bobo!" The fact that there had been a shooting not thirty feet away didn't seem to faze her. Mom-fear had taken over, and this was a million times worse than losing him in Target. "Bobo!"

"He's not up there, honey," Jack said, taking her hand. "We searched the whole house."

Grandpa reached into his pocket and pulled out the little blue sock. "I think I know where he is."

Jack climbed back through the tunnel, through the basement, up the stairs, out the back door and to the tool shed. He grabbed the big brass keyring and retraced his steps, taking the stairs three at a time. Breathless, he dashed through the tunnel and handed Grandpa the keyring. "It has to be one of these."

Grandpa began trying keys, and on the sixth try the tumblers turned. He tugged at the door. "We need the combination!"

Everyone was still. Beth sobbed and pounded on the safe door. Grandma clasped her hands over her mouth and one of her curlers fell out. Richard Miller bent, picked it up, and handed it back to her.

Sam hung his head, tears streaking his face, "I wish we'd never won the damn lottery!" he yelled.

Beth stood up straight, suddenly calm. "I know what it is," she said. "I know what the code is."

Everyone stared at her.

"1215. Miles Frank's lucky lotto numbers."

Jack turned the combination, stopping on each number. The door creaked open and Bobo and Alice Patton's blonde rubber doll rolled out.

Beth cried out and knelt beside her son's still body. "Wake up, Bobo!" she said, shaking him.

"If that motherfucker Miles Frank wasn't dead, I'd kill him again," said Grandpa.

"Mothafucka," Bobo said, reaching up for his mom without opening his eyes.

Chapter Thirty-two

Off To the Liquor Palace!

Many Years Before

a novel by Beth Hamlin, writing as Blaze Bolivar

OLIVIA SHARETTE worked as a waitress in a diner in Nashville. She had aspirations of being a teacher someday, and was looking into taking some classes, but she was in no hurry. She was only eighteen, and time seemed like a blurry thing to her teenage self—something without any substance. She had all the time in the world.

Olivia needed to save up for tuition; her parents wouldn't be any help, so she worked long days, and sometimes nights, in the diner. The nights were tough, though: a lot of drunks came through after the bars closed, and she'd had her fill of old and young men making passes at her. But the tips were good, and she put up with more than her older self would have ever dreamed of putting up with.

Her hair was long and black back then, and she pulled it back into a tight ponytail; her eyes were gray and smokey, and they sparkled with all the keenness of youth. Her red uniform had white buttons up the front and a crisp, white collar. On her feet were bobby socks and white Keds tennis shoes. It was the standard diner uniform and she owned two of them, both with her name embroidered on the breast pocket. One dress was a size smaller and seemed to get her better tips with the drunk crowd. Men could be awful; it was a shame boys couldn't grow up into something else.

One very slow, humid night two men in suits came in and spoke to her manager, Beverly. There was a whispered exchange of hushed words, and Beverly approached the only occupied booth. She leaned in and spoke with the couple sitting there, then handed them a few bills. Olivia couldn't tell how much money it was from where she was standing, but the pair rose and exited the diner in a rush. After the booth was cleared, the men opened the front door, with Beverly standing close by.

In a cloud of bodyguards, in walked Elvis Presley. *Elvis Presley.*

♫

Beth looked up from her computer, took a sip of wine, and reached down to pat Mr. T on the head.

"This is going to be a great one," she said to him. Mr. Tinkles woofed once as three red pens rolled off the shelf and onto the floor.

Beth smiled.

Sam watched his mom offer Grandpa a nectarine for the third time. She'd found a great deal on them and had bought an entire bushel for Bobo's fourth birthday party. They were obviously not Grandpa's favorite fruit, and he politely declined—for the third time.

The Hamlin family had purchased the land on which Miles Frank's house had stood. It had been razed to the ground, the bomb shelter completely filled in with dirt and concrete, and a garden planted. The money that was in the safe was equally donated between the Patton Historical Society and Saint Jude's Children's Hospital. The family planted more roses in the colors that Maria had planted all those years ago, including a new ivory variety called Rock and Roll in honor of Elvis. There was also an abundance of bird feeders and benches, and a playground for the kids. A bronze statue of a little girl blowing a dandelion stood prominently in the west corner of the yard, her bronze hair ribbons billowing behind her. One of the benches was engraved with a plaque which read, "Teachers! Changing the World One Child at a Time!"

Trevor's dad, Glen, sat under a shade tree with Jack, Beth, and BJ's mom as the smaller kids played on the playground (no rusty kid launcher in sight) and the older pre-teens sat huddled in another part of the yard, obviously too cool to participate in playground activities. The yard was bustling with action, and Bobo stood atop the slide holding a lightsaber.

Alice's remains had been buried in her family plot with her parents and sisters, and—other than the occasional red pen of shame showing up in various places—the paranormal activity in the house had calmed.

Jack had the '57 caddy repainted in its original pink glory. He had full plans to attend car shows and gatherings to tell the story about how he had become its present owner. He drove it a few times a week, and kept it in tip-top shape; the glove compartment had become the nook where all of the accumulated red pens were stored.

Grandpa and the Army buddies huddled around the fire pit telling old stories and embellishing new ones. Beth walked over with the last nectarine.

"Dad?" she said, "Please take this nectarine, it's the last one."

Grandpa reached into the box and picked up the remaining nectarine and casually chucked it over the fence and into the cottonwoods. Everyone roared.

Beth looked down into the empty box and then at her father, who hadn't skipped one word or missed a beat in his storytelling.

Bobo hurried over, took Stumpy Joe's hat, and placed it on his head. He climbed onto his grandpa's lap and whispered, "I buried mines in the sandbox."

The tattooed guy from the dollar store didn't own a car. He usually walked home down Main Street after his shift, but today he took the scenic route, which led him directly past the old Patton mansion.

As he walked, the tattooed guy bounced a small rubber superball that he'd found in the back room at work that day. Bounce, step step. Bounce, step step.

He passed an old man in an Army cap who was oiling the iron gate in front of the mansion, and said hello. The old fellow said hello in return, and the tattooed guy kept walking and bouncing his ball. Three houses down, he missed a beat, and the bright orange ball hit a crack in the sidewalk and flew off at an angle into a bush.

"Shit."

He bent to retrieve it and noticed something white and sparkly under the bush; he picked it up. It was a purse, covered in sequins and unusually heavy. The tattooed guy opened it and peeked inside.

"Well, hot diggity damn."

The tattooed guy from the dollar store stashed the coat baby—which Helen had tossed from her car window when she sped off after shooting Miles—into his jacket, the orange superball forgotten. He pumped a fist in the air, jumped, and clicked the heels of his sneakers together.

"Off to the pawn shop, then hello Liquor Palace!"

The End

Read on to preview Chapter One of

THE ORE BUCKET

by Sue Alcon O'Connor

Coming in 2023

AFTERWORD

Dear Reader,

Thanks and congratulations on making it safely through this book and coming out unscathed on the other side.

If you enjoyed this story, please take a moment to leave even a brief review: these are the lifeblood of indie authors who are competing with big publishers, and without reviews, we have no visibility.

A lot of the things you read are based in reality. The monkey story is real. My son Logan had this happen when he was a junior in high school. The vice principal called me. I laughed. I laughed some more. Logan really did say, "I told you my mom would laugh!" Which about put me on the floor. I'd give anything to have a copy of the story itself, but what I included in the book is close. The next year we had to meet with his counselor regarding his plans for his senior year. The poor kid was going to have the same teacher for English. He spoke up and said he couldn't be in her class because of…an issue…last spring. The counselor looked at him, pointed and said, "OH. OHHHH… You're that monkey kid!" I almost peed my pants.

Sam and Ben are a combination of Logan and Marshall, my mischievous boys. Bobo is a combination of my daughter

Gina and my grandson (named after Grandpa Al, who was also real). Gina once got stuck in the TV stand, and we took pictures.

Grandpa and Grandma are real. Grandpa was ex-Army, and at seventy-six years of age and with only one lung, he wrestled a shoplifter to the ground. Grandma cleaned a lot and despised old stoves.

Egypt December is kind of real, and modeled after my friend Faithie. When she was a little girl she said her future child would be named Egypt December. Thank god she wised up and had a Brittany.

No cats or Elvises were hurt during the writing of this book. I like cats. I've made a donation to a cat rescue to ease the pain of fictional cat murder. I also like Elvis, and I'm sure he was a pretty great guy.

Thank you all again from the bottom of my heart, and may Helen and her shotgun ride off into the sunset.

My son, Marshall, to whom this book is dedicated, passed away from colon cancer right before I began writing this book. Please, even if you're in your late thirties, get tested. If you served on a nuclear submarine—do it every year. I'll go with you and hold your hand if you want.

Read on to preview Chapter One of

THE ORE BUCKET

by Sue Alcon O'Connor

Coming in 2023

THE ORE BUCKET

Chapter One

JENNALISE JONES took the money she inherited from her Aunt Belinda and bought herself an old jail. She had no idea it was a jail when she bought it sight unseen, but she found out fast enough. It's not the kind of thing you miss.

From the outside, the building wasn't much to look at—not yet anyway, but Jenna had plans. Big plans that involved most of the rest of Aunt B's money, a small loan, and a Santa-sized sack of elbow grease. Jenna knew she was up to the task. She exercised (sometimes) and was in decent shape, if you didn't count her coffee and pastry addiction, which left her with a few extra pounds. But that didn't bother her or slow her down. She appreciated her curves and liked herself the way she was. Life was too short to live on kale and dry broiled chicken.

Not long before he succumbed to lung cancer, Warren Zevon said that his best advice on living was to "Enjoy every sandwich." Jenna took that to heart and lived her life to the fullest. If that included a slice of cheesecake, personal trainers and nutritionists be damned: you never knew if it would be your last slice, and it better have a raspberry swirl. Jenna wasn't the kind of woman who went out on a date and ordered a dinner salad to impress someone. She balanced out the extra calories with exercise and weights—good enough. As for going out on dates, it had been awhile, and might be awhile yet with all the work she had to do.

The money part of her new endeavor was covered, (thank you Aunt B), and as for the inspiration, Jenna was filled to the brim with innovative ideas. She felt inspired, she was motivated, and truth be told she was just a little terrified. Opening a gift shop in a small town was a far cry from her job as a therapist. With the isolation caused by COVID, she had gone from a thriving in-person practice to a much smaller practice online. She fully planned to keep most of her clients, moving their appointments to the evening or into the afternoon, since her sister Viv had agreed to step in and watch the store for a few hours. Jenna shook her head and smiled to herself: life would be crazy busy, even though she only scheduled three clients a day.

Small town life—Jenna'd been born and raised in Denver—would come with a multitude of pluses, and a few minuses as well. On the plus side, Shay, Colorado was quaint, walkable, filled with summer tourists, and brain-meltingly beautiful. Jenna's sister lived here with her husband and kids, so she'd have family close, and a four-hour drive got her back to Denver to visit her brother and her parents. On the minus side, not one Starbucks in sight, and as far as she knew the only doughnuts came from the supermarket that wasn't really all that super.

Jenna had raised a few eyebrows when she moved in with her tall, blonde-haired, blue-eyed sister who lived on the northside of town, but she was used to raising eyebrows. Unlike her sister Vivienne, Jenna had bright, curly red hair, honey colored skin, and a splattering of the darkest freckles anyone had ever seen. People took notice. Add to that the fact she barely hit five feet on a good day, and that like her Aunt Belinda, she had eyes that made people stop in their tracks: just like Aunt B, Jenna had heterochromatic eyes. One was a rich chocolate brown, the other as green and lush as grass in the shade. Yep, people took notice. Jenna hoped her unique appearance would jumpstart her business, even if customers just came in to get a look at the new girl in town with the unrestrained red curly hair, mismatched eyes, and freckles that looked a bit like the Pleiades star cluster.

She laughed to herself thinking about all the unparalleled cards she'd been dealt. Someone actually told her once that she should join the circus. People always asked if she and Viv had the same father. They didn't, but still, how rude was *that*? Jenna took it all in stride: being unique was precious to her now that she was an adult. Not so much when she was in school—that had been tough at times.

Jenna punched in the key code for the realtor's lockbox, and opened it. She pulled out a key ring that was now hers, along with everything the keys opened, bought and paid for.

It was a dump. That was being kind; in actuality it was a *giant* dump. It was an elephant-sized dump, minus the peanut shells. Jenna had purchased the property for its location, thinking it would be an ideal spot right in the middle of town. She'd only seen photographs, and she knew it needed work, but wow! It needed a *lot* of work.

The rustic brick building was directly on Main Street in Old Town Shay and consisted of two stories plus a basement. She looked around the one room first story, put her hands on her hips, and blew a stray red curl from her eyes. It was certainly big enough to hold the shop she envisioned, but it would take some muscle. Trash and dust littered the floor, along with pieces of boards and glass, beer cans, an old mattress, and some very unsavory graffiti. Jenna placed her hands on her hips and read the walls. "I guess Mallory S. was a slut," she said aloud, with a frown. That would be the first thing she painted over. Poor Mallory S. Jennalise knew what it was like to be bullied.

Soon this area would be filled with cut flowers and plants, honey, homemade jams and jellies, and gifts of all persuasions. There would be local artwork and crafts, jewelry, toys, and books. Through all the dust and debris she could see it already.

Jenna climbed the stairs that led to the upper level. They creaked beneath her feet, and she was extra cautious climbing them since the only light in the place came from very grubby windows. On the landing just before entering the second story was a window that looked out to the west and over the mountains. Even through the haze she could tell the view from this spot would be impressive.

Beyond the landing and through a door was a two-bedroom living quarters; the smaller one would be her office. An adequate-sized kitchen with appliances that seemed older than her mom, and a bathroom that looked as if it needed to be completely gutted—except for the clawfoot tub. That had to be refinished, and it had to stay. There was no way she was parting with that. She envisioned soaking in it with some of the bath salts she'd be selling, with candles also from the shop and with a glass of wine or two. She looked closely at the black stains in and around the tub. That little daydream would have to wait; she had bigger fish to fry, like windows and walls and inventory.

Off the kitchen was a small living room with a fireplace that was surrounded by green ceramic tile. There was a built-in bookcase, and a large bowed window that overlooked a particular jagged portion of the Rocky Mountains. The room was just big enough to hold a loveseat and a chair. Jenna surveyed what would be her new living quarters and smiled. In time it would be perfect.

Remembering that there was a basement storage area, she made her way down the stairs, turned a corner, and stood before a metal door. Fumbling with the keyring, she found the key that opened the basement door, pulled the cord that turned on the stair light, walked down stairs that swayed a little under her feet, and stopped dead in her tracks. Three cells lined the back wall, all of them with iron bars and heavy latches.

Jenna pulled the light cord.

The floor was dirt, and other than a table, two broken chairs, and a wall lined in dusty shelves, it seemed empty. "I'll be damned," she whispered. "It looks as if I bought myself an old jail."

Jenna did a quick sweep-up of trash before Viv, Alex, and the kids arrived. The word *jail* had the whole family dashing to the car to come and see Aunt Jenna's slammer.

Carlos blasted in the front door. "Wow, Auntie Jenna, this place is a *giant* dump." The eight-year-old was so much like her, she had to laugh.

"That's why you're here," she said, "to help me clean it."

"First I want to see the jail," he said, and pointed to his six-year-old sister, Bailey. "Can I lock her in it?"

"Carlos…" Viv said.

"I don't think we'll be locking anyone in it, I can't find the keys," Jenna answered. "I have a ton of keys on this ring, but none fit the jail cells. I'll show them to you, but be really careful on the stairs." She pulled the cord to the bare light bulb and led the family into the basement.

"I'll come over tomorrow and reinforce both sets of stairs," said Alex, as he walked down the rickety steps.

"I'd appreciate that," said Jenna, as she stepped off the last stair and onto the ground. "Welcome to my new home." She gestured with her hands as if she had just led them into a mansion. "A few throw pillows…some candles…maybe a chaise…"

Bailey ran to the center cage and gave the door an excited tug. "If we had the keys, I'd lock my teacher in here!"

"Bailey!" said Alex, shaking his head, obviously a little embarrassed. "We birthed these two, but I think they were switched at the hospital with Ted Bundy's kids."

"Who's Ted Bundy?" asked Carlos. "Is he my real dad?"

"No, I'm your real dad. He's some crazy guy that knew a lot about jails."

"Oh." Carlos grabbed Bailey's hand and they dashed up the steps. "We're gonna see where we'll sleep when we stay over!"

"When I grow up, I want to be just like Ted Bundy and learn everything about jails," Bailey squealed, running upstairs after her brother. "I love this old jail!"

Alex, Jenna, and Viv burst out laughing.

"Should I be worried?" asked Viv, placing her hands on top of her head in exasperation.

Jenna laughed. "I love you guys so much," she said, and hugged them both. Her family might be a little weird, but that was exactly why she adored them. "Thanks for letting me stay with you through the renovation. I know you both have a lot on your plates." She reached up and turned off the light, leading her sister and brother-in-law up the stairs. She turned off the stair lights, plunging the basement into darkness, and closed the metal door.

"We love having you, Jenna," said Alex, "but the first thing we're going to do is get your living quarters in order so you can get the hell out of our hair." He pulled her into a hug, and she laughed again.

Viv took a quick walk around the main level, her knowledge of interior design written all over her face. "You know what, Jenna? This is going to be amazing."

Jennalise smiled. "Let's gather up the little hoodlums and head out to dinner." She squeezed her sister's hand. "Burgers are on me."

Harry Erikson was not hairy. In fact, each time he looked in the mirror, the bald pancake at the back of his skull seemed to grow and mock him like an obnoxious little pal that wanted to tag along everywhere he went. He, however, refused to do a combover, and just let that giant hairy eyeball on the back of his head do its thing. Do your thing, Mr. Pancake, do your thing.

Harry trimmed a few stray, wiry hairs from his red beard, pulled his tee shirt over his head, tucked it into his jeans, and headed to work at the café. It wasn't a long trip—just down the stairs. He lived above the shop in a small one-bedroom apartment he'd designed. It was small and cramped—*cozy*, as relators liked to call it—but it suited his needs just fine.

Harry had been born and raised in Shay, Colorado, and each time he'd head out to the big city he came home appreciating small town life more. He'd spent three days in Denver this past week and had picked up a huge piece of equipment for the store. The behemoth sat in the bed of his 2016 Dodge Powerwagon, and Harry had no idea how he'd get it out. Probably call his brother and a couple of friends, but that could wait for a bit: he had to get the store open and the coffee perking.

He opened the front door to the restaurant and dragged out the sandwich sign that stated what was on today's menu, looked across the street, and saw a curly-haired red-head kid walk into the old Shay jail. She turned, saw him, and waved. Whoa. She certainly wasn't a kid. Just short, really short, with some stand-out, very adult knockers.

He waved back and made a mental note to bring her complementary coffee as a welcome-to-the-neighborhood gift, and get the scoop on why the hell anyone would buy a broken-down jail.

The next day the work started in earnest. Viv and Jenna came equipped bright and early with trash bags and cleaning supplies, and Alex made a trip into the larg-er town down the road thirty miles for everything he'd need to reinforce the staircases. Jenna headed out to her car to get the big broom she forgot, and saw a man across the street pulling out a sandwich sign. He had auburn hair, a red beard, and probably stood about six feet two.

She waved at him. He waved back. Jenna wondered if he knew the history of the building she'd just purchased.

She'd have to ask him…and was that coffee she smelled? The name of the shop was Latte to Dinner. Has to be coffee. Maybe they even have donuts.

Jenna pumped a fist in the air and danced the broom into the front door. Coffee!

The man with the cowboy hat sat in one of Harry's outdoor patio chairs, a cup of black coffee in front of him. The morning waitress, Stacy, came up to his small table and topped off his cup. "Is there anything else I can get you, sir?" she asked.

"I'm good, darlin'," he told her. He crossed his long legs at the ankles, leaned back in his chair, and watched her as she walked to the next table.

The man stared at the old jail across the street. He never thought that the old place would sell. Apparently there was someone stupid enough to buy it. He touched the key ring in his pocket. The keys opened the jail cells in the basement.

He took a sip of his hot coffee and grimaced. He preferred the good old standard Folgers he bought at the grocery store, but he'd gone straight to the café patio when he heard the building across the street had new occupants.

The jail had stood empty for quite a few years. The Shay courthouse had moved into a more modern building in the mid eighties. A couple from Albuquerque had bought the jail in the early nineties but never did anything with it. They hung onto it for twenty years before putting it on the market, and that listing had not gone unnoticed by the man. The internet was a wonderful thing.

Now, there's a red-haired kid running in and out of the front door like a plump spring robin on a manic quest for a worm dinner. The man lifted his sunglasses to get a better look.

"Well I'll be damned," he muttered. The kid was a grown woman. A little too short and curvy for his taste, but kind of cute, he supposed. If you took away the red hair and replaced it with blonde, if she lost about twenty-five pounds, she'd look a lot like that slut Mallory S.— God rest her soul.

▓ ▓ ▓